LAGNIAPPE

ALSO BY LES EDGERTON

The Genuine, Imitation, Plastic Kidnapping
The Rapist
The Bitch
Just Like That (*)
Bomb! (formerly *The Perfect Crime*)
Mirror, Mirror
The Death of Tarpons

Short Story Collections
Monday's Meal (*)
Gumbo Ya-Ya

Writer's How-to Craft Books
Finding Your Voice
Hooked

Sports Books
Surviving Little League (Co-authored with son Mike when he was 12)
Perfect Game USA and the Future of Baseball

Other books on business, hairstyling, etc.

(*) Reissue forthcoming

Praise for Books by Les Edgerton

"The sad wives, passive or violent husbands, parolees, alcoholics and other failures in Leslie H. Edgerton's short-story collection are pretty miserable people. And yet misery does have its uses. Raymond Carver elevated the mournful complaints of the disenfranchised in his work, and Edgerton makes an admirable attempt to do the same. He brings to this task an unerring ear for dialogue and a sure-handed sense of place (particularly New Orleans, where many of the stories are set). Edgerton has affection for even his most despicable characters, but he never quite takes the reader past the brink of horrible fascination into a deeper understanding. In the best story, 'My Idea of a Nice Thing,' a woman named Raye tells us why she drinks: 'My job. I'm a hairdresser. See, you take on all of these other people's personalities and troubles and things, 10 or 12 of 'em a day, and when the end of the day comes, you don't know who you are anymore. It takes three drinks just to sort yourself out again.' Here Edgerton grants both the reader and Raye the grace of irony, and without his authorial intrusion, we find ourselves caring about her predicament."
—*The New York Times*, on *Monday's Meal*

"Les Edgerton has swiftly become my favorite crime writer. Original voice, uncompromising attitude and a pure hard-boiled style leap him to the front ranks of my reading list. He will become legendary."
—Joe R. Lansdale, bestselling author

"Les Edgerton is the new High King of Noir."
—Ken Bruen, bestselling author

LES EDGERTON

LAGNIAPPE

A COLLECTION

Down & Out Books
3959 Van Dyke Rd, Ste. 265
Lutz, FL 33558
www.DownAndOutBooks.com

Cover design by JT Lindroos

ISBN: 1-943402-85-X
ISBN-13: 978-1-943402-85-4

CONTENTS

We were best friends for a long time and then we weren't.

Just like that.

He said, "I know about you and Missy," and there wasn't anything to say after that. It caught me by surprise.

That was when we were getting off the streetcar, coming home. We both got off at Riverbend by The Camellia Grill.

All I could think was he knew this all day and didn't say anything until now.

"Tony," I went, but he had already walked away. I walked behind him half a block, going slow to let him get ahead. We both lived on Burthe, me closer to Carrollton. What I wanted was for him to get past my apartment first. I had an idea Missy was there like she had been lately, and this was the wrong time for him to see her there.

I stopped and had a drink at Madigan's to allow him plenty of time. I had two beers and played Pac-Man and talked to a girl and then I walked home. Missy was there, waiting inside. She had her own key. Her idea.

"He knows," I said, before anything else. She had a drink in her hand. It looked like straight Jack, yellow and mean, so I knew I wasn't telling her anything she wasn't already in on.

"There was a note in my mailbox," she said. "He's got a gun, Frank."

I fixed myself a drink and went into the living room and

sat on the sofa. She came and sat down on the other end. I saw there was more Jack in her glass.

"I bought it for him for his birthday. The gun. That's how I know he has one."

"He wouldn't use it," I said. "You're not even married to him anymore. Why would he use it? He's just hurt. His feelings are just hurt."

She left after a while. We hadn't made love. I said something about calling her up the next day, but that was just what you say to someone in that situation.

We still rode the streetcar together the next few weeks, Tony and I. Of course, we didn't sit together any longer. At work, we were polite when we had to be, but that was it. I kept believing he'd snap out of it, come around, and maybe he would have, but one day about a week later, I came home after stopping at Madigan's and she was sitting on the stoop. She'd already gotten into the Jack.

"I saw Tony," she said. "Right here. Not twenty minutes ago. I said hi to him but he just walked by."

"He was getting over it," I go, and I'm not happy with this. "Another day, we would have sat down and talked it out. Who the fuck asked you to come over? I told you I'd call you." She looked at me for a minute and then threw her drink at me, not like in the movies, but the whole drink, glass and all, and then she left. I didn't call her up any more. That was over.

Tony was worse after that. I think Missy had called him, laid some story on him. He was even more polite. And he would stare at me. I'd look up from the phone, talking to a client; something would make me look up, and there he'd be, just sitting at his desk, staring, no expression on his face at all. Spooky. I'd say goodbye to the client, cut him off, and go to the bathroom and wash my hands or have a cigarette. My hands would shake.

There was a bum, a street person. We always laughed at him, Tony and I, before our falling-out. The street person had layer after layer of clothing on, no matter what the season or how hot it was. We'd lay odds how many layers there were. Five or six, I'd say. No way, goes Tony. Ten, at least.

He had a shopping cart. The street person. He went around to all the trash receptacles in the Central Business District, the CBD, and fished out the newspapers. This, too, was a joke for us. He's keeping up with world affairs, Tony would go, case his country calls for him to serve; be President. No; he's got a mansion on St. Charles and he's collecting insulation, I'd say, and we'd laugh. This was before he found out about me and Missy.

Ninety shimmering degrees of New Orleans heat, and the street person would put on *more* clothes. You couldn't see any sweat on his forehead, ever. That would be the only exposed flesh. He'd have on a woolen stocking hat and a navy blue muffler as well. In September. In New Orleans.

Once, coming home on the streetcar, we saw him peeing. Right on the street. Hung it out there and let 'er rip. People, women, were walking around him, shaking their heads, as if, can you imagine? It must have taken him half an hour to unzip all his trousers. Good kidneys, we said; be able to hold it that long. We couldn't fucking believe it, Tony and I. We looked to see if there was a policeman around. Not that it mattered. This was New Orleans. Once, during Mardi Gras I saw a couple performing fellatio not twenty feet from a policeman and he didn't even bother to watch. Two guys. Maybe if it was a hetero couple, the cop would've been interested enough to at least watch.

There wasn't a policeman anyway. The coast was clear for a daring daylight pee on Canal Street. One woman picked up her little girl and ran down the street, her eyes big, and you could see her jabbering to her kid. We laughed, Tony and I, holding onto each other we were laughing so hard. He was standing there, peeing, big as life, on Canal, during the after work rush hour, his one foot up on his shopping cart like he was worried someone might grab it and run off. There was a huge puddle running down to the curb that people were hopping over. A kid rode his bike through it and a lady was slapping at her skirt like some had sprayed her, and she was gagging. It was pretty funny stuff. This was a couple of months before Tony found out about Missy and me.

And...

We'd get off the streetcar and I'd toss my newspaper in the trash. A morning ritual. Sports was all I read. See how the Saints were doing, what players had injuries. The street person was always there, waiting. I'd look back and he'd be digging it out, putting it in his cart. This was before Tony got mad at me, and after, too. Our problems had nothing to do with the street person's routine. He could care less. Even if he would have known.

* * *

It was about a month after Tony found out about Missy and me and it was on a Monday morning. I hardly thought about him anymore, just ignored the situation and looked through him at work.

Going out of the bus to catch the streetcar, I noticed the Sunday *Times-Picayune* on the floor beside the couch where I'd left it the night before. Why not? I thought, and picked it up. I got the Monday paper out of the machine in front of The Camellia Grill. When I got on the streetcar, I must have been carrying four pounds of newspaper, about two ounces of which I actually read.

Tony got on, a block up the line, something he'd been doing since our little falling out, so we wouldn't have to stand and wait for the car together, and this day, instead of sitting in front like he'd been doing, he walked all the way back to where I was and sat down in the seat opposite. Then, he did something I didn't like too much. He grinned at me and opened his jacket with an exaggerated gesture. There was his gun, stuck in the waist-band of his trousers. The grin abruptly left his face, he closed his coat, picked up his own paper and began reading. I thought: Jesus.

When the streetcar stopped just off Canal, I got off. I didn't look his way, but I was acutely aware of him. He was letting me get off first. I started toward the office, not running exactly, but moving at a good clip. There was the trash receptacle, just ahead, and the bum was already going through it. I went up and placed both my papers in his shopping cart.

"There you go, old-timer," I said. "I brought you Sunday's, too." I shined him a big smile.

It was the morning for surprises.

He came unglued.

He ran the two or three steps to his cart and began screaming at the top of his voice, "I don't want your goddamn papers. Don't put your goddamn papers in my cart!" I could smell him, old piss and the sweetish-sour smell of wine and another smell I couldn't identify right off. Musty, like the underside of a board in a vacant lot. Dirty clothes, I realized. Dirty clothes that had been rained on and slept in. Many times.

"I don't want your goddamn papers!" he was screeching. He shook them in my face.

"Here! Take 'em! I don't need your fucking charity!" He pushed them at me.

It all happened so quickly, I didn't see any option but to take them. I stood there, holding two days' worth of *Times-Picayune*, and he went back to his cart, muttering and arranging his other papers into neat piles. Shrugging, I went to the receptacle and tossed them in.

Then, from somewhere, Tony was there and he had his gun out. I'd forgotten all about him. But it wasn't me he pointed the gun at. It was at the bum. Right at his head. Right *on* his head, matter of fact. He laid the barrel right up to the side of the bum's head and then he said, "Take my friend's papers. Go on, take them." In this calm, conversational, *insane* voice, like he was ordering a BLT on white bread from a waitress.

"Fuck you *and* him." This was the bum speaking, not even looking up or acknowledging the gun, still digging through his papers.

"If you don't take my friend's papers, I'm going to have to shoot you," Tony said.

"Tony," I said, finding my voice and hearing it come out of me from very far away.

"Stay out of this," Tony said, his eyes on the bum, on whom he still has the pistol trained, in a two-handed grip, both arms extended, like detectives in movies do. "This isn't your business. Or do you like bums? You don't like women. We know that for a fact, don't we, Frank? You don't like your friends and you don't like women, not even your friend's woman. All you like to do is fuck them. Your friends and your friend's woman. Only it's not like real fucking. It's more like you masturbate with them. So stay out of this. I'm in charge here. I'm the one with the gun this time. I'm going to show you how to fuck someone in a less painful way."

"Kiss my white ass," said the bum again, still digging and ignoring the gun. He thought Tony was talking to him.

"Okay then, sir," said Tony. "You have left me no choice but to blow you away," and he giggled and pulled the trigger. Only instead of a blast and a bum's head blown to hamburger, there's this little click. And then, there's a cop that gets involved, must have been watching from somewhere, comes running and takes Tony down with a tackle shoulda been on the NFL highlight film, and before you know it, there's a whole bunch of cops and tourists looking over their shoulders, and I'm in a squad car and Tony's been led to another one, giggling and telling the four cops who've got him that it isn't loaded, which they've already figured out for themselves, and he's explaining this and other things to them while they drive him away, and the two that have me are asking me hard-eyed questions about what happened for the hundredth time, and then there's more cops, different cops, and I have to repeat everything to them all over again. I see they've got the bum over against a car, talking to him, and I guess I'd talk to him outside my car, I was the cop, too, with the aroma this bum is putting out, and then it seems I have to take a ride downtown and explain what has happened to some other cops, higher-ups.

When we're pulling away, I hear one of the cops with the bum say, "Fuck this shit. I ain't puttin' him in my car. I got six more hours on this shift to ride in this fucker and they ain't gonna want him downtown no way. Cut 'im loose."

Half a block up the street, I see they've let the bum go, and he's over pawing in the trash receptacle and just as we turn the corner I see him pick up my papers and start for his cart with them.

Well, there was a lot of talking and confusion down at the parish station and I find out they took Tony first to the lockup and then later, over to Charity Hospital for psychiatric, and after a time they drive me back to the office, telling me they might need me to come downtown again and tell my story to the one or two policemen in the parish who haven't yet heard it.

I asked for the rest of the day off and the next day I called in and said I was taking my vacation.

That's three months back and I haven't returned, so I guess I quit. I stayed around the apartment a couple of days, just drinking Jack and watching the tube. Once, a day or so after Tony tried to shoot the bum with his unloaded gun, Missy came by and rang the doorbell, but I just stayed inside until she finally went away. She didn't try and use her key, which I'd forgot she had. If she'd come in, I don't know what I would have said to her. Just hit her, I guess is what I'da done. Tony was right. I didn't much like women, at least not this one. I wanted to tell him I liked myself even less, see if that made any difference. Probably not.

The telephone rang a few times, too, and after a while I unplugged it.

I woke up sober one day, or out of booze which is the same thing, and called an old friend of mine, Randy Duplechette, and asked if he needed any help and he guessed he did, so I went out with him, out through Ponchartrain and into the Gulf. Randy does some part-time shrimping, takes time off from his regular job which is drinking. He has this small, homemade trawler and net, and then I made a deal to sub-contract his boat from him, and that's what I'm doing now, shrimping and selling what I get to Deannie's. That's about over, what with the weather, Randy's boat won't make it down to the Mexican coast where the shrimp are heading.

I don't know what I'll do next.

Tony's back on the job. I know, 'cause I went down to get some things and clean out my desk, and there he was. I said hi, in a quick way as I walked by, but he didn't even look up and that was fine with me. At least, he wasn't pulling that polite act any more. Miz Shelly, the boss's secretary, tried to get some information out of me as she took me back to the closet where they'd stored my stuff, but I didn't tell her squat, at which she sniffed, and then, of course, she had to tell me what *she* knew, which was that Tony had suffered some sort of nervous breakdown and had just come back on limited duty. He was supposed to have some kind of trial in a couple of months, but it wouldn't amount to anything, she said, the way they had it figured. It was just a bum, wasn't it, she said. I just kept nodding my head and clucking my tongue, which made her press her lips together hard, and then I left. I went out the side door so I wouldn't have to pass his desk again.

I haven't seen him come by my apartment after work in weeks, the times I'm home, so I guess he's either moved, or else takes a different route from the streetcar, maybe catches it over on St. Charles now. I saw Lucille Hardy, she used to work in the office with us, down at Madigan's once, a day or so ago, and she says she heard Tony and Missy had gotten back together again, were thinking about getting remarried, not that I asked her for this gossip. It's just something some people want to do, tell you things maybe you'd prefer not to know.

We were good pals, Tony and me, at one time. We were the very best of friends, brothers practically, worked and played together, did everything. Went to ballgames, drank beers and shot pool out in Fat City, ate po-boys at lunch together, things like that.

I may walk down to his place one of these days and see if I can catch him outside if it happens he still lives there, maybe pruning back his oleanders. Maybe just start shooting the breeze and see how it goes. Particularly since it looks like he's got what he wants. By that, I mean Missy.

I'll probably tell him I'm sorry. I am, you know. Maybe we can all get together and talk it out, him, me and Missy. Go back to the way it was, before.

I'm just whistling Dixie here, aren't I?

First published in *High Plains Literary Review*. Nominated for a Pushcart Prize. Nominated for Houghton Mifflin's *Best American Mystery Stories* series.

FELON

I. My Father Died

My father died. I got a phone call the day after. It was Mom.

"I tried all day yesterday to reach you," she said. "Your father passed away."

"I was away," I told her. "I was at a buddy's house for the weekend."

"Who?"

"Never mind. When's the funeral?"

When I drove up to the funeral home and looked at my watch it read one-forty-eight in digits. We were supposed to be there at one thirty. "Fuck it," I said to Donna, the girl I was living with. In a way I was glad. I didn't want to go to my father's service with a whore. My mother would have picked up on it right away and there would have been something. So I waited outside. Sat in the car and smoked. This all took place right after they'd let me out on parole.

"How come you're not a pallbearer?" Donna said.

"How come you're not a D-cup?" I said back. She shut up and moved closer to her own window, blowing smoke out the window.

"Why'm I running this air conditioner when you got the goddamn window open?" I said.

When the procession started out I turned on my lights

and waited for the last car. Then I became the last car. I had no idea which cemetery they were all headed for.

A rent-a-cop came up at the cemetery and asked what I was doing.

"That's my father they're burying," I said.

"Oh," he said, and just stood there awhile looking over at the mob of people gathered around the mound of dirt. There was a tent set up beside it for those who wanted to get out of the sun. I thought I could see my mom but we were quite a ways away so I'm not sure. It looked like her from there but then I'd never seen her in a black dress and she looked different. Maybe it was one of my aunts. From a distance who knows? The rent-a-cop kept standing there about two feet away and he just stared at the preacher even though where we were you couldn't hear anything.

"I didn't know cemeteries had their own police force," I said, trying to keep a conversation from happening. He just muttered something and walked away. I thought he was going to walk over to my father's funeral but halfway there he made a military turn and went instead toward another funeral that was taking place about two hundred yards away. They were planting them all over the place it looked like.

"Shouldn't you go up or something?" Donna said.

"Shouldn't you mind your own business?" I said. "I might've gone up if we weren't late. If you didn't have to comb your hair forty thousand times we'd been on time." She had nothing to say to that. That was good. She wanted to play the dozens I could spot her eleven and still wipe the floor with her ass.

After a while it was all over. The people started getting back in their cars. It *was* my mother, I saw now. She got in the lead car, the one with the funeral home chauffeur and the little plastic flag, and I think she spotted me. She kind of hesitated, looked like, looking our way, and then climbed in the back with somebody looked like my Uncle Clarence. He was helping her, holding her elbow.

I waited until the last car left and then I got out and walked toward the big pile of dirt.

There he was in this coffin. The ropes they'd used to lower him were still there, the ends snaked in esses in the dirt. I stood there for a few minutes looking down at the black casket. I just stood there looking and nothing came up in my mind. No thoughts, nothing.

I just about jumped out of my skin when a voice said right at my elbow, "Your dad, huh?"

It was that goddamn rent-a-cop.

"I guess," I said. "My mom got in a limo so it wasn't her. You got a smoke on you?"

He gave me one and held up his lighter to try and light it. There was a breeze just started up and it kept going out. "Here," I said, grabbing it out of his hand. I got it lit after two-three tries cupping my hand around it.

"Well, my sympathies," he said, turning around and walking away. I guess he was looking for another funeral to bother. I thought I saw some people pulling up clear on the other side of the cemetery and I started to point it out to him but he was nowhere to be seen. Then I saw him come up a small depression and walk to the top of the hill. He was heading for the new funeral.

I smoked the cigarette down to the filter and flipped it down on the casket. It bounced once and fell in the dirt beside it.

There was something I should probably do or say, I thought.

Well, I said in my head, and then aloud: "Well."

Donna started laying on the horn, a long blast and then another and then she really laid on it.

"Well, Dad," I said. "Well, well, well."

Time I got back to the car it was starting to overheat. Steam was curling from the hood. We didn't talk most of the way home, I smoked six or seven cigarettes, not bothering to knock loose tobacco from the lighter.

II. Women

We were clear the other side of Anderson on 69 before Bud even mentions anything about where we're going. We're maybe ten minutes from the 465 bypass around Indianapolis when he said, "South, huh?"

I grinned and squeezed the can of Miller's Genuine Draft he'd handed me, between my legs so's I could pop the top. We had all the windows down, front and back and were cruising at seventy, every so often rolling them up when we went past a pig farm until we got drunk enough we didn't care. That stretch of 69 you could do sixty-five, legal, and they always gave you an extra five. "That okay?"

This was like old times.

We drank all the way down, listening to the radio and then a Waylon Jennings tape Bud picked up at a truck stop outside of Evansville just before we crossed the bridge.

This trip was my idea and I didn't have a clue where we were going. *Warm* was all I cared about.

Together we anted up the pot and we had four hundred and twelve bucks and some silver between us. Three-fifty of that was mine counting what I'd got from the QuickStop in a spur-of-the-moment stickup right before I'd picked Bud up. I didn't tell him about that. No sense in worrying him for no reason. I hadn't bothered to go back to my apartment to get my clothes and things but I wasn't totally a moron either. I'd stopped by the bank on the way to Bud's place and closed out my bank account. That was half of the three-fifty.

"If I'd known the bitch'd cleaned me out I wouldn't have called her and told her I was leaving," he said, soon as he climbed in the car. "I got sixty bucks total, homeboy. If I'd known she went through my pants last night I woulda went over to the hospital, made some excuse and jacked her up for some. I fucked up, calling her first."

It didn't matter. We figured to go as long as our money lasted and find something wherever that was, a job or something, or if we happened on a place we liked before we were broke we'd do the same there. Neither of us gave it much thought. We were both thieves, at least that's what we'd both done time for although each of us had done a few other things too. Armed robbery, strong-arm robbery, dope, things like that, the usual, guys like us. Though that wasn't the only thing Bud got popped for. He got busted for rape with the other stuff but that's another story.

I had my Mossberg twelve gauge and a .22 rifle in the trunk and Bud had brought a Police Special .38 with the numbers filed off which I made him hide in the wheel well in the trunk case we got stopped. Under the spare which was flat. I put my .45 there, too. It wasn't that we were planning on doing a job, it was just that we both knew how to and if worse came to worse, well, it wasn't the end of the line like it would be for some folks.

That night we kept an eye out for a cheap motel close to a bar and found one just across the line into Tennessee, I don't remember the name of the town, some little podunk where the bar and motel up on the highway seemed to *be* the town. Gobbler's Knob or something was probably the name of it, most of them one-horse towns was called something like that. Finger Fucker's Ferry, Joe-Bob's Dell. Weird names, you wondered where they came from, what the history was.

We checked into a double and it was a bit pricey seeing as how the cabins looked like a pack of former slave quarters or something, bunch of little shacks all painted white at one time, peeling and gone to hell by now and practically falling down, but as I say, we were flush and said what the fuck. Twenty-eight bucks and three for the key, get it back when you turned the key in. First thing we checked was the air conditioning and it worked fine though it was loud. Sounded like it was about to blow a gasket but the air was frosty and kicked out in buckets. The sheets were clean too. There was a few roaches but not the big ones you see in Florida. These were hardly nothing, little bitty things. There was a Bible and a phone book that was smaller than my rap sheet.

This was one of those rent it by the hour dumps, couples coming and going all hours and mostly drunk or high whole time we were there and I figure we copped the only double in the bunch, musta used it for the big orgies. Big ol' hillbilly Cadillacs parked all over; '57 two-door Chevies with California rakes, painted either black or red. Only two colors they could use and still be in the hillbilly race driver club probably. Once in a while a '56 Ford would pull in, most likely the maverick redneck. Seemed like every time we turned around that night somebody was spraying our door with gravel trying to impress their little girlfriends but hell, we all done that shit even up north.

Well, we have found the action place we said to each other and jumped in and took turns showering and loading up with the aftershave, turned out in our best threads, me in my truck stop rodeo shirt and then heading over across the highway for the bar which was knee-deep in big-titted gals and guys with beards and cowboy hats. I bet we were the only guys without chin hair. Must have been a local thing and it sure made us stand out. Which was good and bad. Good 'cause the women noticed we was fresh meat and bad cause the local bad asses noticed we was fresh meat, too.

The joint was called the Blue Pony—where they got *that* from God only knows—only it was full of blue neon lights and signs. No ponies though, flamingos that looked more like blue turkeys, cartoon characters and dogs or something I guess were supposed to be dogs. And every beer sign in the world, most of them red. They shoulda called it "Neon City" 'stead of the pony thing. Who knows what goes through a cracker's head?

We didn't have to wait long. Just got our first beers and cracked wise at the waitress, this peroxide burnout couldn't been much more than sixteen when these two Hill Williams—that's what Bud liked to call them—sidled up and sat down at our table uninvited, a big, mean-looking doofus with a scar alongside his chin looked like wasn't put there with no Gillette Blue Blade, and his sidekick, a little wormy kind of character, with a Snidely Whiplash pencil 'stash and a goatee with a vitamin deficiency, kept him from growing the complete, filled-out article.

"You boys are new in town," said the moose. I swear to God, that's what he said, and it was all either of us could do to keep from busting out laughing. I peeped at Bud and he at me and I knew he was having the same trouble I was keeping the snickers down, or asking the guy if maybe he hadn't seen too many John Wayne movies. Before anything else happened, Bud stuck his hand over the big guy's mitt that was on the table, and the guy's hand just disappeared. Just fucking disappeared. I told you, Bud was a big guy. Six-six and about that wide.

Then it got interesting.

Bud leaned over and put his face right up into the guy's mug, up under his Stetson and said real soft, "I just want to make this point, my friend. My buddy and me are just here for a little drink or two and maybe if we get lucky we find some friendly girls. We're passin' through, be gone in the morning. We ain't after *your* girls so if you want to point out which's yours, well, we'll lay offa them maybe. But if it's some trouble you want then it's trouble you got, only this ain't gonna be no brawl like you been in before." He leaned in even closer, his nose not an inch from the other man's and smiled. It was a smile that said: *You need to know I'm a dumber hillbilly than you are, friend. I don't know when to quit.*

He put the mojo to it, squeezing the guy's hand. There was no mistake—something cracked, a finger or a thumb. We all heard it. The big guy had sand, some, anyway. But Lord! the sweat was coming off him, making him blink as fast as he could and his color was white as a Ku Kluxer's dress robe.

Bud patted the other man's hand like it was some mangled pup got caught in a combine. He patted it gently and the man winced and drew his hand away. He sat there a minute staring at Bud—in fact, he hadn't taken his eyes from Bud's—and then he looked away, down, and got up, turned, and walked to the front door. The other guy sat there a minute as if confused, had found himself in the wrong place by accident maybe and then he stood himself up and went out the door.

"Damn," I said.

"Hold up, home-boy," he said. "We're not out of the woods yet."

I realized what he was saying. Hell, I should have known better from my time in the joint. Never front a guy, make him lose face in public. In this case even though Jim-

Bob and Little Ernie had departed, us laughing about the little confrontation would be like laughing at all the others, that's *family*, places like that and there were too many for us, bad as we might be. Well, bad as *Bud* might be although I wasn't exactly no slouch at bustin' heads either. It came right down to it I seen he was right and I wiped the smile off my kisser.

He read the hand right. The locals left us alone and the tension settled down and we had us a few beers, checking out the talent. There was some uglos but there was some good ones too, some that smiled back, gave us a look.

Along about the third or fourth round he finally got around to it.

"It's your girlfriend isn't it? Why we're doing this, why we're sitting here in cotton country instead of over at the North Star on State?"

I admitted it was. "Yeah. I got it pretty bad, Bud."

"Must be. You're still on parole aren't you?"

He knew I was.

"And you didn't even call in to quit your job did you, home-boy? I *know* you didn't get permission from your P.O. t'do this. Fuck, man," Bud said, shaking his head admiringly. "You're a gen-u-wine twenty-four carat fuckup. You're gonna be back there with Dusty and who's gonna save your ass this time? Was it that Donna, that redhead I seen you with at the Three Rivers Festival? Big tits she's proud of?"

I cleared my throat, took a swig of beer, tried to look at him but couldn't quite make it.

"Yeah. I even tried to take the pipe, man. Some shit, huh?" I was embarrassed as soon as I said that. I don't know why I did, except we were like brothers and I figured if anyone could understand, Bud could.

"You're shittin' me."

"No." I thought again about the last few days. "I got me this room at Motel Six, you know the one out on Coliseum Boulevard, out towards Harvester. By Azars. The one has the tittie bar behind it. Three days. Sat around in my skivvies with the TV off and the shades down. Didn't know if it was day or night most of the time. Didn't do nothin' but sit there and eat Jack Daniel's and chocolate doughnuts. Did a bottle a day. Fuck, I don't do a bottle a *week*."

"So, how—"

I grinned, or tried to. "All I can say is I can't shave with my Norelco now. Fucking cord's busted. You got a razor I could borrow maybe?" I rubbed my neck. It was still sore. Then, I did laugh. "I paid a lot of money for that damn thing. You'd think the cord'd be stronger! Think the warranty's good on something like that?"

I looked at him and took a deep breath.

"I was gonna do it again, do it till I got it right, only I laid there awhile on the floor thinking that now I was gonna have to go out and buy something stronger, a rope, and I started to wonder what places were still open had rope for sale on a Sunday and then I wondered that if I was to find such a place would they take a check cause I only had a couple of bucks in cash left and then I remembered I would have to go back to my apartment cause that's where my checkbook was—I could see it in my mind, sitting on the dresser and then I thought—what the hell am I doing? If it is this much trouble then the hell with it! I would much rather spend my time doing something more fun that took less effort. So I did. I got up and turned on the TV. I didn't think about leaving town then—that's the honest to God truth. I did that this morning, driving over to Harvey's but I might have started to think about it last night while I was lying there thinking about what a fuckup I was at killing myself, who knows? Anyway, here I am and here we are and what do you think of that? No, don't answer that. I just want to get drunk and see if we can get laid. I already forgot about what's-her-name.

"Donna."

"Yeah. Whatever." We both laughed.

"Pussy's pussy."

Yeah, there was that. Bud was right but then again he was wrong. I'd always thought that too—pussy was pussy—all cats look alike in the dark—all that shit—and mostly that's true, I guess, but Donna...well, Donna was... well, *different.* I can't think of a better word.

It was all kinds of things, me and Donna. The way she fucked. She screwed you like you and her were the last two motherfuckers on earth and if she coulda got to pick who she was gonna get to play Adam and Eve with it wouldn'ta been nobody else but you. That kind of shit.

She all the time was making you think. This is a good one. This is pure Donna. One time we're vegging out in bed, Sunday morning, the papers spread all over the bed and us and out of nowhere she says, "You ever notice that all the people who park in handicapped spaces drive Cadillacs?" I mean, who *thinks* of that kind of shit? Not me.

"Yeah," I said, coming back. "Being handicapped must pay good."

Then she said something else, added to what we started and we had this whole conversation going—*funny*-ass shit. Half an hour we go on. Talking with her was like talking to another guy, a brother or something. She never needed any of that bullshit fake-ass crap most girls seem to crave, have to always be telling them their eyes were like diamonds, shit like that. We lay there, rapping like a couple of buds and it was even better because you sure can't roll your buddy over and take one. Not me, anyway. It was like having a pard only ten times better because you had the sex too and the sex was only the best I ever had. But that was Donna. She had this other side too, not so good.

"Why'd you break up with her?"

Because of my dad, I thought, but I didn't tell Bud that. I didn't want to bring up the funeral, even think about it. I didn't tell him about the baby she aborted either.

Probably it was our baby she aborted was the last straw, now that I think about it. Dad gone to room temperature and me the last of the line and she goes and offs the baby. Then makes me late for his funeral so I couldn't go up until everyone had left.

Yeah.

"I don't know. Lots of reasons."

That was it. We didn't talk any more about it. I didn't want to now that it was out and Bud didn't bring it up again.

Funny. What I *did* think about was my dad. That was all the time happening—out of nowhere, for no reason, I'd be thinking about my father and wishing he was there, see me in action. See what a cocksman his number-one boy was. That was just nuts, the way that always happened, thinking about my pappy, me a grown man and all. I wonder if other guys think about their fathers when they're pulling a job, a robbery, or going down on some gal. Right. I'm the idiot has the father ghost always popping up at the dumbest times. Wondering how he'd take if if he'd known he almost had a grandson to carry on the name. I wonder what the shrink back at Pendleton Reformatory would think of that.

Don't even say it.

III. Down Again

I finally run into Donna, day before I robbed Smiley's. I was down at Alexander's over on State, came in for the take-out ribs and I turned around and there she was, big as shit, tits hanging half out her blouse and looking like SEX with all caps. It was about three months after we broke up. I didn't know what to expect, it being sudden like that and a surprise, this not being a place where we'd ever gone together so I wasn't on my guard but you know what? I didn't feel anything. Not a goddamned thing.

That was something, that.

I can't say this hadn't crossed my mind, about running into her. Once or twice I even dialed her number but I always hung up before she answered. Maybe I thought a guy might answer and I didn't know how I'd handle that.

"Hi," she said and I could tell she was trying to figure out how I'd react to this, knowing we'd had our violent times and that felt pretty good, knowing she was up on her toes so to speak, but all I said, and this I couldn't fucking believe, all the speeches I'd rehearsed, even the way my eyes would be, *frosty,* was—"You still owe me for the rent."

We stood there a few minutes, toe to toe, just looking at each other, her folding and unfolding her hands down in front of her, her eyes big and wide and...and *bright... glittery*-bright.

"I got your letter."

I just stared, trying to get my mind untracked.

"Oh. Yeah. Well, I thought of you a couple of times. I'da written more, but..." But what? "But, I was hooked up with this girl," I said, not knowing I was going to lie like that. I wish I'd had more time to think of something else, something better. "A black girl. Her name was Saundra. You'da liked her, Donna. You probably wouldn't even try and stab her like you did Patsy."

Oh, man. This was the lamest thing I could have done but how do you haul something like that back into your stupid mouth? You just have to go on with the program once you start some shit like that.

"I had to leave cause her dad didn't like white boys."

Fuck. I wouldn't buy this crap myself. I did the only thing I could do at that point. I walked past her, just barely brushing her shoulder and went on out the door of Alexander's and out into the cold. It was January and snowing and there was gray slush on top of the clean snow, the snow plows having just been by, flinging crap all over everything, the sidewalk, all over my windshield, this piece of junk I'd just bought for fifty bucks, another Ford. I didn't have a scraper so I just used the Styrofoam box my ribs were in, trying not to spill them, but got the fries and the French bread and ribs all mixed up, sauce on everything.

Back in my room I kept getting this picture of Donna and the way she kept folding and unfolding her hands and right behind it I got this image of Bud and the guy in Tennessee, the one whose hand he squeezed until something broke. The whole time she was doing that with her hands, it was like she was doing it to my insides, same as Bud did to that big hillbilly.

Way it turned out, I got shot in the leg breaking into Smiley's over on Vance Avenue and now here I sit in city lockup awaiting transport back to Pendleton. There was a lot of boozy nights and days, I suppose, led up to me making that kind of mistake.

I usually don't go for the sauce that much and I hate guys who blame everybody but who they ought to blame which is themselves when they lose control, take up drugs, booze, whatever, and so I got to do the same. But all I know is I kept thinking of that fucking bitch Donna. I'm not saying it's her fault—I'm not saying that—fuck, I'm a big boy and ought to be able to keep it cool. I'm not even that sorry I lost it there for a while and I'll be damned if I even knew how it happened. I'm sitting in a bar one day, tossing back a quick one and just about ready to leave when I thought, what the hell and I had another one and ended up spending the rest of the afternoon when I should have gone back to work. That was pretty much it for work. It was that second drink did it. Just like that. That's when I started making bets that weren't too bright.

I did a lot of thinking during that period, which is what you do when you drink. Unless you got a compadre wants to sit around getting stinking with you which don't happen as a rule, all you got to do is think. Think and drink.

It's funny. I've read as much as anybody about why guys like me end up spending half their life behind bars and they've got all kinds of theories except for the right one. Doing crimes is like drinking. It's the same, exact thing.

There's a jolt you get when a job goes down. Ain't nothing like it in the entire universe. Better than whiskey, better than coke, matter of fact, it's better than sex in a lot of ways. I sure never got as high after a mattress marathon as I have after I stick up a guy. That sex high lasts about ten seconds but the buzz you get when you just got off some motherfucker's poke can go on for weeks. It's a drug is all it is. The body's own natural drug. Adrenaline. I finally figured it out and that's the secret. Which means nothing's gonna change in society. Only way it's gonna change is take out the gland makes the adrenaline. It ain't even about money only you couldn't convince the do-gooders of that. They got this idea that if everybody gets a big piece of the pie then crime will disappear. They just don't get it—it's not about money or any of those things.

Besides that jolt, there's one other reason guys pull crimes. For control. Most of us haven't ever been in charge of even a little bit of our lives. Holding a .45 on some clown in a liquor stores makes you God, at least for a few minutes. In the back of your head, you know that situation's gonna come to a crashing halt eventually, but for a few minutes you get to be in charge, make the other guy feel the fear you carried around with you all the live-long day.

When I was pulling jobs, when I first started doing burglaries, stuff like that, I had all the money I ever wanted. Give me twenty bucks, I'd say to my mom and she'd fork over thirty. Any time I wanted. Money wasn't why I broke into places. I did it for the high. All the money in the world, all the things that all the money in the world could buy legitimately for you couldn't duplicate that high. Nothing there is can match that 'cept you pull the crime. If you had a million dollars in your back pocket and you got the crime monkey on your back then you'd hold up somebody for his thumbs, for the lint in his pocket. Whatever. Like they always say about guys who wheel and deal on Wall Street—money's just a way of keeping score. That's all it is and until the sociologists and other book freaks figure that out there ain't no way criminals are going to disappear.

Once you've had a rush like that it's only a matter of time before you get around to it again. We're like alkies or dopers, us thieves. Same for other kinds of outlaws 'cept maybe rape but I'm not even sure about that since that doesn't happen to be a trick in my own bag.

You got to get away from anything that makes it easy for you to take up the habit again, get a fix. The court system kind of knows that. That's why they have all these rules when you make parole, like no drinking, no drugs, can't associate with known criminals or other paroles, stuff like that. They know that even if you got the best intentions in the world, you get with other guys who've got the habit same as you, sooner or later one of you is going to get an idea and before you know it, you're out there with a cut-down twelve gauge in your mitts, looking over the counter at the local 7-Eleven at some punk who's stuffing money into a paper bag. It's like being a smoker.

The thing is there just ain't nothing on earth like crime. Slashing and ripping and tearing up, that's a kick can't be had anywhere else. There was nights when I was going good, had the juice going, when I'd rip off eight, nine, ten places in a row. Not even plan none of them. Just do it. I'm God in a getaway car.

I'd be driving around town see a bar all dark and it just drew me in. Park the car a block away, hike on over, check out the layout. No tools, nothing but my smarts. There's those think burglars have all these fancy-schmantzy burglar tools, and sure—there's some do, I have myself, but usually it's nothing that complicated. Most places have glass someplace and wherever there's glass you can get in with nothing more than a rock or a brick. Get in, get out.

Even if there's no glass, at least none you can break through easily, you can go through almost anything. I seen businesses where they had all the fancy locks in the world on their back doors but the wall itself was basically wallboard, something thin like that. A five-pound sledge and a crowbar will take something like that down in two minutes. It always made me laugh I seen a setup like that. They must figure burglars can only go through doors or windows. Hell, if the wall's thin that's the best place to break through at.

I went in a house once, had these big heavy-duty sliding glass doors on the back. I knew the owners were gone and it was out in the country so nobody could hear me break the glass. Once I was inside, I had to admire the locks on that door. Nice ones, must have cost a lot of money. The owner even had a steel bar he'd put down at the bottom of the runner. Guy like that must think people who break into houses can't figure out any other way than to pick a lock to get in. Picking locks only eats up time and gets you caught. Bust the fucker down's the ticket.

The bolder you are the less likely you'll get caught. One time, over in Bremen, this little town south of South Bend, I pulled into this strip center had about seven businesses in it, along about two in the morning. Everything was closed up except an all-night Laundromat. Just across the street was a gas station and there were two state police cars parked by the pumps and both the guys were standing outside their cars jawing, probably about what master criminal-catchers they were. I give 'em a little wave which they gave back and went into the Laundromat. In the back was a coin changer bolted by two steel bands to the wall. I went back out to the car, got a crowbar and hammer and went back in and ripped the machine off the wall. Made all kinds of racket. I carried it out and put it in my trunk, climbed behind the wheel and drove off. On the way by the cops I give 'em another wave and they waved right back. Being bold's the only way to fly.

That was a serious rush. You get a rush like that no way you're gonna be happy sitting home watching *I Love Lucy* reruns. No, you got to have more.

They figure out something a guy can do that will replace that kind of high that's legitimate they can start tearing down prisons. Ain't likely that's gonna happen. Put too many lazy fuckers out of work. What would cops and hacks and judges have to do? Get a real job? Coffee shops would all close up and doughnut factories would start laying off. You got a whole entire economy depends on criminals.

IV. Timing

I've got to come in a few months to stand trial for the thing at Smiley's but first I had to go back to Pendleton and begin serving the rest of my other sentence, the one I was on parole for. My parole officer Brooks came down to see me but didn't say much, just kept shaking his head till I let him off the hook, told him it wasn't his fault, there was just some folks are gonna always be in the joint and that I was one of them. Nothing you can do about it, pardner, I told him and when he left we were still friends. He even left me a carton of butts. Show me another P.O.'d do that.

Vance has always been a bad luck street for me. I got my nose broke in this same bar—probably why I hit it—Smiley's—and my teeth rearranged in the same circumstance. Smiley's changed my smile that time and now Smiley's has changed the way I walk, least till it heals. The bullet went clear through and I found out something. Getting shot in real life isn't anything like you see on TV. On TV, those guys get up after they been hit and keep on doing whatever it was they were doing before, smacking the bad guy, running over the tops of buildings, whatever. Bullshit.

When I got hit I just laid there and bawled like a baby. I admit it. I ain't ashamed of it. I thought I was dying it hurt so bad. I couldn't have walked on that leg any more than I could have flown the first spaceship to Mars. The cops didn't even have to work hard to find me. Just follow the screams to the back room where I'd crawled. I had this idea that if I tried to get up and make it out of there I'd bleed to death, push the blood out faster, something like that. The way my heart was thumping, I figured I'd have all my juice pumped out in about three minutes flat.

Smiley himself popped me. He was laying up on a rafter like he was making love to it, his .22 rifle in his hands. Later, I find out somebody snitched and he knew all along his place was going to get hit that night. Teach you to talk about a job in a booze-joint. It's for sure you never know who your friends are.

Fuck it is what I thought, once the paramed tells me I'm going to be all right. I wasn't even that upset about being caught. You can't do the time, don't do the crime is the motto of every man Jack's ever been behind bars and it was a motto I held to in heart and head. Sooner or later they're gonna get you is what I figured and it was just my time again.

One of the guards, guy I thought was a righteous dude named Robin something, told me the lawyer I was using was a dirtbag, couldn't get the Pope off for a parking ticket but he knew this public defender named Brockman was the best legal eagle outside of F. Lee Bailey and I wouldn't even have to pay the guy, just plead poverty and the court would assign him if I asked.

I bought it, the whole deal—what'd I know?—and fired my lawyer, Mr. Connors and sure enough, it worked just the way Robin said. I told the judge I was broke and wanted a public defender and could I please have Mr. Brockman and the judge smiled and said, why not, that's fine with me, only it's on record you paid Mr. Connors so I'm not buying this poor routine, you'll have to pay Mr. Brockman you want to use him.

A month later, I'm sitting in quarantine at Pendleton and a couple of inmates let me know how stupid I was. It seems Brockman *used* to be a fair lawyer but he'd spent all his time these last few years trying to break the land speed record for getting to the bottom of a bottle and had lost his job and family and everything and the only work he could get was what was doled out to him as a public defender. Robin Jones, that was the guard at the lockup's name, was Brockman's shill. Sent him customers and Brockman took care of him. The guy I fired, Connors, was a for-real attorney, won about eighty percent of his cases which was about the opposite percentage for Brockman.

I ended up paying Brockman the same as I would have paid Connors and the mistake I made was paying him up front. If I'd slow-walked him or told him he wasn't getting his fee until I got cut loose I most likely wouldn't've ever seen Pendleton. As soon as the check cleared—I had to ask Mom for the money for which I'll be forever sorry—Brockman says the best thing to do is forget this not guilty plea crap and plead guilty—waive my right to a jury trial and take a bench trial and he'd get it assigned to this judge who owed him a favor. Just plead guilty and I'd be back on the street in no time at all, he said.

You don't never pay your attorney up front, an old con told me. They don't have to do no work then and most of them won't.

Only problem with that advice was that I didn't get it until I was back in Pendleton. Timing is everything in life.

"Your Honor," says Brockman, and that's the only words he got out without slurring his speech. He was dead drunk but did that matter to the judge?

"My client..." and here he had to look down at the papers in front of him to remember my name. "Mr. Mayes wants to plead guilty but also wants the court to know he's truly contrite over his actions and will never commit another crime as long as he lives if you will but grant mercy in this instance."

The judge was this little ol' baldy peckerwood looked like he was about three sheets to the wind himself and he looks up over the edge of his throne and said, "I look at your record and all I see is an incorrigible criminal. Two to five, including time already served. Next case."

The whole shebang must have lasted all of six minutes. Last I saw of my lawyer, he was walking at a fast clip out the door. On his way to a meeting with Jack Daniel's I figured, way he was stepping smartly, his cheeks twitching. You live and learn.

My leg was on fire that night when I laid down. I couldn't even sit up and play in the pinochle game like I usually do. I hit the rack early, not that it helped, laying down.

Laying there on my bunk in lockup when the card games broke up and the bullpen quieted down, everybody hitting the rack, it started to hit me that I was going back and I thought about what that would mean.

Survival is what it meant.

The main thing was to maintain a low profile. You get nowhere but noticed and dead or hurt in a significant manner if you walk around like some kind of bad ass. Fucking up bad asses or those who think they're bad is what makes reps and reps are what lots of guys are after. Guys in the joint, some of them anyway, are doing shitloads of time and they've got egos like anybody else. Like some dudes who are doctors, say, or musicians or whatever, they're out to make a name for themselves. About the only way a guy who thinks like that can be a big shot is to kill somebody. There's just some cons who love to walk around with everybody whispering behind their hands when they go by. Gives them a rush, makes them feel like they're somebody. I guess that's it. Erasing some fucker is not something that appealed to me, even if it made people want to line up for my autograph, but there's plenty in the joint who want exactly that.

You're smart, you try and become invisible. Blend. Into walls, furniture. You walk into the day room, say, you pick a spot along a wall. Never in the middle of the room. Paint a bullseye on your back you do that. Never in a corner where lines of sight converge. Not in the middle, even along a wall. Somewhere between the middle and the corner, up along the wall. By an object. Not in the open. A trash can, something like that, something that can take the focus off of you.

Never make eye contact. That's definitely a big rule to follow. Never. If you do you keep your gaze flat, unemotional. You don't look away too quickly or hold your gaze too long. A second either way can get you noticed.

You adopt a gunfighter's attitude like in the Westerns. Quiet and controlled, as if you could explode from stillness and wreak devastation. You play-act in your mind, get the mind-set, force your body so it's a top gun's attitude.

Quiet means strength. A loudmouth is a motherfucker who's headed for an I.V. hookup in intensive care, or worse.

When you go into a room the first thing you do is take a photo with your eyes and locate possible weapons. Even with every precaution you can take, some silly mother can still walk up and front you. You want a mop handle or a heavy ashtray, something to use as a weapon, that happens. You assume the worst will happen and be ready.

The main thing is you always try to disappear.

The times you have to pass by a group of guys who aren't friends, you do it with quiet, controlled force, not enough to appear threatening, but with your eyes slightly averted, or better yet, looking through the men like your mind is elsewhere. Like, you're so confident in your badness and abilities you don't even think to be aware of their potential threat.

You never smile with your eyes. There's a trick of smiling with your mouth only and you better learn how to do that. Only with your lips and never a full smile, only a hint. If possible, with a little bit of a sneer, not enough to antagonize, enough to make someone else believe you don't even know you're sneering—it's just the way life has forced your lip to go.

First published in the inaugural issue of *Murdaland Magazine*, by invitation.

Nothing moved. Not at that early hour. Not even a bird or two. It wasn't as if the world had died; it was more like it had yet to be born, like the first day, but not like that either. It was like any other morning.

We undid the boat from its mooring and climbed in, myself last, for it was my job to push us off. Neither of us said much. We didn't want to waken the people sleeping. We whispered when we spoke, which was only when absolutely necessary. The campground behind us was as still as a monk, and we moved as if in a sickroom. The self-imposed stillness was an omen my youth didn't recognize but still respected.

My father was rowing and each squeak of oars on oarlock sounded very clear and loud to us. We looked around at each squeak in the same way a child does when his mother has told him to be quiet and he hasn't been and he expects her anger. Our mothers weren't there, but they might have been. We felt that they were.

It wasn't a long distance to the spot, but it took an extraordinarily long time to reach it, and I could tell he was tired from rowing and holding his breath. There was a motor, but we hadn't used it for fear of the noise.

There were anchors on each end of the boat, and we let

them down an inch at a time, holding our breath until the weights touched the bottom. Then they were down and we reached for our fishing rods and baited the hooks. We were using redworms and a slip-bobber.

The sun was coming up now and neither of us had had a bite since we'd arrived. We felt permission to talk now because of smoke curling back at the campground and the sound of a car honking. Mostly, we talked about the lack of nibbles and wondered if we should change bait or fish deeper. We didn't though, we kept on the way we were, and after a time my father caught a bluegill, a big one about eleven inches long. He caught three more, all more or less the same size before my own bobber went down for the first time, and then I was taking off a bluegill and it was bleeding on my hands and then on my trousers where I wiped my hands. On my blue jeans you couldn't even tell it was blood, it was just a dark, damp stain that could have been water.

I caught a little one and couldn't help laughing. It looked just like Jimmy Porter, my best friend, with his pop-eyes and oval mouth. Jimmy was always opening his mouth and not saying anything either, just like this fish. I'd tell him about the fish later, and he'd say, *well, you're no movie star either*, and then he'd laugh, too. We were great pals. I put Jimmy back into the water and he swam away, crookedly. He swam exactly like Jimmy walked.

Don't throw those back anymore, my father said. *Kill 'em. There's too many little ones and they're starving out the big ones.* He had a little one in his hand, and while he was talking, he laid it on the seat beside him. Taking his big fishing knife, he stabbed down into its head and drew the knife nearly the length of its body. Then he made a cut sideways in the fish. A perfect cross. He threw it over-board. *Now, next time you get one that size, kill 'im*, he said. I nodded but didn't speak.

There were other boats on the water now, although none were by us. Like a pariah, we floated aloof from all. None of the boats would have anything to do with us. The sun was white-bright but not hot, and a baby breeze ruffled the tops of the tiny beginnings of waves. For some reason, it reminded me of the picture of the Sea of Galilee in my Sunday school book. My father's bobber was going down as quickly as it hit the water now, and the stringer was more than half-filled. I didn't feel like fishing anymore. Several small bluegills floated belly-up in the water near the boat, dead from fish-knife wounds in their sides. They wouldn't be starving out the big ones any longer or going hungry themselves.

My father didn't even notice I had stopped casting. If he did, he didn't say anything. There were more fish floating near the boat than before, and some were still alive. The live ones would float motionless on their sides and then all of a sudden begin swimming in a jerky, circular fashion, flip-flopping sideways, and then they would be still again. After a time, the flopping would stop and their bellies would turn up and they wouldn't be a threat to the big ones any longer.

Finally, the stringer was full. We made lots of noise now as we hauled the anchors. Going back we didn't row; we used the motor and the sound didn't seem loud.

The campground was awake and crawling with people when we pulled up to the dock. Some little kids were already splashing around in the water, and their mothers were yelling at them to come in and eat breakfast *right now or else.*

Some men came down to the dock when they saw us come in. There was a regular gang of them, maybe eleven or twelve. *How they bitin',* said one. *Pretty good,* my father said. *Too many of those darn little ones, but the big ones are there, too.* He held up the stringer and some other people saw it and came up too. I wasn't in the conversation, except somebody asked me if I'd caught most of them, winking at my father. I just shrugged.

My father was feeling good now, smiling and laughing at just about everything he said. He laid the stringer down on the dock for everyone to admire. They looked just like those smaller ones that were floating, but some of them were still jerking. They were shiny, like new dimes, and the ones that were still alive kept opening and shutting their mouths. I reached down in the water and splashed some over them, and they shone even more.

I looked at the fish and then at the gang of men on the dock and then I looked for Jimmy Porter, my best friend. I couldn't see him, and I needed to see him. All of a sudden, I couldn't breathe, and I was scared and sick to my stomach, and the lake came up at me, looking like a sea of little fishes, and I was letting go with my lunch, except it couldn't be lunch or breakfast either as my last meal had been supper, but whatever it was, I lost it. The fishes turned into fire, and I must have had a fever because I was hallucinating, at least I guess that's what I was doing, and just then Jimmy Porter's mom came up and asked where Jimmy was. My dad said we hadn't seen him, and she said that's funny, he said he was going with you; I guess he must have taken a hike into the woods or something. If he doesn't hurry he's going to miss breakfast, 'cause I'm sure as hell not going to save it for him.

That's when the fever must have really set in, from what everyone said, that I kept repeating one word and where that came from I have no idea. It didn't make a bit of sense and still doesn't, and I don't think I even knew or realized my father was standing there, so surely I wouldn't have said what they said I did because I love my father. I really do.

Anyway, he grabbed me by the belt, and I was done throwing up. I still felt sick and suffocating and the stringer was still there and Jimmy wasn't. I had this idea he was somewhere in the lake and he swam crookedly with a cross in his side. I guess I was still a little woozy to be thinking the crazy things I was.

Come on, son, said my father, jumping up on the bank. He held out his hand to help me up. I didn't want to take it, but his eyes made me, so I did and stepped up on the bank, and he reached down and grabbed the stringer.

Probably the sun, he said to a man standing behind him. *I better get him up to the camp before he gets any sicker; his mother will kill me.* We walked through the people standing there, my father, me, and the bluegills, all hand-in-hand and walking together.

Jimmy didn't show up, but I was wrong. Foul play, said the sheriff, and me and my sister both got poison ivy from looking in the woods along with the whole campground. They set up roadblocks and everything, but whoever kidnapped him slipped through somehow.

We left the next morning since my mom and dad were best friends with Jimmy's mom and dad, and they did it to help share their grief.

Early, early in the morning before we packed up the tent, I took the boat out by myself, not caring about the noise—I used the motor—but there was nothing to see. None of the fish were still floating where we had been, but it might have been too dark to really see. It wasn't raining, but it was cloudy.

The sun didn't come up all day, even on the ride home.

First published in *The Analecta.*

Brenda Paxton had the refrigerator open, holding it with her hip as she eased ice cube trays out and filled up the two drinking cups on the counter. The cups were plastic, the kind you catch off the floats during Mardi Gras, art nouveau pictures of masks in carnival colors, purple and yellow. She straightened up, letting the door go and reached for the bottle of Jack Daniel's on the counter and splashed a generous amount into each cup and then a dribble of RealLemon. She didn't look up when Daniel came into the kitchen, only pointed to one of the cups and took the other for herself, stirring the ice with her finger and sucking off the moisture before she took a sip.

He said, "Are you ready?" He picked up the cup and sniffed it before taking a sip. "You didn't put lemon in mine, did you? It tastes like you did."

"I know better," she said, sitting her drink on the counter and gazing out the window at the pool. "I wouldn't dream of it. And yes, I'm ready."

"Did you call Tim?"

"Yes. He said to meet him at the entrance. The back one, not the main one."

"You know where that is?"

She shook her head. "I think so. Tim explained how to get there. We can get there off St. Charles on Melpomene. Go in the back way."

Brenda liked a lot of lemon in her drink, to cut the alcohol taste. Daniel Paxton preferred the taste of the booze. He went over to the sink and poured about a fourth of the cup out and then went to where she'd put the bottle and put more Jack Daniel's in the cup.

"Let's go. I want to get this over with. Then you can say you went. I don't know why you had to ask Tim. Kinda funny how he's spending so much time with us, lately. When we gonna sign the adoption papers?"

Brenda looked at him from over her cup, eyes gray and blank. "You like Tim, Dan. He's just lonesome since his wife died. We're about all he has, family-wise. It won't kill you. You used to like hanging around with him."

"That was before Becky died. Now, it's like he's moved in. Christ!" He set his drink on the kitchen table and felt his pockets. "I've got to get cigarettes. Remind me."

When he came back out of the 7-Eleven, he said, "You sure you want to go today? It's a World's Fair. It's going to be here a long time you know. It looks like rain today. Wouldn't you rather go out to Ponchartrain. Go to Bart's, watch the sailboats, have a fuzzy nail?"

"It's okay. If it rains it won't last. We promised Tim. There's no way to reach him now. He's probably at the gate already, waiting."

"So?" Daniel punched in the cigarette lighter in the dashboard. "You his mother? I wonder..." He let the sentence trail off.

"So don't wonder, Dan. You like Tim as much as I do. I don't know what's wrong with you. What do you think? Tim and I? C'mon, get real. Tim's more your friend than mine. I just feel sorry for him, that's all." She turned her head and took a sip of her drink.

He lighted his cigarette and then banged the lighter against the ash tray to dislodge any tobacco before he stuck it back in its hole.

"I think you like him a lot more than I do."

Brenda took a swallow of her drink. She looked straight ahead. There was a muscular man in a tank top just coming out of the 7-Eleven, a six-pack dangling from his fingers. She turned her head to the right, away from the man and over at the shoe store which was closed.

"Don't start, Dan. Let's just go and have a good time."

He stared at the back of her head. He turned the ignition key and the engine caught. "Your mother says you never told a lie in your life."

She turned and looked at him and there was an expression in her face. "My mother's right. What's your mother say?"

When he backed away, he nearly hit the man with the six-pack who was getting into a rusted-out, blue pickup and had the door open. He saw him just in time.

"Damn hillbilly," he muttered. He burned rubber when he left the 7-Eleven parking lot and turned onto Veteran's Highway. He cut across four lanes to get to the turnoff and a car honked at him. He laid on his own horn, held it down. He could feel Brenda beside him, even though he didn't look.

Tim was there, a drink of his own in his hand in a cup just like theirs. He walked up, his smile widening as he made his way toward them, threading between the crowds of fair-goers entering the grounds.

"Hi, Brenda, Dan. Got your party shoes on?"

The drizzle let up, as soon as he said that, and a water-logged sun came out.

* * *

There were all sorts of people streaming through the gate. It seemed to be some kind of service entrance. High school bands in their uniforms, carrying their instruments, were on either side of them, and people in work clothes, their names stitched over the pockets, some carrying tools and other objects were coming through. They walked past the little white-washed building that was some sort of check point and were twenty yards into the compound when a blue-uniformed young man with a badge on his shirt came running after them.

"Hey! You! You can't come in here! This isn't the entrance. You got a pass?"

Brenda did an amazing thing. Daniel and Jim could only stand there, their mouths hanging open.

"Narcotics," she said. "We're Narcotics." As she spoke, she reached into her purse and brought out a badge. Daniel knew what it was. It was her Auxiliary Badge. Her father was a policeman, and she was in the Auxiliary. So were her mother and sister. And most of her cousins. The badge had no authority, except it helped out on speeding tickets, depending on the officer.

She flashed the badge quickly and just as quickly put it back in her bag.

"Narcotics?" The young police officer, a young man barely in his twenties, stopped in his tracks and pulled off his hat, scratching his head.

"Of course," Brenda said. "We're Narcotics. This is where they told us to come in at."

"Well..." The policeman seemed uncertain. "What are your names?" He ran to the guard shack and trotted back, clipboard in hand.

Daniel and Jim hadn't yet said a word. Daniel opened

his mouth as if he were going to say something to Brenda, but the officer was back before he could.

"I'm Detective Brenda Vacarro, and these men are Detectives Sam Spade and Charlie Chan."

The young officer read down the list on the clipboard. Something was not right; you could tell by the expression on his face, but it was plain he wasn't sure just what it was.

"You're not on here."

"Let me see that." It was Brenda. She snatched the clipboard away from the officer. Jim looked at Daniel and rolled his eyes slightly. Daniel smiled, just a bit, and then got a sober look, his lips pressed together.

Brenda handed the clipboard back to the policeman. "I don't know how this happened, Officer. Our captain was supposed to inform you people. Somebody messed up. I suppose we better phone him, but he isn't going to be happy about this. We're late as it is. We're supposed to hook up with the others over by the Australian exhibit."

The young man looked at the clipboard again, as if expecting their names to have magically appeared by now. He looked at Brenda, and then down at the clipboard again, and then said, "Well, they're supposed to call down here and give us your names. You're right. Somebody must have screwed up. I'll let you in this time, but from now on, make sure the watch captain calls in first."

Only Brenda and Jim thanked the young man. Daniel was already walking away, into the fairground.

They went right to the Australian exhibit. Everybody had been talking about it. It was the fun place at the fair, the wildest bar. There was a huge wooden statue of a kangaroo outside, that's how they found it. Everybody'd been talking about the statue, too.

Brenda and Jim had Australian beer. Daniel had a Jack and water. He said something about beer being something you drank at bowling alleys. His remark was ignored—the other two were still howling so hard they had tears. Daniel looked mad and didn't say anything as the other two went over what had transpired back at the gate.

"Brenda Vacarro!" Jim laughed so hard he choked. "And Sam Spade and Charlie Chan! I don't believe it! Which one of us is Charlie Chan?" He held his stomach.

"That would be Dan. Don't you think he's inscrutable?"

They both looked at him and burst out laughing again.

The only thing he said was, "You were smooth, Brenda. I'll give you that."

A couple of drinks later, he relaxed, and even called Jim "Sam" a time or two, and they went to four or five other bars. "We'll do a pub crawl," said Jim. Each exhibitor had a bar featuring national drinks and cuisine. They got a map and made it a contest, to see how many bars they could have a drink at.

Once, they passed by a little lagoon that had been set up to imitate a scene in *The African Queen*, with the actual boat that had been used in the movie, and they got to go on board. Brenda slipped on the gangplank and since Daniel was leading and Jim was bringing up the rear, Jim caught her, just under her arms, preventing her from going into the water. "You need to take a coordination pill," he said, and smiled, and Daniel said something about "blondes," but he looked at the two of them longer than he meant to. Soon after, they decided to call it a day, but to leave from the main entrance in case the same policeman was still on duty.

After waving goodbye to Jim, they walked down the street until they found their car. It wouldn't start. He'd left the lights on.

"I told you it was going to rain," he said, acidly.

"That's why you left the lights on?"

"Well, sure. If it hadn't rained, they wouldn't have been

on in the first place, now would they."

"Maybe so. Maybe I should have reminded you they were still on. Should I have? This is my fault, I take it."

Daniel didn't answer. He tried the key several move times with no response other than a clicking. It was really down.

"Guess I'll go find a gas station."

It cost twenty-five dollars to send a truck out and give the battery a jump. He made the truck stay until he was sure it had charged enough, and then at first, the man wouldn't take a check until Daniel said he'd put five extra on it for him. The man asked for a credit card and Daniel didn't tell him they only had the one and it was maxed out.

They didn't talk most of the way home, and he smoked six or seven cigarettes, not bothering to knock loose tobacco from the lighter. The only thing he said was, "Gave Jimbo a good feel, didja? Funny, I didn't think it was that slippery." Brenda stared out the window on her side and didn't answer him.

They were getting ready to go to bed and Brenda was in the bathroom, brushing her teeth. Daniel was already in bed, the TV on, a black and white movie. He couldn't pick up the thread of it, half-watching the picture and half-listening to the sound of his wife brushing her teeth.

"Thought you never told a lie," he shouted, above the TV and running water.

"What?" She stuck her head out of the doorway, toothbrush in her mouth.

"I said, I thought you never lied. Brenda Vacarro. This afternoon. At the fair."

"Oh," was all she said, disappearing back into the bathroom.

* * *

"What's the movie?" she asked when she came out.

"It's about this guy whose wife fucks around on him. I think I've seen it. I'm sure *you* have. I'm going out to the pool."

He got up and went out to the kitchen and fixed himself a drink. He used one of the same cups they'd taken with them that afternoon, rinsing it out with hot water first. He went back into the bedroom and grabbed his trousers which he'd left on the floor. Brenda didn't say anything to him and he didn't say anything either. He noticed she had changed the channel, was watching something about seals and polar bears. He went downstairs to the pool outside and sat in one of the lounge chairs. In a few minutes one of the girls that lived in the downstairs corner apartment came walking through the passageway from the parking lot, a tight black dress designed to show off cleavage hugging her curves, blonde hair piled high on top of her head, a few strands hanging down around her ears, high heels he bet were all of four inches.

"Just getting in, huh? Night on the town with your girlfriends, I bet. Me, I just got in from the World's Fair. You're in the end apartment, aren't you? I've seen you around."

She came over and sat in the chair beside him. He'd seen her sunbathing several times on the weekends, but had not spoken to her before. They talked for a little bit and he found out she did bookkeeping for an insurance company over on Veterans Highway, and then out of the corner of his eye he caught a movement upstairs at his own apartment window. It was Brenda, pulling aside the curtain and looking down. He smiled slightly and settled back in the lounge chair. The curtain closed.

"Why don't you go get yourself a drink and join me," he said to the girl.

"Could you bring me one too?" he said as she got up. "I'm getting low here. Anything would be fine, even beer."

He looked up at the closed curtain at his apartment window and hoisted his Mardi Gras cup, like he was presenting a toast. He was sure Brenda was watching. There was a little corner at the bottom of the curtain, looked to be pulled open. This time, he showed his teeth when he smiled, and for just a small part of a second he felt something funny inside, like something had pulled loose, but then he forgot it, concentrating on what he was going to say to the girl when she returned. Conversation was something he had to work at, to get it right. It took a lot of effort to appear casual. Especially when one was excited, the kind of tingle you got when you boarded a cruise ship. You knew where you were going, but you were anticipating something even better when you reached your destination.

First published in *Maize.*

He was already two steps away from the car by the time the door slammed shut and all the way up the walk he kept looking for her, expecting the front door to burst open. The nearer he got, the more he slowed down, until the last ten feet or so when he suddenly quickened his pace, reaching the steps in three long strides. He turned the knob and threw the door open. She wasn't there.

He found her in the kitchen, standing over the sink, the water running over something she held in her hands. Lettuce. His smile returned.

"Guess you didn't hear me come in, huh?" He slipped up behind her and put his arms around her waist, nuzzling her on the neck. She smelled damp and warm and something else. He couldn't figure out what it was. It was vaguely familiar. Someone else used to have that smell. Who was it? He couldn't remember.

She didn't exactly push him away, but she didn't turn and kiss him either. She kept turning the lettuce over and over in the running water.

"Have a good day?" Her tone was matter-of-fact, the same as a supermarket clerk's "Have a nice day."

He released her and took a step back. He looked at the back of her neck where his lips had been and thought he could see a little redness. He remembered how easily she bruised.

"Yeah. It was okay. First day back, you'd think it'd be rough, but it wasn't so bad. I got kidded. A lot!" He went over and sat down at the kitchen table, still watching her. She had yet to look directly at him.

"About what?"

He laughed. He could only see part of her face, but he thought her lips turned up a bit.

"You know.

"I do? No, I don't. Did you do something weird?"

He got up and sighed. "I think I'll take a bath. I'll be in the bathroom."

He was going out of the room when he heard her say something. It sounded like *You didn't call me*, but he wasn't sure. He slowed his step for a second and thought about asking her what she had said, but kept on going toward the bedroom instead.

He kept the door to the bedroom open while he ran the water. He would have liked the water a bit warmer, but when it felt comfortable, he turned off the hot side and let the cold run by itself for a minute before twisting it shut. Then, he changed his mind and ran the hot water for the same amount of time. He'd brush his teeth first. By then, the temperature would cool down.

His gums were tingling and bleeding a bit by the time he put away his toothbrush. The whole time he scrubbed, he kept glancing back into the bedroom, and once he thought he heard the floor creak but there was no sound after that, so it must have been his imagination.

Lowering himself into the bathtub gingerly, lest he slip and fall, he made a face as his buttocks touched the water. It had cooled off quite a bit. He put his hand on the hot water tap but then removed it and slid down deep into the water until all of his stomach was completely covered. He picked up the bar of soap in the receptacle and put it to his nose, sniffing it, and then put it back. Not yet. He'd wait a minute or so.

He heard something, a noise, and he sat up sucking in his stomach and flexing his pectorals, not enough to cause a cramp but enough to harden his chest.

She walked into the bathroom and for the first time looked at him, just briefly, and then at her own reflection in the mirror.

"What'd you say?"

"I didn't say anything."

"No. Out there. In the kitchen. Did you ask me something?"

"No."

"Oh, that. I just wondered why you didn't call me at lunchtime. It's no big deal. I was just wondering."

"Oh, honey, I was tied up in a meeting and didn't even *get* lunch. Well, I did...*later.* One of the girls brought me up something. An egg sandwich or something."

She didn't reply.

He splashed water up on his chest. His skin was tightening as it dried and the water felt good.

"Well, I'm sorry."

"About what?"

"Not calling you. First day apart and all that. That's what this is all about, isn't it? Not calling you?"

"I don't know what you mean. I just thought you would call. It doesn't matter. I hardly thought about it." She turned on both faucets in the sink and lowered her face, splashing water on it. She let the water run until she had reached for a towel and dried herself and then she turned the faucets, one in each hand, hard.

Then she surprised him. She stepped over to the toilet, beside the tub, wiggled her blue jeans and panties down and sat down.

"You're going to the bathroom?"

"Girls do that, you know. This *is* the bathroom, isn't it?"

"Yes, but...you've never gone to the bathroom while I was in the room!"

"I just never had to before when you were in here, maybe. Does it bother you?" The sound of her urine streaming into the bowl made him flinch. He watched her face which wasn't *mean*, exactly, more...*set*, than anything.

"No. A little. You just never did it before."

"Well, don't let it bother you. I imagine you'll find out a lot of other things about me you don't know. Same with me. Like today. Like you not calling me. I just thought you would." She plucked a sheet of toilet paper and wiped herself. "I guess we're married for real now."

She rose and pulled her garments back up and buttoned and zipped her jeans. She pulled the lever and flushed the toilet, and then leaned over the tub and trailed her fingers through the water. "It's too warm," she said. He recoiled as the skin of the water's surface broke, sending ripples around his naked body and realized what he'd done, but it was too late. He made his voice conciliatory.

"Are you coming in?"

"What for?"

"Well...because you always do. Least you have been."

"Have been? Oh...you mean the last two weeks. That was in the Catskills." She looked at him.

"It was before, too. When we were dating."

"Well, that was then and this is now. We're married, now, remember?" She left the room.

He waited another minute or so and then reached for the hot water spigot and turned it on. When his skin began to redden, he shut it off, reached for the soap, and lathered himself from neck to toe. He sank back down into the water, rinsing, and at that precise moment, she walked back in.

"You already soaped."

"Yeah. Oh…I'm sorry."

"S'all right. Water looks pretty hot. Hot and dirty." She turned and left again.

Ten minutes later, dried off and dressed in shorts and a T-shirt, he went out to the living room. The table was set, but there were no candles and she was already half finished with her salad.

They didn't say much, except, *pass this*; *may I have this, please*; *this is good*, and then, by unspoken mutual agreement, they carried the dishes into the kitchen and stacked them and retired to the bedroom.

This night he kept on his underwear. It felt strange wearing underwear after two weeks without any at night. She undressed and put on a nightgown he hadn't seen before. It was brown and hung to her ankles. He lay in bed on his back while she got herself ready for bed, staring at the ceiling, but he could see her out of the corner of his eye.

"Good night," she said, getting into bed and turning over on her side. She turned off the nightstand lamp.

"'Night." He stared at the darkened ceiling.

Long, silent minutes passed and then he felt the bed move and heard it squeak. He didn't turn his head to see what she was doing, but rolled his eyes as bed he could. She got up and walked to the bathroom and turned on the light. He couldn't tell what she was doing at first, and then he heard the shower go on. A shadow blocked out the light from the bathroom.

"I'm going to take a shower, Dave. Will you join me?"

For some reason, illogically, the memory of her smell earlier came back to him, and with it, an older memory. He recalled where he had smelled it before. It was a coppery kind of smell. He didn't know what zinc smelled like, but that's what he thought of whenever he smelled it. He hadn't smelled it since he'd been a boy. It was his mother that had smelled like that sometimes, always when he'd go into her room and she'd been laying on her bed, yellow tissues all around her. A coppery, zinc-y, damp, salty kind of smell.

He got up.

"We've never taken a shower together."

They were standing face to face and she was nude. For the first time that evening, she smiled at him.

"I know," she said.

She leaned over and pushed in the cigarette lighter at the same time that he turned the ignition key. He turned to his right to check behind him before he backed up, his eyes meeting hers briefly as he turned. She looked away, quickly.

Out on Coldwater Road, they were almost hit by a car that came from out of nowhere. The car swerved around them, honking its horn. Remembering what the counselor had said, brief moments before, he just turned the radio up louder.

"That's good, Jake," she said, plucking the lighter out and sticking her cigarette into the little stainless steel depression. "You're a good little student." She blew out smoke in a little snort.

"Well, *one* of us is trying," he said. From the corner of his eye, he saw her turn her head to stare out her window, her cigarette held aloft in two fingers like it was a dart she was about to throw.

At the first stoplight, he said, keeping his face straight ahead. "What was that thing about blue jeans? Why can't you just say what you mean, instead of...whatever that is you do. You know what you do." He felt, rather than saw, her smile.

"You don't get it, do you, Jake. You don't, do you? Go in the closet, check it out. You don't have one single pair.

In eight years, I've never seen you in one single pair. Doesn't that say something to you? You want me to be plain? *That's* plain, buster. How much plainer could it be? That's Norman Rockwell plain."

When she got out, she said, "I don't think this is working, Jake. You can go back, next week if you want. I have to think about it."

Instead of going to work, he went to the Ayres Department Store.

He said, "Yes, you can help me. I'm looking for a pair of blue jeans. Thirty-six waist, I don't know the length. That's dumb, isn't it? I mean, the length hasn't changed, not since I was eighteen, nineteen years old, probably, but I don't remember what it is, whereas the waist...well, I can guarantee the waist has changed! That, though, I remember."

When he wrote the check and watched as she took information from his driver's license, he said, "I can't believe how much these cost. These used to be cheap. What happened?"

On the way home, he passed the Blue Moon Bar and stopped off for a beer. It was too late to salvage any of the work day and he didn't feel quite like going home just yet. He made a point of sitting next to the brunette who was already at the bar when he went in. Any other time, he'd of sat at least three stools away, but not today.

"I just bought my first pair of blue jeans in years a while ago. Man, why didn't someone tell me!" he said, and waited for her reaction. Her reaction was, she got up and moved down to the other end of the bar.

* * *

Later that afternoon, when he got back home, she wasn't there. There was a note, scribbled with red crayon on the back of the monthly phone company envelop. He lifted it and smelled it. They were those crayons that smelled when you used them. Somebody, Julie, he thought she'd said, had them at work. Weren't they cute, she'd said. The envelop hadn't been opened yet, so he didn't throw it in the trash.

I ran out with Katina and some others, it said. *I just need to talk to someone before I go nuts. There's a Mexican dinner in the fridge. I'm sorry if I was a bitch, I don't seem to be able to help myself.* It was signed "Love, M."

Just her initial, not her full name. And, what did she mean, signing it "Love?" Nothing, he decided, after thinking about it for a full minute. It could have been a rubber stamp, just something a person does automatically, or because they've been doing it that way so long they don't know any other way. Maybe, it was like leaving the door open a little way, or maybe just unlocked.

He went into the bedroom and tossed the shopping bag with his new pair of blue jeans on it and sat down and removed his shoes. When he got his trousers off, he threw them over the exercise machine that stood against the wall and put on the jeans. Walking over to the closet, he opened it and looked at himself in the full-length mirror glued to the inside of the door. She'd said, about a year before: What I need is a mirror here. A mirror here would sure be handy. Well, she was right, turned out. This mirror was in the right spot, all right. She knew what she was talking about.

He didn't know what to think, what he was expecting to see. He felt the same as he had before he'd put them on. Was he supposed to feel different, have some sort of change come over him? He twisted his body and looked at his rear end, first from one side and then the other. That looked okay. So, now what? Was he exciting all of a sudden? Unpredictable? Transformed, like the Man of Steel? He didn't think so, but maybe he needed an outside opinion. He felt confused, as if the rest of the world was on a different time than he was, maybe operating at a tenth of a second ahead of him; like he was behind glass, watching.

When it got to be midnight, he got off of the couch and went over and switched off the television. In the bedroom, he took the blue jeans off, and carefully folded them. He looked in the ashtray on top of the dresser and collected all the little tags and stuck them in the pockets and put the jeans back in the store bag.

Tomorrow, he'd return them. Maybe he'd get a pair of those gabardines he liked so much. Jeans cut off the circulation, he'd found.

Before he climbed into bed, he looked to see where she'd put the remote control and found it on top of the dresser. He took the pillows from her side and added them to his own two and got into bed, only he kept smelling something, finally figuring out it was her fragrance, her perfume on the pillows and he reversed their order, putting his on top and it was better.

It felt sort of funny, watching television in bed. Only vegetable-heads watch TV in bed, she'd said when they first got married, and so, of course, they never did it, that becoming one of those marriage rules.

It felt funny, but good. All-Nite Movies, said the promo on the third station he clicked, and then the title of the one coming up. It was one he'd seen years ago, starred Charles Bronson. He remembered how much he liked it.

He wondered what was on afterwards and decided against going back out to the front room to check the *TV Guide*. Maybe it was a Bronson Festival if he was lucky.

That'd be great. He didn't feel the slightest bit sleepy. In fact, the way it was, the way he felt, he could probably stay up for days and days, just lay here in this bed and watch movies, one right after the next, watch the goddamn sun come up in the morning, wouldn't that be something?

He got excited, just thinking about it. The thought of being awake when the sun came up made him feel young, more alive somehow. Maybe he'd hang onto those jeans after all. Maybe all it took was to wear them for a few days, get used to the feel.

At one o'clock, the phone rang but he ignored it, and after a while, it quit, and at five a.m. he glanced over at the clock and figured he had probably another half-hour before the sun came up.

Maybe he'd grow a beard, starting right now. Blue jeans and a beard. Now, that would be something.

He had a life other than football—he went to classes, went out on dates, worked on the Indiana Toll Road in the summer, replacing broken windows in toll booths, had a declared major in General Studies, which meant he hadn't really declared at all,—things like that. If someone asked him, which they often did because of his size, he told them he was a football player. That was the way he identified himself, even in the summer when the season was over.

Football season had ended, so he worked part-time in a liquor store near the campus. The owner liked to hire football players for two reasons. One he was a fan, and two, he liked football players behind the cash register because of their size.

His size hadn't discouraged the man standing in front of him who had a handgun pointed at Big Red's solar plexus. He hadn't introduced himself to this robber, a small black man, but the gunman knew his name.

"Give me everything in the register, Red," he said, from behind his gun. "Or else."

Red didn't ask what "or else" meant. He gave over the money, the bills, stuffing them into a paper sack the way the armed man told him to. Luck, for the owner; he'd just cleared the drawer of everything but eighty dollars for change, putting the rest in the floor safe. He did this every hour, more often when it was busier. It was part of the job description.

The gunman was weaving, drunk, no doubt. He dropped the money, most of it, and waved his weapon at Red, saying, "Git out here and pick it up, Red."

While he was picking up the bills, the thief said, "I oughta shoot you. You seen me."

That kind of talk made Red nervous. He tried to reason with the man.

"Oh, nosir," he said. "I didn't look at you very good." He made up his mind not to look the man in the eyes any more. He would look at the man's ear when he spoke from now on.

"Yeah." The robber grunted. "Maybe. Git me some booze. Git me a turkey."

Big Red didn't know what he meant at first, which panicked him since communication was so important in this interchange, and then it dawned on him the man wanted a bottle of Wild Turkey.

"Git me two," the man said. "It's on sale." And he laughed. Red tried to, but all he could manage was a clue of a grin. He grabbed another bottle of Turkey from the shelf and handed it to the robber who was weaving more now and trying to hold onto both the gun and the two bags. He dropped the money bag again.

Briefly, he considered rushing the man, knocking the gun out of his hand. Tackle him, leg-whip him. It'd be easy, he thought. The guy was a little bitty guy, not even half his size. Drunk, too, probably slower than hell.

He didn't though.

The man dropped one of the bottles and when he bent to pick it up, he tipped the money bag and the bills spilled out again.

"Pick it up, Big Boy," he said, and Red came around the

counter and did as he'd ordered.

"I oughta kill ya," he repeated, and Red said, his voice breaking, "Nosir. Please, sir. I don't know what you look like. I won't tell you've even been here. Please don't hurt me, sir."

The man dropped either the money or the liquor at least twice more, each time making Red pick it up, and he kept saying, "You seen me. I oughta shoot ya," and Red couldn't fight it anymore, the tears beginning to roll down his cheeks. "Please," he said. It's all he could think of to say.

The man stared at him; the All-Big Ten defensive end, nominee for the Outland Trophy, possessor of sixty-six tackles in the season just ended, twenty-one solos, team MVP, and he just shook his head.

"I usta yell for you," he said. "I was at the Purdue game. Put the QB out, broke his collar bone, you did. Ran the ball back for a touchdown. You was great, man. Lookit you. You got snot all over your face. You a mess."

He stepped closer to Red and brought the gun up, aiming it at the bridge of Red's nose. "You just a punk. You act tough, but you ain't. You nothin but a baby."

Red brought both his hands up, covering his eyes. It was all he could do to stay on his feet, his knees trembling.

"Look at you," the man said, laughing. "You pissin' your pants!"

It was true.

"Git in the bathroom," the man said. "Git in the bathroom and sit on the stool for ten minutes. Come out—bang, bang."

Red heard him out in the store, heard him drop the booze again. He stayed in the bathroom for more than a half hour, long after he heard the front door bell tinkle. When he did come out, he peeked around the door and listened for more than five minutes.

He locked the front door and walked to the office in back, for the phone. He picked it up and started to dial, then hesitated, held the receiver out and away from him for a minute, and then replaced it on the cradle. He left the office and went to the front and turned off all the lights except the night light. He went to the door and flipped the Open/Closed sign around, unlocked the door, went out, then locked it and took the key off his keychain and pushed it through the mail slot.

He played a game of pool in the game room with a guy named Danny who was in a couple of his classes who kept asking him who he was going pro with and things like that he didn't feel like talking about, so he laid down his cue and went on up to his room. Somebody yelled from downstairs that his boss from the liquor store was on the phone and he yelled back to tell the cocksucker he quit and the guy downstairs yelled back up to tell him himself, what was he, his goddamned messenger; he was hanging up.

Red went over to his bed and laid down, clothes on and all, and started to read an old *Sports Illustrated*, and then he fell asleep and slept so soundly he woke up late and missed his first class.

He threw a book at the window, breaking it, and that made him even madder, so he kicked his desk and the leg broke.

He started thinking about his old dog at home, Pork Chop, and he got to missing him so much, he decided to call home, and worse luck, his dad was there instead of his mom, and sure enough, he said,

"Hell no, you can't come home! And do what? Lay around here all day and drink beer? You've got the draft coming up, don't fuck up now. Dallas, alla them guys gonna be there. Get your ass to class and don't be running up any more of these long-distance bills!"

He missed his next class and the one after that, just sitting in his room, and decided to make the last one, Kiddie Lit, an easy course he should have taken freshman year but put off, but the prof pulled a surprise quiz and he flunked it, didn't know any of the answers, and then he felt so low he walked clear to the other side of town, to a townie bar where he wouldn't run into any other students.

He drank so many shots of tequila he threw up, outside in the parking lot. The next day, Saturday, he laid around in bed all day, and then it was Sunday and his head felt much better and he stayed in all that day, reading the sports pages and snoozing. Monday, he felt clearer and decided to go to his first class. A girl he had wanted to ask out came up to him after the lecture and started talking to him, asking questions about the upcoming draft and he said, "Oakland," and told her why, their defensive scheme was suited for someone of his build and abilities, and one thing led to another and they ended up back in his dorm room, naked. Only he couldn't get it up.

After a while she left. She was nice about it, even wrote down her name on a piece of paper and her room number over in Ballantine Hall.

His father would have been proud of him if he could have seen him that night. He had his sociology book open and a yellow highlighter out and no music on, not even the radio.

But the words just kept swimming by his eyes and he couldn't focus. The words might as well have been hieroglyphics. Downstairs, somebody yelled up that his weight coach was on the line and wanted to know why he wasn't over lifting, was he sick or something?

He grabbed his letter jacket, went downstairs, and walked past the kid holding the phone. He went out to the parking lot, climbed in his car and cranked over the engine. When he got to the same townie bar he'd visited the night before, he walked in and looked for the biggest guy he could find and saw a guy who had to go six-three, maybe six-four standing at the far end of the bar. He doubled up his fists and began the long walk toward him.

First published in *Blue Moon Literary and Art Review Magazine*, Spring/Summer Issue, 2010.

Plainly, the man had never visited a hairstyling salon before. It was evident from the way he approached the reception desk, eyes darting around the room, picking his way gingerly as if afraid of making noise on the tiled floor or creating a disturbance, avoiding any of the other waiting patrons' gazes. He cleared his throat and gave his name to the beauty queen behind the desk, a long-maned, scrunch-styled, purple-eyeshadowed young lady, who talked between bursts of chomps on her chewing gum.

"Have a seat over there," she said, waving in the vague direction of a row of minimalist furniture that looked like chairs. He picked one apart from the others.

"Coffee?" spoke the charm school graduate from behind the desk. He declined in too loud a voice. His cheeks pinked at his error, and a youngster in another waiting chair giggled and whispered something to the lady beside him. The man reached over to a pile of magazines on the table before him, selected an Elle and opened it. For minutes, he sat there, staring at the picture of a woman in a white bra and panties, without turning the page.

"First time at the Chez, I'm right?"

He nodded, sharply, up and down, the way a five-year-old would, first day of school. He was seated before a mirror edged in gold foil, and in the mirror he could see himself and a young man whose name he had learned was Charles.

"Yes."

The stylist nodded sagely. He was adorned in parachute pants and a silver shirt, made of some kind of shiny material. The pants were black and baggy, and he had three gold chains of varying thicknesses and lengths around his neck. A tiny gold earring set off the ensemble.

His hair was black and curly and hung past his shoulders.

"Well, if you'll just put yourself in my hands, I think I can give you what you need." He began combing the man's hair with a gray comb, curved at the end, first one way and then the other, glancing back and forth from the man's head to the mirror, and making little clicking and sucking noises with his tongue as he combed.

"I'm not criticizing, but this hair is a mess. It needs layering badly." He stopped combing and looked into the mirror, his eyes hypnotically locking with the man's eyes in what could only be described as an earnest look. "Who did this?"

At first, the man didn't know what the stylist was talking about, and then it came on him what the question was about, and again, his cheeks flamed red. "Jim cuts it."

"Jim?"

"Yes. Jim at Jim's Barber Shop."

"I see. Jim." There was a silence of several seconds, during which the man managed to break off eye contact with Charles.

"Just do whatever you want. That's what my wife said. 'Just have them cut it the way they think it should be cut.' That's what she said."

"And right she is. We're not *good* here—we're the

best!" He laughed. "I'll have Inez prep you. Inez! Yo!"

He turned and crooked a finger at a young black girl who came up, almost at a run. "Inez, this is Mr. Brown. Get him ready for me and use the conditioner in the green bottle. And…" he paused and Mr. Brown saw the stylist's eyebrows raise in a way he had never seen done before,"…shampoo him at least twice."

Ten minutes later, he was back before the mirror, waiting for Charles to take a last drag on a cigarette he was holding in his index finger and thumb and stub it out.

He began combing and cutting, sectioning off hair and placing clips in the hair to separate the sections. He worked quickly and in a confident manner. Hair fell steadily onto the floor. He talked as he snipped.

"I can't *believe* this haircut! This Jim a friend of yours?"

The man said nothing, only stared at the edge of the mirror.

"Well, this is your lucky day, getting me. We're all good here." He leaned forward and lowered his voice. "But I'm the best." He straightened back up and stepped back, eyeing his handiwork with a critical eye.

"Don't worry, this is going to look great. Say, is something special coming up for you to desert old Jim and come see me?" He snorted, not noticing that Mr. Brown nodded his head, just the slightest bit.

"Well, if this isn't for some special occasion, it's a shame. You'll have to do something tonight after I get done. Take the wife out for dinner or drinks or something." He winked at the mirror.

"It's a special occasion," said Mr. Brown, his voice husky and strained, but Charles didn't notice the tension with which he spoke.

"Man! This is really chewed up!" Charles shook his head, great sorrow in his eyes. He combed the hair again, and once more strands began to fall to the floor.

"The reason we're so good here, is that we go to millions of shows. Hair shows, you know. Just this week we have to go to a show." He sounded irritated. "It's gonna cost me four hundred bucks, time I'm done.

"I'm giving you a professional look. A businessman's cut. All you'll have to do is blow dry it for about five minutes after you shampoo each morning. Easy as falling off a log.

"I'll show you how. You do own a blow dryer, don't you?"

Mr. Brown didn't say anything, but it didn't matter. Charles just went on talking and cutting.

"If you don't, get one from Debbie at the desk. We've got a sale on right now. Twenty percent off. You've got to have one.

"A good shampoo and conditioner, too. Don't put crap on your hair. I could feel a waxy buildup before you got shampooed. It's the junk you're using. Throw it in the trash and get your shampoo from us.

"The reason I was late for you was that Madeline was late again. Fifteen minutes! I shouldn't even do the bitch. She's a good tipper, that's the only reason. I tolerate her. People don't understand appointments. They think if they have a ten o'clock appointment, it means they should get their hair cut precisely at ten o'clock. Assholes! S'cuse me, but that's just the way I feel about it. Some people have no concept of time or respect for the other person's time. In Europe, if you have a ten o'clock appointment, you might not get in the chair till noon. That's the way it should be here. All a ten o'clock appointment means is that you're next in line, reasonably close to ten o'clock. People here have no concept of what appointments are designed for. Americans!

"I went to Europe last year. London. For two weeks. I saw some hair, I can tell you! That's why I'm so good. I go to shows and I go to Europe. I'm going this year, too. Next month. Italy. Milan, I think. Is there a town named Milan?

"My friend thinks I'm going to take her with me when I go. Can you imagine? She's crazy if she thinks I'm taking her to Italy. Not with all the babes over there! Man!

"I'll break up with her if I have to. Take her to Italy!"

He stopped for a breath and laid down his comb and scissors on a little table on wheels behind him.

"I'm done cutting. You can see the shape already. It's gonna look good, isn't it? Just wait.

"Say, how is it you came here to the Chez? Got something important coming up? I mean, there must be a reason for you to desert old Jim and come see Charles! Anniversary or something, right?"

"Something," Mr. Brown said, just audibly.

"Right. Gotcha. Well, partner, you're gonna love this. When I get done blowing this out, you're gonna wanna leave the old lady and kids and go find some sweet young thing! Hey! Maybe I'll introduce you to Vicky. Get her off my back! Ha, ha!"

Mr. Brown stiffened and started to rise from the chair, but stopped and settled back down into it. Charles didn't take note of this, nor did he see the look in the man's eyes. He just went on talking. He had a huge silver dryer in one hand and a black brush in the other and he raised his voice to above the sound of the dryer. His movements with the brush were quick and deft.

"Just kidding, pal. You look like one'a them happily married types. I admire you, but me? No way! Live with one woman ten years? No way, José! What's that they say? 'So little time; so many women?' Ha, ha.

"Betcha you're surprised, me picking you out as the

happily married kind. It's a gift I got. I think it's called empathy or somethin'. Yeah, empathy. I got it in buckets. I can tell what a guy does ten seconds after I seen him. You, my guess is, work in a factory. Make ding dongs or tires or somethin'. Am I right? I thought so. You're an easy one, but know what? Women are even easier. I can just look at a woman and tell you if they want to get laid. Like any of 'em don't.

"Well, this is it. What was your name again? Black? No, wait...Brown. That's it, right? Sorry about that! I get so many people in here it's hard to remember names. Takes me two times, then I never forget. I'm taking this course to remember names. They say to associate something unusual with the person's name and you'll always remember it. I just need to come up with an image for your name and I've got it. I'll never forget it then. I better not! I paid three hundred bucks for this damn course! I know—I'll think of bowling when I think of your name. Get it? Factory worker, bowling league, B for bowling and B for Brown. Wow! This shit really works!

"There. How's that? Do you like it like this—look in the little mirror until you see yourself in the big one. Yeah, that's it.

"Well? I didn't lie, did I? You never spent fifty bucks more wisely, Mr. Brown. There! See? I got it—I got your name. Nailed it.

"Say, thanks for coming in, Mr. Brown. You pay at the desk. You can leave the tip in your check and they'll see I get it.

"Say, you never did say what your special occasion was. Was I right? Your anniversary? Twenty-fifth or somethin' Or," he started laughing, "don't tell me it's your league's bowling banquet! I'll crap if you say that's it!"

For the first time since he had first sat in the young

man's chair, Mr. Brown looked straight at the stylist. His shoulders were squared back and his eyes were hard and when he spoke there was no quaver in the sound, only strength, and beneath it, barely controlled anger.

"It's a special occasion. It's a funeral. Tomorrow. My wife's. She always wanted me to come here when she was alive. I never did until now. It's in her honor." He turned and walked away.

At the desk, he counted out fifty dollars in various denominations, a twenty, a ten, two fives, and ten dollars in ones, and handed it across to Debbie, the receptionist.

"Did you want to leave Charles a tip, sir?" she asked.

"No," he said. He turned and walked toward the exit, but before he reached it, he had run his hands through his hair.

It looked closer to the way it had when he had walked in.

MY FATHER AND ROBERT FROST

One day I found a volume of poetry by Robert Frost in the prison library at Pendleton and checked it out.

Back in my cell, I read: *Home is the place where, when you want to go there, they have to take you in.*

When I made parole, I called my mom to tell her my good news. I found out that my dad had never read Robert Frost.

At least not that poem.

First published in *Blue Moon Literary and Art Review Magazine,* Spring/Summer Issue, 2010.

"I was bumrapped you know."

We were sitting on the balcony of the Seaport Cafe on Bourbon Street in the French Quarter in New Orleans, two hours after we'd driven across the Lake Ponchartrain causeway. Knocking back Pearl beers and shots of Jack and watching the tourists down below. It was two days before Christmas, four days into our trip South.

Bud was drunk. I'm a sipper but Bud likes to slam 'em down like it's ten minutes to closing, even if it's high noon.

I'd heard this story a thousand times. Every day in the joint. Every time something would get him down, some hack give him some shit, Bud would trot out his sadsack bumrap tale. Thing was, I knew he was telling the truth.

"I'm fucking this babe," he says and I can finish the story, word for word, I've heard it so much, but I keep quiet and watch the tourists and make like I'm listening. There was a guy in a Santa Claus outfit staggering up the street, a go-cup in his white mitten. It felt about eighty degrees out, so I figured in that outfit it must be near a hundred. Santa must have got into the *good* egg nog, way he was stumbling around.

"I'm fucking this babe, what?—about three-four months, maybe longer. I'm eighteen she says; that's what she told me a hundred times. I figure she's lying, her boobs were still growing an inch a day I swear! But I go along with the program. She *acts* eighteen. Hell, in bed, she acts *thirty-eight*. One night, we're done burying the kielbasa for a while, we're up in my crib and we must've dozed off watching the boob tube. Next thing I know, the door's busting down and this little bitty guy, couldn't been nobody else but her old man—same hook nose—comes flying in bustin' the door down and starts popping me with this little toy gun. A twenty-two. Fucking shorts. Not even long rifles, pukey-ass shorts. Can you believe that? You believe a guy tries to shoot a guy my size—hell, *any* size—with twenty-two shorts? Fucker's nuts."

The waiter came by and Bud reached out and grabbed his arm.

"Do it," he said, pointing to our glasses.

The Santa was almost to our block now. I noticed he kept going up to the doors of the strip joints and peeking in. Maybe he was looking for Missus Santa.

"It turns out she's *fourteen*, for crissakes! I knew she wasn't eighteen but I'd've guessed seventeen, maybe the back end of sixteen. But *fourteen?* That freaked me out. Freaked her out too, way her old man came in like J. Edgar Hoover. Scared her, she started screaming I'd raped her. Came up with this story about how I'd held a knife on her, picked her up at the bus station. She had quite an imagination, I'll give her that. In some ways, I don't blame her. Her father was little, but *scary*, even with that little pissy-ass cap gun. She'd already told me some stuff about him, how he usta nail her when she was sleeping, whale the crap out of her and then make her gobble his knob. I nailed 'im, gave him a shot broke his jaw, but somebody, nosy neighbor probly, had already called the cops."

He did his shooter and took a big draw on his beer.

"Yeah, I don't really blame her for what she did. I blame the jury. And the judge. They shoulda seen what was going on, just some little chippy got caught by her daddy and was trying to get out of a mess. She was hard, son," he said, looking at me to see if I was believing him.

I was and what I was thinking was about all them myths about guys in the joint. Ever time you see a movie about the penitentiary or read a book, there's this thing they got to put in, this bullshit that says everybody doing hard time claims he's innocent. That's pure horseshit. I knew maybe two thousand guys, time I spent in Pendleton and Bud's the *only* one I ever knew said he was innocent. Everybody I ever met in there was *proud* of being an outlaw even if they weren't.

I figured out where that crap come from. Even though nobody claims to be bumrapped—least to other guys inside—you *always* claim you were wrongfully convicted when you talk to straights. I bet Charlie Manson does the same thing. You talk to counselors, the parole board, *anybody* but another con, you tell them the system made a big mistake, your case.

So, what happens I figure is the guys that make these movies, they go interview cons for "background" and of course, the guy they talk to says, "Hey, I shouldn't be in here. I'm innocent, man. Was some guy looked like me, my fucking evil twin maybe." 'Cause the thought is that somebody who has power will believe them and set them free.

Pardons. There's lots of pardons the public don't know about. The governor gives out a couple three-four dozen a year. Big sentences, like the ten and a quarters you get for rape, for residence burglary, they all get cut loose with a pardon from the governor. Six-to-eight, six years, eight months Indiana says you got to serve on a ten and a quarter and then you're eligible for a pardon. Eighty percent get it first time. You think a guy whose only shot at freedom is a pardon is going to tell somebody, "Yeah, I did it." Yeah, sure. They feed you all this stuff that all they want to see is evidence of remorse but that's a bunch of bull. Admit you're guilty, you can kiss that pardon goodbye. Long as you get them to thinking there's even a slight doubt of your innocence you got a shot the governor's gonna sign that paper.

People don't even know this goes on. They think a pardon is only doled out to a couple murderers every hundred years or so. That's the ones make the news. More often as not, there's a big deal in the papers about some guy who's whacked his wife for sharing her love peach but has truly repented for his one slip and wants to rejoin society as he's a changed man. The newspapers put it out that the governor's really agonizing over it but at the last minute decides he can't, in good conscience, let this poor soul go loose in proper society as he has to pay the full penalty for the terrible thing he's done. This gets a lot of votes; the straights think, hey, this is one tough hombre we got heading up this state. If they knew he probably just signed a dozen and a half pardon orders to ten and a quarters the day before they'd shit purple bricks but that shit never gets in the paper.

There's lots of misconceptions like that. Makes me mad. I give up going to movies about prisons. I haven't seen one yet that come close to the truth.

That's why I believed Bud when he said he was bumrapped. He even said that to all us other cons which is why I believe him. Even those guys who truly were innocent—and there's some in the joint that are, I know—even those guys would never claim a bumrap to another con. Another con thinks you're not a lifelong hard case he's gonna be all over your ass.

"Yeah, Bud," I said. "I believe you, man."

"Fucking judge," he went on. "Most I shoulda got was

statutory rape, give me a one to ten. Asshole judge goes on about how I deflowered this poor little mutt, probly ruined her entire life—shit, she was turning tricks when I met her and rolling half her tricks in a New York second—says the only thing his conscience will let him do is sentence me for first degree, which is the big one."

That's why Bud wasn't on parole. He got one of them pardons after his six-eight the governor gives out like Halloween candy. Cost him five grand, his mom paid and we both know where half of that went, the half the lawyer didn't stick in his own Swiss account. Anybody ever wonders why some sumbitch would spend a million dollars to get elected to a job that pays forty-two G's a year should spend some time in the joint and the math would clear up fast.

Bud was chuckling but it wasn't a laugh of joy. "Little bitch, she's slick. Comes into court wearing this little gingham number with lace on the sleeves and her hair done up in one of them Shirley Temple perms. She had on fucking patent leather shoes. Christ, she looked twelve! I'd been on the jury *I'da* voted to convict. That's what fried my ass."

He went on and on some more but I was shutting him out now. I'd heard the story too many times. Besides, that Santa down below us was fun to watch. He was drunk as a Holstein got in the silage, staggering all over the place, his drink sloshing out of his go-cup making parts of his suit darker like blood. The sky was the same gray as the sidewalks now and it was cooling off fast. Santa lurched over to a group of tourists, two couples and a little girl belonged to one of them and reached over and patted one of the women on the ass. I woulda liked to pat her myself. She had on those things used to be called hot pants and she looked hot all right. She let out a little yell we heard clear up where we were and her husband or boyfriend or whatever clipped Santa, got him right on the button and down he went, his drink spraying every man Jack in the party. There's yelling and screaming and then this cop comes running up. He was in plainclothes like they mostly are in the Quarter and he puts his foot on Santa to keep him there and starts talking to the man. Pretty soon—he musta called someone on his beeper—here come two squad cars and they loaded up the whole bunch and took off. Couple of the cops had to whap Santa in the ribs with their sticks first.

"Bet he's out picking sugar cane for the state tomorrow," Bud said and I grinned.

"Yeah," I said. "Kinda destroys your faith in Santy, doesn't it?"

He looked at me and we both said it at the same time, laughing.

"Not!"

Just then, two lookers walked out from under the balcony we were on, must have been eating inside and Bud gave out a whistle and they stopped and looked up.

They waited for us to make our way down to the street.

"Those're hookers, you know," I said to Bud. He just grinned.

One of them was a blonde, the kind does it at home in the kitchen sink, the other had a nose that had seen a fist at one time, had the kind of crook you can only get from being broken. Her eyes were striking, though, emerald-green which really stood out in contrast to her hair which was so black it had bluish tones to it.

"You're a real flirt, aren't you?" the one with the nose said.

"Fuck a buncha flirting," I said. "Flirting's like driving down cul-de-sacs. You waste a lot of gas and don't never get to where you're goin. Me, I like to hit the open road and get right to my destination. Run the red lights, all the stop signs if I hafta."

Turned out they were a couple of hookers like I'd thought. And yeah, we got down, had us some fun, copped us each a B.J. in a courtyard off St. Peter's. A couple of times while the ladies were going at it, tourists would pop in, see us and pop right back out. The last time that happened, the girl was with me just turned her head a little to eyeball the Nosy Parker and came up for air for just long enough to yell at this guy, "Fuck off, man. Can't you see I'm working here!"

It was that Santa. They must have cut him loose. Some shit, huh?

First published in the spring issue, 2009, *Flatmancrooked—First Spring.*

He jumped up, as did the boy on the other side of him and the boy on the other side of that boy. There was no one to his right. He was the last.

"Okay, two minutes, guys. We got this one if you don't fuck up. Keep it away from Number Forty-Two. Foster. Jerry, you get the ball on the in-bounds and dribble till they foul you. Let's go!"

He stuck his hand in the circle, but failed to make contact. "Team!" he said, or some such noise; it didn't matter as long as the coach noticed he said something.

He returned to his seat, taking care not to catch any-one's eye in the stands. He felt ashamed, as he did always.

"What's that guy doing in the huddle?" he imagined someone saying. "Coach hasn't put him in a game all year." He could feel the laughter.

Indeed, someone just behind him, two rows away may-be, let loose with a belly-ripper. He felt his ears grow hot.

"Let's go!" he yelled, looking straight ahead. His jaw muscles twitched and his stare was catatonic, not focused on anything, but seeing the floor as a blur.

Two minutes. In two minutes, win or lose, they would be back in the locker room, quiet or loud, depending on the outcome. Someone would turn the first shower on, pro-vided Coach Willis didn't make them sit down for a chewing out first, and he would have to make the decision he did after every game.

To take a shower.

Or not.

It was coach's orders: Everyone Takes a Shower, Whether You Played or Not. But he felt so horrible, standing in the steam next to bodies that were red and sweaty and bruised. And happy. They were happy whether they won or lost, most times.

He'd take his shower and try to be invisible. He didn't want to be noticed and have somebody say the obvious. Why are you in here? It had happened.

If he tried to sneak out without a shower and the coach caught him, it would be worse. The coach would be vitriolic. And loud.

He glanced at the clock. One-twenty-two in digital numbers. Eight-point lead.

Two by Jerry. And he was fouled.

Nothing but net.

Eleven-point lead.

He stood up and shook his fist like everyone else along the bench was doing. He sat back down as the other team inbounded the ball and started back up the court. It had been a long time since he had tried to get the coach's eye in a situation like this. Once, right after the season started, he had even gone down to him, scuttling on his knees, like a crab, so the other players on the bench could see, and had begged him to put him in the game. The coach had jumped up in the middle of his request and yelled something to the players on the floor and then sat back down. It was only then that he seemed to notice him.

"Siddown, Dorey," he said. "I'll let you know when I want you to go in."

His name was Corey.

Fifty-three seconds. Fans were leaving. The other team was trying to set up a shot, when Ted stole the ball away from one of their guards and raced up court. Jerry ran in tandem, the other players trailing. Back and forth the ball went, the last pass back to Ted who went up and put it in against the backboard.

Thirteen-point lead.

Forty-nine seconds.

He could feel how dry his uniform was. The player next to him had a wet jersey. So did the one next to him. And next to him. All of them had wet jerseys. It made the color different, redder. His was the only pale red jersey on the bench. It always was.

He had no hope for a letter now. He had not played in a single game all season. The only way he could get enough minutes for a letter now would be for the coach to start him and play him the whole last game.

He wondered for the nth time why he had stayed on the team. Because he liked the game. He loved practice, the feel of the ball against his palm, the way his lungs ached after a fast-break, the feeling of elation on the rare occasion of a snagged rebound, or the rarer event of making a lay-up. He even liked the way his body felt as he griped his way around the perimeter of the court, running laps. Like he belonged. Like he was involved in something male and secret. The pride in knowing that out of the entire school, only twelve boys could be on the basketball team.

Thirty seconds. Half a minute. Forever in a basketball game.

"Dorey!"

Seventy-seven to sixty-three. Fourteen-point lead. Thirty seconds to go. All in digital numbers. Like this: 77-63 00:30.

In a dream, Corey stood, facing the other end of the bench, and put his forefinger to his chest. Me?

"Yeah, you, Dorey. C'mere."

He trotted down to the coach. For a second, he considered correcting the coach about his name, but decided not to.

"Yes, Coach?"

"Get in there for Swan. Take Number Forty-Two out. We play them again next week in the sectional."

"Take him out?"

"Yeah, dummy. Hurt him. When he goes up for a rebound, loft him. You know how to do that, don't you?"

"Loft him?"

"Dammit, Dorey, loft him! Get under him when he goes up. Flip him when he comes down. Maybe he'll break something. Get your ass in there."

Loft him, he thought, turning from the coach and walking toward the scorer's table. Hurt him.

"Don't forget to report in," yelled the coach from behind him. "We don't want a goddamned technical!"

Report in, loft him. Number forty-two.

He walked up to the scorer's table, turned and faced the timekeeper, hesitated, and turned again and walked back the way he'd come. He didn't bow his head, but he didn't really take note of the fans yelling and hooting at him, nor at the coach who stood up, red-faced and screaming. Screaming six inches from his own face, what he was saying, he didn't note either.

Past the coach and into the green double doors and down the corridor and into the first room on the right. The locker room. Walking past the rows of benches and lockers, dropping his uniform; first his jersey, now dark red under the arms, and then the red satin pants, and then he had to sit on the end of the first bench and untie his shoes and remove his socks.

The shower felt good. It soothed his aching muscles.

First published in *Aethlon.*

THE DEATH OF TARPONS

Here in the marshes the water was shallow, at the most four or five fathoms deep, and on the average, about waist-high. Long, bleached fingers of sand, sparsely covered with tough, slender salt-grass lay maze-like, swelling here and there to a height of a foot or so and then gradually receding back into the water, providing a natural dike system that kept the movement of the sea to a more tranquil pitch than that of the booming surf further out. Fishing country, miniature, cigar-shaped islands and dozens of channels and tiny bays dotting the landscape as far as the eye could take in, until the beach proper and the waiting sea appeared. Far off, in the opposite direction, lay cypress swamps, and beyond that, north and east, pine forests, and beyond that, civilization.

Pencil-legged kingfishers, the geeks of the animal kingdom, and delicate sandpipers angled slowly and gracefully across the bays, secure in the calmness of the water where they searched for food. With each imperious and regal, halting step, majestically and methodically they worked the bottom, searching, cunning eyes alert for the sudden movement of tiny, steel-gray mullet or baby blue crabs, which they speared with swift, iron beaks.

Far overhead, seagulls floated like quotation marks over the whole scene, silent curlicues against the huge canvass of the firmament, silent, except when every now and then one would flash-drop with a kree-kree-kree and plummet into the lapping waters below, curved wings folded for aerodynamics, close to the breast, and emerge, bright sparks of sea showering, a silver flash of color in a curved, cruel, impersonal beak.

Sandfiddlers scuttled sideways in the sand, their one, ridiculously large claw poised nervously in readiness for the unexpected, danger or food, whatever presented itself, a bird of prey, or the larger, fiercer blue crab, or, more happily, a dead fish tossed aside by the waves. Everywhere in the marsh, life hunted the opportunity of death, steadily, relentlessly, matter-of-factly, as the white, formless, Texas sun mounted in the sky, forever chasing the star that kept just ahead of it on the other side of the planet.

An ancient, hump-backed tarpon cruised through the salt liquid of his world, his huge tail barely switching from side to side as he hunted, eyes piercing through the shadows for schools of fish. Incredibly strong, but slowed by his years, he was unable to catch the sleek, swift mullet of his youth, yet still able to overtake the slower sheepshead and red snapper, and it was on them mostly that he now fed.

Behind him, at a respectful distance, trailed a smaller version of himself, perhaps even one of his own progeny. The younger tarpon was an aberration. Tarpon are not normally social fish; they prefer to hunt and live in solitude, but this particular youngster had been sounded by an alligator when he had wandered too far up a coastal bayou and was so lacerated by the reptile's teeth, he was unable to hunt as he had before. By good fortune, he had come upon the old tarpon days before, just after the ancient warrior had had the good luck to destroy a small school of yellowfin tuna, and discovered that by hanging back just far enough, he could pick up morsels the elder fish had missed or not wanted. His prehistoric brain had just enough intelligence to tell him this was a good thing, and so he adapted, the last week, laying to, just off the old tarpon's stern, feeding on his leftovers and regaining his strength. From time to time, the old tarpon would wheel and make a run at him as he was aware of the upstart, but the older fish was too slow to catch the younger on a short run and then, he didn't seem so much to care that he was being shadowed and used. The younger tarpon was now almost fully recovered from his wounds, but still swam behind the other, enjoying the gift of ease a symbiotic relationship provided.

The old tarpon was close to death and he knew it in the way animals know these things, through a slowing in the blood and a calling from somewhere up ahead, but he wasn't yet ready to concede and roll over just yet.

A slightly-luminescent greenish mold covered his back and was spreading its way toward his belly and up toward his massive head. When it reached and finally covered his gills, he would suffocate, a slow, laborious death from which there was no escape, a victim of the mysterious slime that appeared now and then in these waters, one of the by-products of civilization and its attendant gift of pollution. Younger fish usually escaped it, the mold confining its spread to the older of the species, almost as if it were a judgment against them for having lived too long. Or, maybe it was a plague of mercy, ending an existence that had turned undignified.

All paths eventually converge at one point or junction, and the tarpon's path too, would meet with another's, his fate to be sealed therein and the golden circle of his life completed. As he slowly worked his way up and down the narrow bayous and frequent bays, he was minute by minute, mile by mile, drawing nearer to the point of convergence. Time and space were diminishing, like the two hands or a watch reaching toward each other until finally, they would be as one, for one full, impregnating second, embracing for one full tick of the clock, in mutual climax as it were. So the tarpon and his future would embrace. The other tarpon, there only to garner easy food, would be Greek chorus to colossal events, significant from a tarpon's point of view and also to the human animals who were a part of their destiny.

Far away, even now, a boat of singular significance, carrying two people, a boy and an old man, moved in the whiteness of the same Texas sun toward a bay not far from where the tarpon hunted and lazed in the warm salt water of a no-name bay off Bryan Beach.

The boat thumped and humped against the waves of the sea as its motor sang a ragged roar of song and the old man steered into the sea's furrows, strangely akin to what a farmer does across his landlocked fields, humming a tune with no words and older than his oldest forebear. The young boy sat in the bow, race-memory genes recognizing the song, and smiled a strange smile, a smile without mirth or warmth, feeling the sun and salt breeze move across his face like the soft caress of a large, invisible mother's hand.

It was a small boat to be traversing the waters there in the open sea just off the breakwater, but the old man at the throttle seemed to be confident of his ability to pilot their way and the young boy seemed to trust the old man.

Long, swelling waves plumped against the sides of the craft and curious gulls swerved far overhead as the boat knifed ahead on its unwavering course.

An impartial observer, even such as one of the seagulls circling far overhead, with unlimited access of observation into the contents of the boat, would have noticed almost nothing untoward about the dinghy. Fishing rods, pieces of tarp, tackle boxes, two fishermen, nets and a cooler hold-

ing probably soft drinks and maybe beer, and certainly a sandwich or two. Much was as with any other boat that had passed this way in the past half century or so, save one thing: something the boy held tightly in his hands. Should a curious gull pass close by and use his exceptional powers of sight, he would note the boy's arms to be purplish and bruised, and that would perhaps cause him to brake with wings flung wide, fighting to stop his downward flight, but what was in the boy's hands would no doubt force such an inquisitive seagull even closer, and such a bird would be able to see that what the lad held was black and gray and made apparently of cloth, and could be laced up, although it wasn't.

The seagull wouldn't know what the object was of course, but a human would, provided he were old enough, or learned enough in the study of antiques. What the boy was clutching so tightly was a pair of spats, and they were a present to him from the old man who steered the craft. He was the boy's grandfather. Just at the point where the seagull would be getting as close as possible to see, the boy would lay down the objects, stuffing them under the seat and pick up a piece of shrimp from the baitbox, and fling it to the winged observer, a reward for the inquisitive gull.

The old man would yell at the boy then, scolding him for drawing scavengers to the boat.

"Hey, Grandpa!" I had to shout to get his attention above the crash and hiss of the waves as they struck the bottom of our moving boat.

"Are we 'bout there?"

Grandpa put his tanned, wrinkled hand to his eyes to shade out the sun and looked far ahead and to his left. The seagull I had thrown a shrimp to banked and soared back into the sky, high, high, until it disappeared.

"Over there, Corey. Way over there where those islands are. Good tarpon country." I saw his smile. "Never caught a tarpon, didja? You wait."

I smiled myself and reached over and touched my fishing rod for luck. Grandpa turned and spat over the side.

I was amazed even to be here. After Dad had driven me back home, I had showered and gone straight to bed, I suppose in a state of shock. I hadn't let myself think about what had happened; I couldn't. It hurt too bad. It was more hurt than I was capable of handling just yet. It wasn't the beating so much—he'd whipped me before; no, it was the emotionless, cold way he'd gone about it, like it was a piece of work to be done, dispassionately. Something new was added, something dangerous. I could feel it inside me, a black chunk of anger, and sorrow, and fear, and I kept it there by refusing to think about it. Sooner or later, I would have to deal with it, but this wasn't the time. Something had slipped a cog, inside, and I couldn't face what everything meant. Soon.

It was dark in my room and dark outside and Grandpa was shaking me awake. "Come on," he whispered. "Be quiet and don't wake anyone. I'm not supposed to be here."

I obeyed, not fully awake, slipping out of bed and standing, clearing my head. "We're going fishing," he said in the same whisper. "Wear something comfortable and bring a light jacket."

He had parked in the alley so as not to wake anyone. I had forgotten to note what time the clock on the nightstand read, but I estimated it to be around four in the morning. He had Grandma's car. I wondered why he had hers and not his own, but I didn't ask.

We drove over to a friend of his, Smiley's, and he just went up and banged on Smiley's door, four o'clock in the morning or not, and I kept behind in the car like he'd told me to. Smiley wasn't too fired up about being wakened, I could tell, even without hearing what Grandpa and he were saying, but then he seemed to calm right down and I saw him shake his head up and down, agreeing to something. He was. His wife, whose name I had forgotten, appeared in the doorway for a brief moment, her hair in pink curlers, wearing the awfulest pink nightgown I'd ever seen, and then she disappeared back into the house.

Grandpa and Smiley went around to the back of the house and then reappeared, Grandpa driving Smiley's old Nash Rambler with his boat hooked on back. He was lending us his boat and fishing gear. It was all so strange and alien and so unlike Grandpa, but still I kept my peace. I had thoughts of my own to mull over, or rather, not to mull over. Still, something wasn't right. Grandpa would let me in on it when he was ready.

That had all been a couple of hours earlier.

I touched my fishing rod again. Luck. It was Smiley's South Bend bait caster, but for today, it was mine. We'd picked up bait and Dr. Peppers and Jax beer and sandwiches and ice and were all set.

We turned from the open sea and entered a wide channel. After about ten minutes, cruising at about five knots, the channel suddenly opened into a bay with other channels emptying into it like green aortas into a giant heart. Little islands, spits of sand actually, long and narrow, lay here and there, everywhere in the bay. Grandpa pointed the bow at the largest.

Running the boat ashore onto it, we jumped out into

knee-deep water and hauled the craft up onto the sand and grass, then reached in and gathered up our borrowed fishing gear, laying it down in the sand and assembling the gear and baiting our hooks.

We had entered another world. Birdlife of all kinds and colors flew by or fed within a stone's-throw. Electricity and automobiles were a thousand light-years away. Monstrous fish leaped temptingly in the waters just yards away, landing with pregnant splashes as they fed on their smaller cousins. The morning sun sparkled in tiny pin-points on the gently rippling waters, skiffing up as light breezes blew this way and that, and muted bird-calls tickled our ears as our senses drank in the exotic beauty that was all around us. I felt I could never see another person or a town again the rest of my life and be perfectly happy.

Grandpa baited up with a small squid and told me to use one of the shrimp.

"See what they're bitin'," he said, wading out until the water was just past his knees. His feet must have been more tender than mine. He winced as he walked, and then I realized that it couldn't have been the cool sand beneath the water that pained him. I followed him out and flung the heavy weight of my line a little to the right of where Grandpa had cast his.

"Pull your rod tip up and then slack off and reel in," he suggested. He used his own rod to show me, using exaggerated gestures. "Keep doing that but don't do it too fast or you'll spook 'em."

We angled together, side by side, like two Dodge City marshals working Main Street, for more than an hour without a bite. Another hour slipped by and the sun rose higher. The first freckles appeared on my face. I couldn't see them but knew they were there from past experience. Grandpa said, "You didn't dry off good, Corey, your last shower. You're getting rust spots." It was an old joke of his and I always laughed. After a while, he went back to the boat and stuck on a hat he had left there. Still another hour passed with no bites.

After a long time, we kicked up a conversation. I had my shirt off by then, and my bruises were visible. Grandpa didn't say anything. I knew he was waiting until I chose to bring it up. I wasn't ready to.

"How'd Houston go? Are you gonna be all right, Grandpa?"

He kept his eyes on his line, pulling the rod to him deliberately, and then reeling in the slack, doing this several times in the space of a full minute.

"I'm not going to get well, Corey. It's a bad cancer, son, not the kind they can make go away."

A terrible silence ensued, almost heavy with a weight that pressed down, making me feel as if I had been transported to an identical world somewhere else, but one with a totally different system of gravity, where my weight had climbed to over a ton.

"That's what I found out yesterday, Corey. They give me a few months, at best. Three, maybe. Maybe less."

I sneaked a peak at him. Far in the distance, a blue heron flew, his long, stiff legs straight out behind him. He was flying straight for Grandpa's head and would have struck him if it had been a one-dimensional universe. I waited until the heron's outstretched beak stuck Grandpa's head and then passed by before I spoke.

"You scared?"

He didn't answer immediately.

"Sometimes I am, and sometimes I'm not. Most times I don't want to live much longer. Don't see the point. There's a lot of pain, Corey."

Both of us were using each other's names now, almost

as if extreme politeness were required.

"I don't like pain either, Grandpa. If I had pain all the time, I wouldn't like it either."

He looked at me like he was studying something in me, his head cocked like a sparrow hearing something foreign or dangerous.

"I know you're in pain, Corey. Maybe a worse kind than I have. There's a difference, though. Remember our talk the other day?"

I wasn't sure which conversation he meant, but I nodded like I did. I'm sure it was about Dad. Dad and me. That's what we always talked about.

"The kind of pain you have may stay with you for a long time, Corey, but it will get easier, and not only that— there's going to be some good times for you and they're not that far off. Remember what I said about children and suicide? That a child's idea of the future is that it's just going to be more of the same condition, same feelings he's experiencing at that moment? If the feeling is one of hurt, the child assumes the rest of his life is to be nothing but a continuation of that condition. If the feelings are happy, the child sees nothing but joy down the road."

I nodded.

"Neither are reality. I know we talked about this, but I think it's important for you to understand this. Life is a series of ups and downs, downs and ups. One of the things that allows you to cross over from being a child to becoming an adult is when you can grasp that concept. How about it? Do you see what I'm talking about?"

"I think so, Grandpa."

"I hope so, Corey. I have the strangest feeling you're going to need that knowledge in the very near future. I know where you got those bruises and cuts."

"You do?"

"I can guess. Your father."

This was going to be a conversation of honesty. It was the only kind possible with Grandpa, but it made me uneasy. Skirting the edges of truth seemed preferable, more comfortable.

No, it didn't. That was a dumb thought. I'd learned better.

The truth hurt, sure, but it was a clean hurt, and then it was over. Lying about things, especially lying to yourself, kept the hurt alive and festering.

"What'd you do? What made him that mad?"

What did I do? I made him a birthday present.

"He thought I stole something. Money."

"The money I lent you?"

"Yes."

He sighed. He had just reeled in again. He reached back with his casting arm until the tip of his rod almost touched the water behind him, and then he flung it out with a mighty pitch. His bait went out a long way, much farther than he had cast it before. He jerked back on the rod tip, reeled in the slack, let it lie for a second, and then repeated the whole procedure.

The tears just started rolling. Hot, fiery tears that coursed down my cheeks and into the water. I was adding my own salt to the water is the thought that went through my head and I wondered, right after, am I going crazy? I feel this pain and yet I can feel pleasure, like the pleasure of this fishing trip? I began to talk. I told Grandpa everything, all of it. I saw he had stopped cranking his reel. He looked out to where his bait lay, as if intent upon it, but I knew he was hanging on to every word I spoke.

"It wasn't the beating that was so bad. It hurt, I guess, but hurt the most was knowing…"

"…son?" His voice was so, so gentle.

"Knowing. I don't know...just knowing that he was never going to love me." As I spoke this, my voice dropped lower and lower, a small voice to little more than a whisper, and I realized as soon as I said it, that that was what I had been keeping inside, hidden even from myself. The truth. The truth that had been there all along, the truth that I had always been afraid to bring out into the light, a truth that was so awful, so crushing that I'd known it would devastate me beneath it, annihilate and utterly destroy me.

But it didn't. It hadn't!

On the heels of the bittering sorrow, deep, wrenching sorrow, came following an elation, acerbic, joyful elation, sweet in the center and sharp and biting and stinging on the edges, but an ecstasy all the same.

The worst was over.

And I had survived.

I had survived the surety that my father didn't love me, never had. Never would. It was crushing, oh—it was the most debilitating blow ever I had absorbed—but I hadn't folded, hadn't died, hadn't even broken one tiny bone! Not physical pain or death, that was unimportant, I hadn't died inside. I was alive and I was hurting and I was okay. I had to tell Grandpa something.

"Grandpa, while he was hitting me, all I could think of was things you told me. You and Grandma. I thought about that present you gave me. The family heirloom. Those spatterdashers. I kept remembering what you said, that they were something that prevented spatter from dashing you and, that you only wished you had some kind of spatterdasher for the heart you could give to me. That's what I kept thinking about the whole time he was hitting me. The spatterdashers." I looked into his eyes for the first time since I'd begun.

"Silly, huh?" I had stopped crying sometime in there

and my eyes were dry. I threw out my line again. It went out farther than it ever had. Grandpa hadn't touched his reel since I'd begun talking. Now, he did, reeling in sharply for a minute and then letting the bait fall back to the bottom.

"No, Corey, it isn't silly. I think that's what I gave them to you for. I had a feeling the time was drawing near. How do you feel about things now?"

"Just...better, Grandpa. Nothing stupendous, I guess. I just feel better. I'm all right now." I was, too. The ache was still there; it hadn't gone away, even now, but for some reason, I knew I had passed a crisis of some sort and done all right. I was going to be okay. I liked myself right then, felt pride in myself.

"It wasn't the spats exactly, Grandpa."

"No? How's that?"

"It was what you said about them. About them being a symbol and what the symbol was."

"And what's that?"

"People who love you. Love me." I said it so low, I didn't know if he'd heard me. "Like you. And Grandma." My voice raised, got louder. "And Mom. Maybe even Doc."

"Destin."

"Yeah. And Destin. There's others. Lots of others. Friends at school. Cousins. Aunts. Uncles."

He reeled in his line. His bait was gone, stolen. He reached into his pocket and pulled out a clear plastic bag. In it were several other squid. He took one out and rebaited. He glanced at me and then threw out his line.

"You're going to be all right, son. I think you're going to be all right. I have to be sure." He was talking to himself more than to me, it seemed, but the way he said the last sentence I knew he wanted an answer to something.

"What else, Corey?"

"Dad isn't going to change," I said, surprised at what I was saying, knowing as I spoke that these were my true feelings. I went on, but it was as if someone else had taken over my voice. "It isn't my fault he doesn't like me. I act the same around you and Grandma. And Mom and Doc. And none of you hates me." I went on talking, and as I spoke, I felt something growing inside me, a new kind of knowledge about myself. It was the same kind of feeling almost that I'd had when I first understood algebra, or when I first kept my two-wheeler up by myself. Before, I could do the problems, but only through memorizing the process; all of a sudden came a moment when I knew how the goddamned stuff worked. The same way when I didn't fall off of my bike. Suddenly, I knew how to ride, not just the principle or the mechanics, but the balance, the feel. The exultation that there would be no more skinned knees, no more disapproving remarks from my father who was teaching me how to ride, and best of all, freedom. I had my own transportation, my bike. I could go anywhere I wanted, places I couldn't reach on foot. It was odd; I remembered just then the feeling I'd had when I made my first wobbly ride on my repainted red Schwinn, and I was having the same rush of emotion now, only sweeter, better.

"I can stay up, Grandpa," I said, and then blushed thinking he must think I was talking like an idiot.

"My spatterdashers are you, Grandpa. And Grandma. And Mom and my friend Destin. And Doc. And people I haven't even met yet."

I was crying again, but it was a weeping of joy, and the tears tasted sweet, not salty. I felt transported, a sense of ultimate freedom and independence. And a sense of loss. I could go on now, deal with my father, but things had changed, forever, irrevocably, between us. It didn't matter what he did from now on. It wasn't my fault he couldn't see me the way I was. Others could. Only my father hadn't been able to know me. I could see that now. That was what I had always hoped for, that a moment would come when he would see me for me, when he would know how I loved him, openly, without reservation, without qualification, just loved him for being my dad and nothing else. His love for me, I saw, if love was what it was, had always been subject to *terms.* He'd love me if I was this, or if I behaved that way, or if I had these interests. Never just because. Maybe at one time, right after I was born maybe. Or even in my early years, when my personality hadn't yet emerged, when it was unclear what kind of person I'd be. When I'd started being me, he'd lost interest, become disappointed. I didn't fit his idea of a son, I wasn't mechanical, actually enjoyed books and ideas; therefore, I was not a son, not the son he wanted. He'd never understand the kind of love I had for him. The kind of love that didn't require him to be a certain kind of father, act in a prescribed way.

It wasn't the loss of what he wanted from life that made him what he was. It wasn't even Mom, with her religious fanaticism. I could see now that Mom hadn't turned to religion; she had turned away from him. It was her way of being able to live with him. He had showed her the same brand of love he had me. She hadn't measured up to what he wanted or expected either. When she saw that, she was devastated. Maybe she had never been able to articulate her despair; maybe she had never seen her relationship clearly, but in her heart she must have known where she stood. Her religion had become her savior, her spatterdashers.

It's the wrong way, Mom, I wanted to say. You chose the wrong way. All of a sudden, I needed to talk to her. I needed to explain to her that I understood. I needed to tell her that she didn't need religion. Not the religion she had.

She just needed to know she was all right. That I loved her. And Grandma and Grandpa and Doc. And others. Plenty of others.

Dad was the outcast, I'd tell her. He didn't drink, but he was as big an alcoholic as Destin's father had been. He and Destin's father were a lot alike. There was one difference. I didn't have to wait until he was dead to be free. Not anymore.

I think at that moment, crazy as it sounds, I loved my father more than I ever had in my life. For I could see him. And I could see me. I saw him for what he was, a blind, frustrated, *hurting* man who was incapable of any feeling for anyone save himself. I didn't ever expect him to love me back. It was okay, though. I had the right kind of love that wasn't contingent upon anything. I could consciously decide to love him regardless. And I did.

Some of this I explained to grandpa. Not all of it; some of it was private. But enough for him to know that I was all right. And that from now on I would always be all right.

For a long while, we were both silent, reeling in and casting out, rebating our hooks when we had to, each wrapped up in his own reverie.

"You know, Corey, you asked if I was afraid to die. Well, I was, plenty scared, but now I'm not. It wasn't death itself I was afraid of, I don't think, but I felt like I was leaving you unprotected, alone and in danger. I don't know, exactly—I was worried. About you. There's nothing to worry about any longer. You're going to be fine. I told you once before: I see great and wonderful things for you. I see them even more clearly now. You're a fine young boy, and soon you're going to be a fine man. I gave you my spats, but you gave me something equally good: the peace to die. I've accomplished what I was put on this earth to accomplish."

He reached into his pocket and took out the plastic bag again. I had just reeled in and my hook was bare as well.

"Here. Try one of these. I've got a hunch that squid's the answer." He spat on the slimy gray blob and handed it to me. I did the same before impaling it on my hook.

For luck.

At this moment, as if on cue, the old tarpon swam into the bay from a side channel, still looking for a slow sheepshead or a wounded sea trout. Behind him, twenty yards off his port stern, followed a smaller tarpon.

He hadn't been able to catch anything all morning, the old tarpon. The mold on his back glistened dully as he broke water almost on top of the young boy's bait, and then he spied the squid and gulped it down with one instinctive motion, slower than he would have a few years back, but still with incredible swiftness. To his rear, the younger tarpon saw a meal for himself, a small squid about four inches in diameter, lying on the sand bottom. He didn't see the faint outline of the steel leader attached to it, like some alien kind of antenna.

"You got one, Corey!" Grandpa's yell reached me at the same time as the shock of the fish's strike, and I heaved back like he'd coached me, with all my might, feeling the crunch of steel hook meeting solid bone, and then the tarpon's strength swept through the line and into my arms, as he lunged against the sharp pain that burst in his jaw.

I knew instantly it was a tarpon, even without having every hooked one, just as I knew he felt pain, even though everyone said fish couldn't feel pain. I had replayed this scene so many times in my head, it was like watching an old familiar movie.

"Ummmmph!" grunted Grandpa, and I saw his own rod bend, to the breaking point it seemed, and then I was too busy playing my own line to watch him, other than to make sure we didn't foul our lines.

Up, out of the water, exactly as he had in my dream, leapt the great fish, gleaming silver and green in the scorching Texas sun, and the sound was of a giant sucking noise, and then a subsequent, immediate slap, a cannon ball striking the water, sending a geyser ten feet straight up, and then the tarpon was sounding, down five full fathoms, into the very sand it seemed.

"I can't budge him!" I yelled.

"Wait him out!" yelled back Grandpa. "I've got my own problems!"

Indeed, he had. His tarpon, for tarpon it was as well, was smaller, but what a leaper. Up and down, jumping and twisting in the sunlight, he leaped three times in rapid succession before making a long, straight run. I just kept the line taught against the monster on my line and watched Grandpa play his smaller one.

"I've got 'im, now," he said, singing the words. "He's too young, doesn't know how to shake a hook. Thinks it's all brute strength." And just then his line went slack.

"I'll be a son of a gun," he said, respect in his voice. "That sucker sure fooled me. He came back on the line and lost it! For a fish that wasn't too smart, he sure got educated in a hurry!" He laughed, and I felt relief that he wasn't too disappointed. He sloshed his way to my side.

"That was a beauty, Grandpa," I said, in admiration.

"Yeah, it was, wasn't it. But look at the one you got. I never seen one bigger. Don't lose him. I'll help you."

I resisted the urge to horse the tarpon toward me.

"That's what he wants," said Grandpa, uncannily reading my thought. "You do that and he'll be laughing at you six miles away. This one's no rookie. Maybe he taught the other one. This isn't the first time this one's been hooked. You've got to outsmart him, you want to catch him."

Long minutes folded into one another, ten and then fifteen and then it was drawing close to half an hour, and still the tarpon didn't budge. I kept the pressure on, praying I didn't have any weak places in my fishing line. Mentally, I urged my antagonist to move, even though my heart was thumping double-time in anticipation of what I'd do, wondering if I'd be up to holding him. What would he do? Then he stirred. I felt him just before he gathered himself for a Herculean effort. I'd outwaited him and he'd used the time to gauge me as a foe. I knew he could tell he was stronger than I, that I was but a boy. I started to hand my rod to my grandfather, amazed that I had managed to hold onto him this long; it was crass impertinence on my part. Grandpa pushed the rod back at me, refusing to take it, making me deal with the huge fish.

Then, quicker than I could think, the tarpon was coming, coming, hurling himself through the water, toward the surface and he was liked a crazed Brahma bull I had foolishly thrown a rope around. I glanced around, wild-eyed, thinking for a second that I must be crazy to stand here in the same water as this animal—he was coming to kill me and there was no place to go—and then I knew that wasn't likely, or even possible, or was it? There was no way I could ever hope to land this leviathan. Closer and closer to the top he came, and more and more fearful my heart beat, and then he broke through, smashed through, shooting into the air like he was a blue marlin and not a tarpon at all, and the force and fury of his great leap was more than I could bear or handle. I dropped my rod, but Grandpa got to it before I could, reaching swiftly into the water and thrusting it back at me, my hands reaching and clutching only by instinct and not the wish of the boy whose hands they were. Everything happened in slow motion, seconds were minutes, and I had the rod back in my shaking fists just as he struck the water. It had seemed as though he would remain suspended forever, shaking his shaggy head to and fro ferociously, a mad, angry, furious shaking, like a street mongrel shaking a freshly caught rat. Never had a fish jumped so high. Never had a fish been that huge. When he smote the water, the sound and splash was that of a meteor dropping out of the heavens. He was easily sixty-five yards away and even so, drops of water struck us where we stood.

"Jesus Christ!" I breathed, unaware that I was cussing in front of my grandfather.

"That's a fucking *fish*," was his own response. "I *never*!"

It was all I could manage to hang on as the marvelous monster headed toward the mouth of the bay and the open waters of the Gulf. There was something different about this run, though. He was still strong, still all I could handle, but with a different feel.

"He's got air!" shouted Grandpa. "He's done for now. He shouldn't of jumped. Now you can horse him in."

And I did.

The tarpon fought, flinging his tail and head about valiantly, even more. Once or twice I thought him perilously close to shaking loose, but I hung on, even through a last jump, but now his strength was waning rapidly, this jump a pale imitation of the other, and what should have been a long, hard battle became instead a rout.

Five minutes later Grandpa reached down with his gaff as I reeled toward the sandbar where the boat was beached, and together we pulled the monstrous fish up into the shallow water, all the fight gone out of him.

"How we gonna get him in the boat, Grandpa? He must go a hundred eighty pounds!"

"More like a hundred and forty," he said, "and we don't get him in the boat. What for? He's no good to eat. We have to let him go. He'd swamp our boat. Take some of his scales. That'll show everyone how big he was."

Suddenly, he bent down and lifted the tarpon's head out of the water and began dragging it up onto the sand, next to the boat.

"What're you doing, Grandpa? Aren't you going to let him go? What's wrong?"

He finished pulling the tarpon all the way up until the fish was clear of the water. He pointed. "Look there, Corey, See that slimy stuff on his back?"

I nodded, not understanding.

"That's a mold, son. When a fish gets that, he's a goner. Nothing you can do to save them. It's a death sentence. In a day or so, he's going to begin suffocating. Might take one day, might take a week, but he's gonna die, sure as shootin'. And it'll be one hell of a way t'go."

He pushed at the tarpon's great heaving belly with his toe. "We'll just leave him here. He'll be dead in a little while. Lot better'n dying that other way, with gafftops, crabs and other trash fish chawing pieces of him while he's dying. That's not the way a fish like this should go."

He picked up his fishing tackle and mine and placed the gear in the boat, and began pushing it out into the water. I watched for a second and then asked, "Why don't you hit in him the head then? Isn't that faster? More humane?"

He came back to stand beside me and looked down at the tarpon, whose sides were heaving, almost as if he were breathing. "Looks like it would be, doesn't it?"

He wiped the sweat from his brow with his forearm.

"I don't think so though, Corey. See, he's like he's drowning now. A long time ago, I almost drowned, over to Garner State Park, and believe it or not, it was easy, peaceful-like. I never forgot it. It was like going to sleep. I remember knowing I was dying and afterwards everybody said I was fighting like gangbusters, but I don't remember it that way at all. It was just so damned peaceful. I remember thinking the whole time I was under, that, well, her I am, dying, and it's calm; it's not bad at all. Not like I'd ever thought dying would be. It was a hundred years ago, when I was the Boy Scouts, but I can remember every single detail just like it happened an hour ago."

He paused in his reverie for a moment, his eyes far away at a place only he had ever visited, and then he said, "I always kinda thought that would be the best way to go, happen it was your time. No, Corey, I think this is the way for this old tarpon to die. This way, he dies with dignity, slain by warriors like himself."

He gave a bitter snort.

"Far as smacking him on the head and putting him out of his misery, well, sir, I've done that to fish before, a lot, and now that I think about it, I guess I never did think about it too much—I just always did it cause that's what my pappy taught me to do. The theory was that that was more humane. I don't think so, though. I been hit on the head myself, more times than I would have asked to have been, and every single time it hurt like holy hell. No, sir, I think we'll just let this old boy kinda drown out here in the air.

"See?" He nodded at the heaving body of the tarpon. "He looks at peace, don't he? He's thinking about what a glorious life he's had and he's glad he doesn't have to fight any more. He's dying and he knows it. He welcomes it. He gets a chance to kinda go over his life, remember the highlights, the good times, and then he's gonna go to sleep."

He grabbed the gunnel of the boat. "Let's get out of here, son. Time we was heading home."

In ten minutes we were back in the open water of the Gulf, the sun at our backs, and the wind jacking up a little. I was glad Grandpa had made me take a jacket. I got into it. I sat in my place in the bow and thought on what had happened that day. This was a day like you always hope birthdays to be, memorable and auspicious, but they never are. This one was. Only, in a way, this *had* been my birthday. I was sure not the kid I had been yesterday. A lot had happened and I was changed. So I guess it was a birthday of a kind.

I started to say something to Grandpa, but saw his eyes and decided against it. He was somewhere, but it wasn't in the boat. Then his eyes seemed to catch focus, and he looked up, blinking as if he wasn't sure where he was at first, as if he'd just dropped in from another planet or something. His guard must have been momentarily down, for I saw pain in his eyes, intense pain. He opened his mouth and spoke, something that was strange at the time and only later made much sense.

"Whatever happens, Corey, I know you'll understand, won't you?"

I shook my head, lost as to his meaning, only I felt I had to pretend I knew what he was talking about, and it was the funniest thing—at the exact moment I nodded, I felt a bond pass between us that was the strongest thing I'd ever felt in my life. It was physical, that feeling.

"I wouldn't ever put you in a situation I thought would hurt you. You know that, don't you?"

Of course I did. I told him I did.

"Good. I thought so. You know, Corey, that tarpon was a lucky old bird. He had a good life, I bet, and some great times, but when it was time to go he just went. Animals know a lot more than humans sometimes, I think. I kinda like that tarpon. I don't think he much liked living the way he was, with that mold all over him and everything. He got lucky. He got to go out the right way, not wallowing in the shallow water, half in and half out, crabs eating him alive."

Grandpa'd slipped back into his reverie. He had addressed me, and he was even looking at me as he talked, but I could tell he didn't even know I was there, not really. He seemed like he was summing up something or making some kind of decision. I think even at that time I knew what it was he was deciding, but I didn't want to think about it, forced myself not to think about it.

I grew edgy as he talked, began to hate the way his words sounded, ominous, why, I don't know. It was the way he was saying the words as much as the words themselves, like he was in church or something, like he was some kind of elder deacon or something. I didn't listen to him, couldn't say anything to him. I wasn't there to speak, only to listen. Something had hold of both of us and all I could do was hold onto the sides of the boat and listen to him as he spoke. The wind kicked up even more, and gray furze that wasn't really clouds, just raggedy bits of dirty rags, moved between the sun and our boat, making the sun fuzzy and indistinct. The wind chilled and whipped from first this direction, then that, then another. I hunched up inside my jacket, shivering, but it wasn't the weather that chilled me as much as it was my grandfather.

It smelled like a norther.

"Y'know, dying's no worsen being born. We don't really know what's coming each time, but the first one turns out okay and I don't see no reason to not believe that so will the second. Dying, I mean." He mused a minute, and then whatever was on his mind left him, and he was back to being Grandpa.

"You ought to have your life jacket on," he said. I shrugged, and put it on. It was an odd request, I thought; we hardly ever wore life jackets, then dismissed it.

We were just coming into sight of Bryan Beach and the waves were rougher near where it got shallower, although it was still deep here. There was a bad undertow at Bryan Beach. We weren't allowed to swim out far when we came here.

He must have been daydreaming, because somehow the boat got turned out to sea and then at cross angles to the waves. That's dangerous, I started to say, but just as I opened my mouth to speak, the boat struck a giant roller and the sea rushed up and over us, blinding me for a minute and requiring all of my strength just to hold on. Blindly, I went down on my knees and reached for the seat before me and clutched it. The motor quit and the boat swung around with the current. We were all right.

Only I was alone in the boat.

There was no sign of Grandpa.

"Grandpa!" I screamed. He was nowhere, vanished. I scrambled to the stern where he'd been sitting. *Get the motor going, find him*, my mind urged. I reached his seat and stood up, a foolhardy, dangerous thing to do. Grandpa will be mad, he sees me, I thought, my mind confused. I looked everywhere for him.

Then I saw him. He was just beside the boat, only a foot beneath the skin of the water's surface. I watched, paralyzed, as his head came up, broke water, and then sank again. He was caught in the undertow. Dimly, I could hear the roar of the surf and, I thought, voices, and realized we were drifting toward shore. *Hang on, Grandpa*, my mind pleaded. I'm not sure if I said the same thing aloud or not. I think I did but I don't know.

With a lunatic's wild eyes I looked about for the life preserver. It was right by my foot. I reached down and grabbed it, and then my fingers slipped and it fell. The boat lurched, enough to cause me to stumble, and all the time I was looking down at the spot where Grandpa had gone down and then back to the preserver. I reached down and found it by feel, never taking my eyes from the water.

Where was he! I had the life preserver in my hand, ready to throw. There! I saw him just beneath the water. He was coming up for the second time. I clutched the preserver with a fish hawk's grip, ready to spring into action.

He came up, fast, and it was the weirdest thing: I thought of the tarpon and his tremendous leap, and then his head broke the plane of the water and popped free, then started sliding back and this time he began to tread water, not making a sound, not choking or sputtering or yelling or anything. There was just this pause, everything, the whole world just stopped, the wind quit, the waves froze, nothing breathed; it was the space of the click of a camera shutter, but it lasted as long as I wanted to hold it. I have never before or since encountered anything like that moment, although those who have been involved in wars, in shooting wars, where the bullets were whizzing about them, over their heads, next to them, say a similar thing happens to them, where time slows down and then just stops, and that's the way this was. I knew what was happening and I knew it was only a brief part of a second, but I had the power to hold onto it for as long as I liked. It was my decision to make to let time start up again when I desired; as long as I retained my concentration the moment would last. Then something happened, I blinked, and for a second forgot where I was and what was happening and as slowly as everything had been before it all began accelerating now to catch up, getting the universe back on track.

A wave crashed into the side of the boat and I drew my arm back to heave the preserver. He was two feet away, I could reach out and touch him with my hand if I chose to, and he started to slip back down in the water. Just before he went under, he seemed to stop once more, suspended, as if he were the last drop of ketchup in an empty bottle, and our eyes met and locked. It must have been for only the narrowest of seconds and time didn't slow as before, but it seemed forever, and I reached down with my arm and he shook his head the tiniest, imperceptible bit, side to side, a trace of a smile on his lips and I pulled my arm back. And then he was gone.

First published in *The Analecta.*

"What's that?" he said.

There was no answer, so he said it again, louder.

"What're you doing?"

Her face appeared in the bedroom doorway. She had her blue robe on and her hair wasn't combed.

"Did I wake you?" she said.

He grunted, didn't say anything, but pressed his lips together, the left side of his mouth indenting into a sneer.

"I'm vacuuming." She held up the hose for proof.

"Oh? I thought space craft had landed. I was just going to check the back yard."

She laughed pleasantly, and stood in the doorway, watching. He stared at the ceiling, feeling her eyes on him.

"I didn't think you'd hear me, in the living room."

"How far apart are they?" He turned for the first time and looked at her.

"Ten minutes. Mostly. Sometimes, they go down to five, but it's not regular."

"How do you feel?"

"Good. Okay. I just couldn't sleep. I was uncomfortable. My hips hurt."

"Should we be going now?"

She thought for a second and then said, "No. I don't think so. They're not that bad. More like menstrual cramps."

"Do you have to keep that running?"

"Oh. Well, I just want to finish. I'm almost done."

He turned his face back to the ceiling and brought his arms up, placing his hands behind his head.

"It's your burst of energy, you know."

"I guess."

She went back to the living room and he shut his eyes, but he knew he wouldn't be able to get back to sleep. He might as well get up.

"What're you doing?"

"Coffee. You want some?"

"I better not. I shouldn't eat anything now."

He put away the coffee container and switched the button on. Water began to drip and then run. In a few minutes it was done perking, and he poured a cup, adding the tip of a spoon of sugar and a half spoon of Cremora and took the cup into the living room where he sat on the big sofa. The vacuum cleaner was off, but still stood in the middle of the room, its cord making S-patterns across the rug to the outlet. Its hose hung down like an elephant's trunk searching for peanuts. She sat down also, on the small sofa across from him, and curled her legs up beneath her, her gaze on his face.

"You want to go?" he said.

"No, Adam. It's not time yet. It could be hours. I'll know when."

He snorted and drank some coffee.

"Yeah? This is your first, you know. Maybe you'll be different. Maybe you'll have hardly any pain. Maybe you'll end up having it in the bedroom."

"Maybe," she said, and then, "I'll know. Trust me." She put her legs down on the carpet, twisted, and then drew them up, positioning her body the opposite way.

"I guess," he said, putting his finger into the coffee and then sucking on it.

They were both silent for a while. He sat there, staring blankly at the coffee table between them, occasionally picking up his cup and sipping, but never breaking his hypnotic gaze at the table. He felt her looking over at him.

"Know what the Indians used to do?" he said, looking up, finally.

"Indians? What Indians?"

"Any Indians. *All* Indians. What's it matter, what Indians? That's not important. It was just...Indians."

"What'd they do?"

"When the woman's time came, the *squaw*, they put her in a special tent, a *teepee*, and the other women took care of her."

"Where were the men? Her husband?"

"I don't know. Out hunting, I suppose. In their own tent, maybe. Waiting."

"Is that what you want to do?" He caught a different note in her voice, and knew he'd stepped on dangerous ground, but he didn't reply.

She put her legs down, leaned forward, her chin on her hands, elbows on her knees and stared at him, a little smile on her face.

"I believe I will have some of that coffee," she said.

She got up, swaying from side to side as she did so, and went into the kitchen. After a while, she came back out with a cup in her hand and sat back down on her sofa.

"What Indians were these?"

"What? Oh. Who knows? All Indians, I suppose."

"That doesn't make sense. Do you know how many tribes of Indians there were?"

"No. A lot, I suppose."

"A lot!" He heard the vein of anger in her voice. "A lot! There were hundreds of tribes, maybe thousands. You think all these thousands of tribes did the same thing?"

"I guess. I dunno. Probably. What's it matter? It's just something I read once. They didn't name the tribe. I forgot the name."

"Was it the Indiana Indians? Crees? Iowas? Florida Seminoles? The ones that lived in New York? California?"

He drank down the rest of his coffee and lighted a cigarette. It sparked when he lit it and a live ash landed on his bare chest, sizzling a hair. All he had on were his briefs. He slapped at it and then rubbed the spot. It stung.

"I don't think there ever were any Indians in California. I never heard of any. All they had in California was Spaniards and taco stands." He tried to joke, change the mood of the conversation. "James Fenimore Cooper never mentions California Indians. Just ones in Canada and New York, the Great Plains. No California Indians."

"Well." Her voice dripped sarcasm. "If James Fenimore Cooper never mentioned them, then they don't exist. That's proof enough for me."

He sighed and stood up. "Want some more coffee?"

She was looking down, staring at the coffee table, her hair falling in her face. He couldn't see her eyes but suspected she was crying.

He came back with his coffee and sat down.

"I bet the California Indians didn't send their pregnant women out to teepees," she said, looking at him with a look that dared him to refute that.

He'd hoped she'd let go of the topic.

"I guess not."

She threw her coffee cup at him. It was still half-full and the brown liquid went everywhere, missing him, as did the cup itself, staining the wall behind him, the couch, and the rug. He just sat there.

"You bastard." She said it low, the words hissing. His expression stayed the same, noncommittal.

"Look baby, I'm sorry. I didn't mean anything by this Indian junk. It was just something I read. I thought you might be interested."

"I want to know if the California Indians put their women in teepees, buddy. Call somebody."

"Call somebody?"

"Is there an echo in here? Yes. Call somebody. Call the library. Call the Bureau of Indian Affairs. Call the governor, the president. Somebody. I want to know."

"Janet, it's…" He looked at his watch. "It's one-thirty. One thirty-three. A.M."

"I don't care. Call somebody."

He crossed the room, sat down beside her, put his arm around her, felt the way her body stiffened at his touch.

"Go away."

"Sweetheart, I'm sorry. I don't know why I had to bring that up. You know I want to be there when it happens. It was just something stupid I read."

He felt the warm liquid of her tears on his arm and pulled her to him. She remained stiff but didn't resist. He brushed her hair away from her face with his other hand and wiped her tears from her cheeks with his fingers. He could smell the salt of her tears.

"Baby, I'm sorry. I don't know what got into me." He stroke her hair, hugged her closer to him. "Yes, I do. I know why I told you about the Indians."

"Why?" Her voice was muffled, sweet.

"I'm scared."

"You're scared?" She turned and looked up into his eyes. Her eyelashes glistened. The hardness left her mouth and a bit of warmth crept into her eyes.

" *You're* scared?"

He nodded.

"You don't want to send me out to a teepee?"

He nodded again.

"You want to be with me? You want us to have a baby? Together? You're not sorry you had to quit high school?"

Again, he nodded.

"But you're *scared*?"

"Terrified."

"Come on," she said, removing his arm and standing. "Let's clean this mess up and get packed. This last one felt like the real thing. It's happening."

He went and got the suitcase from the hall closet.

But first, he put away the vacuum cleaner.

I told Manny the whole story. We were staying in, on a Saturday morning while everyone else went to the movie. Sat up at the front table, playing double sol and eating Keebler's Chocolate Chips and smoking tightrolls, Camels. Doing the prison day off thing.

"I was hung up on her, bro," I said, trying to explain it to him. "She owned my ass."

"I been there," he said and the way he said it I knew it was true.

"We were broke up and I was taking out some other ladies," I went on. "One weekend, a Sunday, I must have had four different babes come over, different times, got laid each time. I was having a ball but it was crazy. No matter how much fun I was having, I still couldn't get Donna out of my mind. I was fucked up, man.

"Anyway, the last chick left about eleven that night and I went to bed. To sleep." Manny cracked up, leaned back in his chair and laughed with his head tilted back and his mouth wide open.

"I guess you weren't gonna pound your trouser worm," he said.

"I guess not. I was just getting asleep when the doorbell rang and I got up and it was Donna. 'I got to talk to you,' she said.

"'Fuck, Donna,' I said. 'I'm just about asleep. We're

over, sugar. Why don't you just leave me alone.' 'No,' she said, 'I've really got to talk to you.'

"'Well,' I said, 'I'm just about asleep and if I don't go right back to bed I won't be able to. I oversleep and lose this job my P.O.'ll violate me.'

"'Okay,' she said, pushing her way in. 'You go back to bed. I'll come with you and we'll talk in the morning. It's really important.'"

I looked over at Manny. "You know how it is when you're just about asleep? I told her, all right, come on in but we're not doing anything, Donna. I just want to go to sleep.

"Well, she came in and I went back and climbed in bed and she came in a minute later and crawled in with me, buck naked. I meant what I said though, I wasn't going to fuck her. I turned over and closed my eyes, tried to get to sleep again. About five minutes later the doorbell rang again.

"It was a girl I'd seen a couple of times that week. Patsy. 'Patsy,' I said, 'I've got company.' 'Oh,' she said, 'Well, that's cool, I guess. I'll see you tomorrow then.' And she left.

"When I came back into the bedroom, Donna jumped up and asked me who that was. Nobody, I said, just a friend. She's gone. Donna ran to the front door and must have seen her walking away. She came back and she was hot.

"'You fucking that girl,' she said. I said, 'No, I'm not but that's none of your business anyway. We're broke up,' I said.

"'That's it,' she said, slamming around and throwing her clothes on. 'I'm outta here.' That was the original idea, I said, back to her, and she went out, just about busting the door.

"That's it, I'm thinking and went back and laid down. But then I thought I heard voices and got up and opened the door and sure enough, there's Patsy sitting in a chair by the pool and Donna's giving her the business, screaming at her.

"'Donna!' I yelled down. 'Get your ass out of here right now or I'm calling the cops.' I didn't say anything to Patsy even though I knew she didn't have a clue what was going on but I knew Patsy was cool. I figured if I said anything to her that'd fire Donna up again and I'd just tell Patsy the next day what went down and she'd understand. Well, they both get up and head for their cars. Patsy always parked on one side of the complex. I watched for a minute, saw Donna was heading in a different direction and went back inside. I lay back down but then I got to thinking—I know this bitch—Donna—I better be sure she's left.

"I went to the front door again, and sure enough, Donna's dogging Patsy, walking right behind her, yapping at her. I ran out of the apartment along the catwalk. All I had on were my jockeys. There's a little space where you can look out at the parking lot and I ran to that. Patsy's up against a car and Donna's got her face right up in Patsy's. I ran downstairs and around the corner and just as I came around the corner, I see Donna's fist come back and she smacked Patsy. She smacked her hard, dude. I never seen a *guy* hit another guy the way that broad hit her. I ran over to them and just as I got there Donna's raising her hand to smack Patsy again. Only she wasn't hitting her. She was stabbing her. It really didn't register though. I got there just as she was coming down with the knife and I grabbed her arm with one hand and Patsy with the other and shoved them apart. Donna went down on her knees and then started coming up, trying to cut me. I ducked my stomach back and at the same time she missed I grabbed the hand with the knife and hit it against my knee. This all happened fast, man. Really fast.

"She lost the knife when her hand hit my knee and my first thought is…*find the knife.* I know if I get the knife first she can't hurt me. We're both scrabbling around looking for it—it was dark in that parking lot—and I find it first. It was this big-ass switchblade—in fact, I'd given it to her a long time ago as a present—and I find it and pick it up and she sees I've got it and she took off running. I'm standing there with this switchblade and I tried to close it and couldn't as it's bent in two-three places. I just stand there until I see the reflection of her lights go on in the other parking lot and hear her tires burn out and then I walk over to Patsy who's standing up against a car.

"Well, this sounds weird, but it's the truth, Manny. I've got this knife in my hand and everything but it still doesn't dawn on me that Patsy's been stabbed. It just happened so fast. Patsy didn't know she'd been cut, either.

"I walk up to her and say, 'Are you all right?' She's got this white silk blouse on and chinos and I see little tiny sprinkles of blood on the blouse, looked like somebody'd sprinkled red salt out of a shaker, or tabasco sauce… yeah…more like tobasco sauce. 'You been hit,' I said. 'You got a nosebleed.' 'No,' she says, 'she missed me. I ducked and she hit me in the back.'

"She turned around and, man! Her whole back was solid red and blood was running down her pants like she was peeing herself. 'You been stabbed,' I said, what had happened finally dawning on me. 'I have?' she said. She didn't even know it herself."

Just then, the dorm hack came by, motioned at us to come over. He was taking the count. Even though he knew us, he made us tell him our names and he read the numbers off our shirts, made checkmarks on his clipboard and then left, probably to take a nap downstairs where his desk was.

We went back and sat down at the table.

"You sure you want to hear the rest of this?" I asked Manny.

"Fuck, yes," he said, grinning. "This is some wild bitch!"

I went ahead with the story.

"Well, I wanted to take her over to Charity Hospital, but she said no. She wanted us to go up to my apartment and get a better look at where she'd been stuck. We climbed up the stairs and I'm thinking she's not that bad, being as how she can go up stairs and all. When we get to my apartment I took off her blouse and all I can see is an entry wound about this big—"I held up my fingers to show a width of about an inch and a half or so, "—so my mind says the knife only went in a couple inches and hit a bone. That's what bent the blade, I'm thinking. Anybody knows you can bleed a lot from even a small cut. The blood's not running any more, it's kind of just bubbling a little. I bandage her up with a bath towel and some electrician's tape I had and then she says maybe I ought to take her over to the hospital as she's feeling a little woozy. That's smart, I tell her and we go downstairs.

"I drive her over to Charity and pull up to the emergency room entrance and the rent-a-cop comes out and they get a wheelchair after I tell them the score and wheel her in. I don't see her until the next morning.

"I tell the rent-a-cop what's gone down and he calls the real deal and when that guy gets there, a uniform, I tell him the same story and give him the knife. I tell him where he can probably find Donna. Look over at the Godfather in Metairie I say. How's the girl got stabbed, he asks and I tell him I don't know, I don't think it's that bad and give him my reasoning about hitting the bone and all. But check with the doctor, I said.

"Well, he doesn't check with the doctor, just leaves and they pick up Donna the next morning and all she gets charged with is simple assault, not assault with a deadly weapon or attempted murder or any of that, only I don't know none of this until the next day.

"About an hour after I bring Patsy in, I'm sitting by my lonesome in the waiting area and in comes this lady and man. The man looks exactly like that guy used to be on *Miami Vice*, the TV show? You know, the captain? The one with all the acne scars? Remember? Anyway, this lady comes over to me, no howdy-do, nothing, and she says, 'If my little girl dies, you die, and this guy will kill you.' She means the scar-face with her. It must be Patsy's mom I guess, which it is, and I try to explain how it isn't my fault—that if it wasn't for me Patsy probably would be dead as Donna was fixing to stab her again when I broke it up.

"'Don't matter none,' she says. 'If she hadn't been at your place she wouldn't have got stabbed to begin with.' I guess she'd already talked to the cops or the hospital or somebody, got the lowdown on what happened. You couldn't reason with her. This guy she was with, later I find out he's connected, would of done what she said, terminated my ass. Him, I never talked to. In fact the whole time, the four hours we sat there the only ones in the waiting room he never said a word to me or her. Just sat there mugging on me with no expression on his face. It was creepy.

"I went to the john a couple of times and each time I'm thinking, Should I just take off now, go to California or something? See, I was convinced that if Patsy died her mom meant business. There was no doubt in my mind. The only thing kept me there was I still thought Patsy wasn't hurt all that much.

"Shit. It was serious all right. Along about daybreak this doctor comes out to talk to us. 'We think she's gonna make it,' he says to Patsy's mom, 'but it's still a little shaky.' Turns out the knife went all the way in, almost came through the other side. It did hit a bone and that's what saved her. 'We were looking to see if the blade hit the lung,' he said. 'If it had even nicked it, we couldn't have saved her. Her lungs would have filled up with blood and she would have basically drowned.' As it was, they had ended up giving her four whole units of blood and the doc said she died on them twice and they had to bring her back from the dead. They had to wait until the blood clotted and moved away from the lung to get a clear picture. The x-ray showed it had missed but how he didn't know. It was a miracle.

"For her *and* me. Once we found out she was out of the woods, we all left. Before we did, her mom turned to me and said, 'You're still on the hook, Mayes. She might still die. If she does, you're dead, mister.'

"Way it turned out, Patsy came through fine, although she was a little sore."

"So why'd you try to kill yourself? I don't get it."

"Wait a minute. I'm getting to it." I seen Manny was getting antsy now that the bloody part was all over so I speeded up a couple of the in-between details and cut to the grand finale. "Patsy gets out of the hospital, sore but okay and we even started dating kinda heavy although we had to fuck real easy or else open up her wound again. Her mom decides she likes me and she tells me what she told me in the hospital was for true—I'da been dead meat if her darlin' daughter'd croaked. She says she's glad she didn't cause now she likes me but somehow that didn't make me feel a whole lot better. She's an okay enough gal, but every time I see her I still get a little nervous.

"Anyhoo, a couple weeks go by and then I start getting phone calls at work from Donna. She don't say hello, kiss my ass or nothing when I pick up the phone, just starts talking like we hadn't ever stopped. 'I drive by your work every day when I get off,' she says, 'and I point my gun at you while I'm going by. One of these days I'm pulling the trigger, motherfucker.' The first time or so she pulls this I just sort of laugh it off, but after a solid week of these kinds of conversations I had enough and called the district attorney. 'Nothing we can do,' he says, 'until she does something, but I made a note of this and if she ever actually shoots at you or anything like that we'll pick her up.' That made me feel about as good and safe as finding out I got blood in my urine. I thought once or twice that maybe I ought to do her before she does me, but when I start scheming about how to carry that off, I realize I'm still fucked up over her."

"You still fucked up over this crazy bitch after the shit she done?" I didn't realize Manny's eyes could get that wide. The way he looked and the way he said it made me think maybe it was me that was crazy. "How can you even want to be on the same planet with her?"

"Because I'm stupid?"

I wasn't a hundred percent joking. I stared at the end of the cigarette I had going.

"Yeah. It's somethin', huh? Go figure. You want me to lie about it?"

"Naw, man. It's just...well, I don't figure you to be pussywhipped, that's all."

"You wait, Manny. Anyway, I didn't know what to do. I knew she was just about wacko enough to pull some stunt like that—drive by and shoot me—it wouldn't be hard—

I'm working in front of this big plate glass window two feet from the street—and then I get this phone call from her."

"What'd she say?" He was all ears.

"She said, 'I just want to tell you why I came over that night.'"

"That's right. You said she said she wanted to talk to you about something."

"Yeah. What it was, what she said was that she was pregnant and that she murdered it. That's the words she used."

"You mean—"

"Abortion. She had an abortion. Man, I'm death on abortions! She knows that, the bitch!" Thinking about it all over again brought on some of the same feelings I'd had then.

"I started thinking about this baby boy—I *know* it was a boy—and, man, I lost it. I started drinking then, went out and bought a bottle of Jack and hit it hard. I'm thinking all kinds of things. You know, 'what coulda been' kinds of things. Me and her. Me and her and our baby boy. I just kinda went out of my skull. It probably didn't help I laid up in this motel room out on Esplanade for three days doing nothing but slugging down Jack and going crazy in the head. That's when I did it."

I told him about the Norelco razor cord and it breaking when I tried to hang myself with it. I don't know why I was telling Manny all this. Maybe to get it all out, make me feel better. Only it didn't. Make me feel better, that is. I felt worse. I felt just like I had during those three days only I didn't have any whiskey to help take the edge off. I know one thing—if I'd been on the bricks right that minute I wouldn't be qualifying for any of those white poker chips they give out at AA.

Time I went to bed that night I'd got it back under control somewhat. Only thing is I kept seeing Donna's fucking face and I hated the way I felt. Like I still wanted us to be together.

Ain't that some shit?

If having Donna on my mind wasn't enough, that fucker Boles came back, the one I stabbed up on the roof of the laundry. You'd think a guy had thirty-some laundry pin holes in him would have sense enough to check outta this sorry life. I was cutting a guy's hair when Manny came over and told me. He'd been up front, talking to the guard on duty that day. They put him in the infirmary. The guard thought he'd be there at least a week before they put him back out in the population and gave him limited duty. Probably put him in the library for a while the guard told Manny. That made sense. Put an illiterate in charge of Angola's priceless Zane Grey paperback collection.

There was no question I had to get to him. It was obvious he hadn't snitched on me yet but I knew it was only a matter of time.

It's hard to move around in prison. In movies, it seems like guys come and go pretty much as they want. All they have to do is bribe a guard or some trusty. That might be the case in Tinseltown, but at Angola it was a different story. You couldn't take a crap without a pass. And what're you supposed to be bribing guards with? Packs of cigarettes?

I was still trying to cook up a scheme when the situation changed just three days later. For the better. Boles got released from the infirmary and just like that guard had predicted he was put in the library. He'd be much easier to get to there. I just had to dope out a way to get there without getting caught. That meant I couldn't get a pass to the library since that'd leave a record on somebody's pass sheet.

The smart thing to do was get to Boles quick. He was still weak from his wounds. Also, he hadn't talked yet. If I waited too long he'd not only be stronger and harder to take down but he might have a change of heart and snitch me out.

My man Dusty came through though. Just like in the movies.

"I got something for you," he said when we came in that night from chow.

"What?"

"You got to fix that guy over at the library, right?"

He knew I did.

"You told me you might need some help sometime with this guy."

I was surprised he remembered and then I wasn't. Dusty was no lame-o.

"So what you got?"

"Here."

He put a piece of paper in my hand. It was a pass. *Free-walkin'* passes we called 'em. Only trusties got this kind of pass. It allowed you free movement wherever you wanted to go inside the walls. The best thing was it didn't have your name on it. A solid gold pass, especially for what I needed it for.

Dusty told me one other thing.

"Do it tomorrow morning," he said. I wanted to know why then. "'Cause, stupid, you're gonna need an alibi maybe and I can give you one. I've got to take the barber shop towels over to the laundry and I'm going to ask for you to help me. You got twenty minutes to do it in. I got a friend at the laundry I already talked to. He's gonna say you came in with me, dropped the laundry off."

It's things like this let you know who your friends are.

All I did that night was have one nightmare after another. Practically every night I had a dream—nightmares most of the time—while I was behind bars. On the bricks I never dreamed.

I woke up after about the tenth dream where I was being chased by Donna with her fucking knife, my heart beating like I'd been doing amyl nitrate poppers and I'm laughing like somebody in the Squirrel Factory and there was some fucker in the back of the dorm ripping out these horrible sobs.

I felt the sweat chill as I threw off my blanket. I yelled, "Somebody put a dick in that asshole's mouth!" I barefooted it over to the window and looked out and the cooking crew was heading across the quad to the mess hall in their whites so I figured it was four-thirty since that's when they went over to start destroying breakfast.

There was no use trying to get back to sleep. They'd be rousting us for wakeup in another hour anyway so I went and got my shaving gear and took a shower and shaved, brushed my teeth. Nice, I thought. You could actually take a shit without ten thousand guys screaming ten feet from you. I'd have to remember that and get up early from now on.

I sat on the stool longer than what I needed, just thinking. About the dream and Donna and Boles and all kinds of shit like that. Just sat there getting madder and madder. It wasn't like I was building a hard-on so's I could jack up Boles, later on. I never needed that shit. You know, get mad so I could jump on somebody. That kind of shit's for punks. The best way is to not even think about it. Just do it.

That's the onliest way to do anything major. 'Specially

when you got a choice, got two roads you can take. Like I could whack out Boles or I could do something else. Like nothing. Just not do it at all, see what happened then.

Fuck that. Boles was going down. I couldn't believe a guy could get stabbed that many times and still live. What was he, some kind of vampire? Thirty-some holes this punk gets with a straightened-out laundry pin and he's over working in the library like he just got over the flu. I shoulda put a wooden stake through his motherfucking heart is what I shoulda done, prevented all this happy horseshit.

It's like a stickup. Most outlaws I talked to got busted 'cause they plan too much. Figure out what to do if this happens, that happens. The best way is not even know you're gonna do it till it happens. Like, you're in a supermarket, buying a deck of butts, whatever and on the way out you see all the checkout girls heading with their money trays to the office on account of the next shift is there. Before you walked in, robbing somebody maybe was the last thing on your mind. You see that, all them trays stacked up on the desk in the office, the safe open and the smartest thing you can do is walk over, pull out your piece and tell the guy in the tie to bag it up, hand it over. Zip, boom, bang, you're out of the place and cruising down the road before you even know what you did. Just like that.

I never once in my entire life got caught on a job when I did it like that. The ones I keep getting busted on are the ones where you cased and planned and schemed for eleven-teen years before and always—*always*—the one little thing you never thought of happens and the next thing you know is you're trying to wipe black ink off your fingers with that one little paper towel they always give you and you feel you're waking up from a bad dream. Into one that's worse.

I'm thinking all this and then I just did it. Dropped a

sheet over all them other thoughts about Donna and even Boles and just went into another part of my mind.

We were walking out of the dorm after breakfast and Manny was saying something to me. In fact, he was almost screaming before I noticed anything.

"What?" I said, wondering why he was yelling at me and then Dusty who was walking with us, said, "Leave him alone, Manny. He's in the zone."

He gave me a look and took a quick glance around and then his hand touched mine and I knew what it was. I slipped it into my shirt. Without looking I could feel it was a knife, a regular hunting knife, not some piece of shit that had been jury-rigged from a piece of metal from one of the shops. This was a serious killing weapon. What he did, what I had in my hand, registered, not in the front part of my mind but in the back, where I was.

We got to the barber school and I just went on back to stand behind my chair instead of screwing around with the others. A couple of the guys walked by, said something and I just nodded. I don't have a clue what they said to me.

Then Mr. Dillsie came to the door of his office and yelled at me to come up front, help Dusty with the towels. I could see Dusty behind the glass. There were five large sacks. I grabbed three of them and Dusty the other two and we went out the back door.

"Run," Dusty hissed, once we were out of sight of the school. "You gotta book, man!"

We ran all the way to the laundry and his man was standing outside waiting for us. "You got fifteen minutes, maybe twenty," Dusty said. "Go!"

I threw down my sacks and took off again, heading up toward the quad, around the chow hall and luck was with me. I didn't pass a single guard, only one inmate. I kept my head down and I don't think the guy even noticed me. The library was two buildings down from the chow hall and nobody was on the walk in front of me. Clear sailing. This was the best time. There shouldn't be anybody else in the library except for the librarian for at least another hour.

There wasn't.

I went in quick, closed the door behind me. I could feel the knife where I'd put it under my shirt, the handle stuck down behind my belt.

At first, I thought nobody was there and then I heard something sounded like a book drop back in the office. I walked back and went into the room. He was there, bending over. He straightened up, a book in his hand and looked at me.

"Boles," I said. I could see the fear in his eyes.

"I didn't snitch you out, man," he said, laying the book down on the desk in front of him and stepping back. He moved kind of stiff-like and I guess I would too, I had that many holes in me.

"I know. I couldn't be here if you had, could I?"

I pulled out my knife.

"Why you gonna do this?"

"You know why."

He took another step back and was up against the wall. I started toward him.

"Oh, man." His voice broke. He put his hands up, palms facing me and began edging along the wall toward the door. "Man, you're safe. I'm not going to tell who did me. If I was gonna tell I'da already done it. I'm sorry for what I did to you, man. We're even. Don't you see we're even?"

In a way, he was right. I'd had the same thought myself. The pain I'd put him through almost certainly matched what he'd done to me. In one way the score was settled.

I didn't even feel the same anger I had when he'd raped me. The day I'd shanked him up on the laundry roof the mad had disappeared, vanishing a little bit with every hole I put in him until it was all gone. There was no revenge left in my heart, none at all. It was just pure-d empty of everything, all malice.

I walked over to him and he just stood there. I don't think his knees would let him move. His eyes told me that. I stopped inches from him. His hands went down to his sides.

"You won't talk? Ever?"

"Oh, man! No! I swear t'God! You're safe, man. I just want to do my time, get the fuck out of here, that's all."

I believed him. I could hear it in his voice.

"You don't even know my name, do you?" I said.

"No." He was telling the truth.

"My name's Jake Mayes," I said. Then I stabbed him. Who knows why? Just like that. It started in easy enough, then hit something solid so that I had to push harder on the handle before it went all the way in. I looked him in the eyes the whole time. It seemed like it lasted for hours, us standing there, and his eyes changed, just the least little bit, in realization of what was happening, I guess, and his eyelids started to quiver like he was trying to keep from blinking, as if once he blinked it was all over and then all the bones just seemed to go out of his face. I reached up with my other hand, grabbed his shirt and eased him on down to the floor. His eyes were still open. He hadn't blinked but he was dead.

I got back to the laundry and Dusty was still there talking with his friend. I knew I had been gone longer than I should have.

"What you doing?" Dusty said, when I came up.

"You're walking like you got all the time in the world, moron. C'mon, let's get the fuck out of here."

The other guy turned and went back inside the laundry and we started walking back to the barber school. On the way, Dusty asked me questions. "You get rid of the knife? Anybody see you?"

Back at the school I had a customer waiting for me. Dusty did too. The guy wanted a flattop. I got out the triple ought blade, rinsed it in the sterilizing solution. When I got done, I stepped back and looked. It was the best flattop I had ever cut. It was a fucking masterpiece, it was. You could land a plane on that flattop. I just laid down my clippers when the steam whistle blew. I knew what that meant. I looked over at Dusty and he at me and he held his hand down low so nobody else could see and gave me a thumbs up. I just nodded. Ice-cold, that's the way I felt. Frosty. Peaceful. When that whistle blew, something happened inside. Time, as a concept, just disappeared. Just blew away in the wind, went over the wall.

A couple of months later, my old rappy Bud came down from Kenner after his trial and Dusty got him into the dorm with us. It was Kimmie he'd killed, got him sent back, but he told us it was an accident. She was giving him some grief, yakking that he was always out too late, lame crap like that and he'd tapped her.

"I didn't even hit her that hard," he said. "I hit her lots harder lots of times. It was just a freak accident."

"Fucking life's a freak accident," I said and we all laughed, me, him, Dusty and Manny. We were all outside on the ball field, sitting at one of the picnic tables, eating Oreos and smoking tightrolls, playing dominoes.

This was as good as it gets I thought, looking around. I

saw a bird fly up to the wall and then it was gone, flew over the side. That was all right, I thought. Good fucking riddance. This was okay too, sitting out in the grass with my buds. The green, green grass of home. No fucking broads hassling us, just good friends sitting around, having us a ball. I started to think of Donna but got that shit out of my mind. Thinking about broads is what fucks up your time in here. All I want to do now is my time.

Eight more years, thanks to Boles. Yeah, they found out it was me. Fuck it. Like I give a shit.

I can do eight years and snooze all the way through it, now that I got Donna out of my skull.

Got my head on right, now. I'm in the zone, man, the zone we all been looking for since the minute we were born. In the zone, you're a man nobody fucks with. You're the fucking Master of the Universe. People step aside when you walk by. You stare at any motherfucker you want, all day long, you feel like it. Cracks me up, way these chumps try and become invisible, they see me coming down the tier walk.

Invisible *this*, I say in my head, when I walk by, and then I do whatever the fuck I want, whatever I feel like doing. Just what-the-fuck-ever. *Just like that*, amigo.

First published in *High Plains Literary Review* and in Houghton Mifflin's *Best American Mystery Stories*, 2001. Nominated for the Pushcart Prize.

CENSORSHIP AND
WHY I LOVE CHARLES BUKOWSKI

Like most of you in this room, I've always written, always had to write. I had this thing inside me that said I had to be a writer. Notice, I said *had* to be. Not "wanted" or "yearned to be." *Had to be.* There was no choice in the matter. God looked down and saw this little runty red thing laying in his bassinet, sucking down a PBR with a formula chaser, and He said, "I need another writer for my Grand Scheme," and Bingo! There I was. A writer. When God Himself says you're gonna be a writer, then, boy, you better be a writer. You play the hand you're dealt.

I didn't have any argument with that. I mean, who argues with God? Except, maybe Francois Camoin. But I didn't have the advantage of being French and cynical and all that like Francois did—I didn't even know where to begin to buy a beret or a black painter's smock or an attitude. I mean, for Christ's sake, I was a kid in Texas. None of those things could be gotten in Texas. If you couldn't barbecue it or shoot it, fuck it or ride it, forget it. Not available west of the Pecos.

So I had to be a writer who grew up in Texas and my opportunities were pretty limited because of that.

Unfortunately, I was the product of a traditional American education. I say "unfortunately" because the literature

I was exposed to in that system included what might be termed "safe" writers. Thackery, Milton, Shakespeare, Melville, Whitman, Steinbeck, Faulkner...you know the list. It's the list we've all been exposed to.

I tried. Believe me, I tried. But my models for writing were all wrong, in a way. They were guys like Balzac and Dickens, Henry James and Jonathon Swift. Ladies like Louisa May Alcot. Great writers, sure, but from another planet as far as I was concerned. I grew up in a bar, saw my first man killed when I was twelve—shot six feet in front of me. I was the night dispatcher for my grandmother's cab company when that happened and had to phone the police. Nothing like that ever happened in *Little Women*, near as I could tell.

One by one, I tried all the genres and styles I became exposed to and one thing or the other doomed each experiment. I mean, I loved the books I read and of course I tried imitating them in style and content, but even though they were wonderful books, they weren't about worlds I inhabited. I guess I assumed you weren't allowed to write about the planet I happened to find myself on.

I just didn't realize you were allowed to write about real life, at least life as I knew it. It was my first brush with censorship, although I didn't know it. Our local public library, which was my only source of reading material just didn't carry anything in the contemporary realism category. Looking back, I know now the head librarian hauncho probably felt those kinds of books would damage my tender and developing character, so even if they had such books on their shelves, they were kept from youngsters like myself.

So, for years, I continued writing what I thought was the only kind of stuff that could get published and little by little became more and more disillusioned with writing and literature in general. Perhaps if I had gone to college at an earlier age, I might have discovered there were books out there to which I could relate, but I didn't. I was in the Navy and then in prison, and in those kinds of environments you just don't run across literature that's much different than what you'd find on your average high school English recommended reading list.

I quit writing for a number of years, because, frankly, I was bored. It was by chance only that I came upon a writer who relit the literary fires.

Charles Bukowski.

Wow.

Lights went off.

This guy was doing things I didn't know you were allowed to do. He was writing about life, about real life. Nitty-gritty, down and dirty life. Lots of it was funny, most of it was sad, but it all touched me, way down deep there in that literary G-spot all writers (and readers) are forever trying to connect with.

I read another guy about the same time that turned me on fire inside as well. Kurt Vonnegut. I read this interview in the *Paris Review* in which he said, "Literature should not disappear up its own asshole, so to speak." Big spark of understanding there. Ol' Kurt said exactly what I had been unable to articulate for a long time, ever since I started reading the "masters." The old boys (and girls) had some good stuff going for them, but it seems like literary sphincterism had set in by the time I came along, all these deified contemporary writers were sitting around contemplating their own navels, it seemed. I was reading all this stuff about upper-middle class angst. Really jazzy stuff, like how some guy was sorrowing because all he had out of life was his Chrysler agency and ten million bucks and was searching his soul and was in this big blue funk because he hadn't gone off with Easy Sally that time at the senior prom way back in H.S. Every book I picked up at that period seemed to have a similar theme. I just couldn't identify. Hell, I never was able to afford a *used* Chrysler, let alone an entire agency, and I *had* run off with Easy Sally—yeah, I was that guy, the one in the leather jacket and the slicked-back hair—really! I had hair, back then— and believe me there isn't a lot of angst to be used for material in the writing trade when you're sitting in the trailer and Easy Sally is looking like Even Easier Sally and you don't know where your next PBR is coming from and the TV is flashing those little tornado warnings across the bottom of the screen and you're trying to quiet the little rascal on your knee that has your last name but the propane delivery man's hook nose. I just *knew* somewhere deep inside my bones I couldn't fake writing a whole, entire book out of what it meant to be the Executive Vice President in Charge of Sales for Southeastern Florida for the Tidy Bowl Corp and sorrowing over the lost babe of his childhood or the sad fact that he'd chucked it all and gone off to paint Tahitian sunsets. Or that his wife had. Crap like that.

All of a sudden, here's this guy Bukowski writing about shit *I* knew about. About whores and hustlers, winos and fathead bosses who were always worried their wives would go to bed with the help so they got their mad out in the open right away.

I picked up a book of his, a collection of stories called *The Most Beautiful Woman in Town and Other Stories.* I loved those other stories. It was like sitting down with a homeboy or your rap partner in the joint and swapping lies. Better yet; it was *entertaining.* All of a sudden, I remembered why I had first started writing. To make someone laugh. Or cry. Learn something about another human being. Just *feel* something. Feel what I was feeling. Here was this guy, Bukowski, and he was doing exactly what I'd always wanted to do.

Bukowski's stories weren't about middle-aged English professors who were all in a fret because their wives no longer get excited sitting around listening to them conjugate French verbs and deducing that their lives, the meaningful portions of them, anyway, were over. Some of these guys, it seemed, took four hundred pages to figure out why the major babe in their life was leaving. They were *bored,* Jack.

I know this was billed as a lecture on censorship and you may be wondering where the censorship angle comes in. Well, where it comes in is that not only were folks like Bukowski not being published by so-called "respectable" presses in this country, but other books by writers like him were not generally available to people like myself. They weren't talked about by our English teachers, they weren't on the shelves of our hometown libraries—or if they were, they were kept from our view and knowledge. In other words, there was a form of censorship operating that kept this kind of book from me and others that exists today and it is this and other forms of censorship, overt and covert, that I'll get to, by and by. I want to show what it is about Bukowski that turned my whole life around. Well, not my *life*—I mean, I still have to mow the grass on Saturday and take out the garbage—but this story saved my *writing* life, which is, after all, the only life worth having.

The story was "The Fiend." You may have read it. If you did, you either became a fan of Bukowski's or you hated his guts. Personally, I became a fan.

Basically, it's a story about a middle-aged guy named

Martin Blanchard, who's been defeated by alcohol. He's lost his wife and family, *two wives, two families,* actually, his job, *everything. Twenty-seven* jobs he's gone through. That's a lot of jobs. This guy's just your basic average slob who can't leave the juice alone. He's reduced to living in this squalid apartment, four flights up, and drinking wine. His only source of income are his unemployment checks and money left in parking meters. Badly educated, yet he listens to classical music, preferring Mahler.

He begins to notice this little girl outside playing. He begins to notice she has on these interesting panties... and...you guessed it, he finds himself masturbating. Afterwards, he feels relief. *It's out of my mind,* he thinks after he gets off. *I'm free again.* Only, he's not. It's just the beginning of a new obsession, a perversion. For the first time in months, perhaps years, he has an interest. It repels him, but he can't resist it, either.

At first, he thinks it's just something weird that overtook him and now it's out of his system, but after he drinks his last bottle of wine, he sees the little girl outside in the street and begins to get hard again. He decides to go to the store to replenish his wine supply and as he walks outside he notices the little girl and the two little boys have gone into the garage across the street. He finds himself walking into the garage behind them and shutting the doors.

He then proceeds to rape the little girl, in very graphic detail. When you read this part, if it doesn't make you sick, you're probably beyond the kind of help counseling can give you at this late date. All the while he's committing this heinous act, the two boys are asking him questions. They express genuine curiosity and don't seem to be overly-frightened, exhibiting more of an amoral attitude than anything. Bukowski does something quite skillful here. Instead of having the two young boys be scared shitless, he shows them to be mainly curious about what Martin is doing to their friend. These kids are witnessing something pretty horrible, but then they're just kids, and there's an amoral innocence about their reaction that blurs the morality. Raping a child is without doubt a truly horrible crime, with no redemption in such an act, but since it's hard to whole-heartedly condemn the two boys the reader is moved into an area of moral ambiguity that creates a kind of complicity with the boys. The reader then becomes, like the boys, a kind of voyeur to Martin's act. This also helps humanize the monster Martin is, inasmuch as any such person could be seen as having human qualities.

The kicker for me in this story was a line a little earlier on in the story, as Martin is kissing the child, just before he rapes her, and the narrator says, *"Martin's eyes looked into her eyes and it was a communication between two hells— one hers, the other his."* When I read this line, it was as if I'd been struck by literary lightening.

What I have always thought good writing was about was *people*, all kinds of folks, and what made writing about people *good*, was that it showed you something about them. Something you didn't know or were confused on or were ignorant of. And not just politically correct folks, either. In fact, preferably *not* politically correct folks. Is there a more boring bunch in the solar system? You see, I was in jail, I was an alcoholic, I was a drug user, I was all those kinds of dudes that aren't allowed to buy a house in Westchester County—well, that's not right, exactly, according to my New York friends, most of the citizens in Westchester *fit* that description—but you know what I mean—and I knew they weren't all weak or stupid or worthless. They didn't all start out that way. Something happened along the road. Some of the most intellectual conversations I've ever heard were in soup kitchens. I met a guy once who used to teach physics at M.I.T., one fine Thanksgiving Day at the free turkey blowout the Salvation Army was hosting in Baltimore. This guy could make hydrogen bombs in his sleep and probably cure cancer if he got a year off the sauce.

Anyway, back to Bukowski and his story about the child rapist. Bukowski doesn't excuse this motherfucker, nor make him out to be anything but the monster he is, but he does show us something about the guy which we probably wouldn't have known in any other way. He shows us there's a human being running around inside the guy someplace. A somewhat *troubled* human being, but one of us at any rate. And this is what literature should be all about. Showing us to one another. The good, the bad, the ugly as well as the downright perverts.

All his stuff isn't good. In fact, a lot of it stinks. Kind of masturbation-on-the-page type of stuff. He considers himself a genius—well, he *is*, actually—and Bukowski seems to have thought that everything he had a thought on was important because it came out of his brain. Not true. That virtually everything he wrote got printed may not have been his fault, but more the fault of publishers who bought into his self-created myth.

Almost any other writer that this same story would have occurred to, would have taken the point of view of anyone *but* Martin's. The little girl herself, the boys, the cops who came and arrested him, the parents. An adult who discovered the crime. A fly on the wall. To write this kind of story from the POV of the perp, in my mind, is the stuff of literary courage. It's very dangerous stuff. It you don't bring it off, it almost makes the writer appear as if he excused Martin for what he's done, which would have made Bukowski an even bigger monster than his character. What he's been able to do is present Martin exactly as he is—a hideous member of the human race...but amazingly, yet...*still a member of humanity.* It's interesting in one respect, too, in that Bukowski wrote this story in the third person, while most of his other writing is first person and confessional autobiography. It looks as if he wanted to make sure readers didn't confuse the narrator with the author, which, if he did, renders him just a little less courageous. I don't want to think of him that way, so I'll give him the benefit of the doubt.

With that one little sentence, "*Martin's eyes looked into her eyes and it was a communication between two hells— one hers, the other his,*" Bukowski gives us an insight that is deeply profound. And that, in my opinion, is what great writing is all about.

It takes enormous courage to be able to write about the kinds of people Bukowski does. Readers, even intelligent readers, tend to associate the writer with the narrator. In my first semester, I wrote a story about a character who was a criminal, and I had the concern that the reader of the piece would want to know if I had been a criminal myself. I addressed my concern to my first advisor here, Phyllis Barber, and she said, "an intelligent reader will never ask if a piece of writing is autobiographical, so don't worry about it." Well, Phyllis meant well, and in a perfect world, this would be true, but believe me, even very intelligent readers at least wonder if the stuff they're reading comes from the writer's own experience and even the brightest of readers will wonder if very negative or dark stuff is what the author really thinks and feels. It's just human nature. It'd be nice if readers accepted work labeled as fiction as just that—fiction—but the truth of the matter is, there's something of the prurient in all of us that makes us hope that the stuff on the page—*especially* the dark, forbidden stuff—is derived from the real experience of its creator. It gives most of us a delicious little shiver of horror to be standing this close to depravity without actually having to get any of it on ourselves. There is some part of almost all our souls that craves the darker side of life. We are alternately titillated and repulsed by immoral behavior and I think that is the reason books and stories and movies about bad guys are so well-attended. We can satisfy this baser part of our souls in a safe and acceptable manner, so long as they get put in their places in the end.

Most of my own writing output has been about such people, and without exception, those who read it and are acquainted with me, will come up and ask, in almost an embarrassed fashion, "Was that yourself you were writing about?" Up until just recently, I would usually answer that, uh, no, I just *know* some people like that. I've usually taken the coward's way out. Just recently, I've begun to admit that, yes, I've done many of the things that show up in my stories. I've been a criminal, done time, sold drugs, been involved in various sexual aberrations, broken many and diverse laws. I don't do them any more—well, not as *many*—I'd be room temperature by now if I'd continued doing some of the things I used to. And, I'm a different person than I was when I was involved in those things. That's why I've usually lied when asked if the author of my work was the same as the narrator. Most folks, no matter what they say, will assume you're still that kind of person and that kind of reputation will keep you from getting some of the nicer rewards of our civilization.

The thing that writers like Bukowski represent to me is *truth.* As a group of animals endowed with a superior intellect—as compared with, say, monkeys or tse-flies—and if we do indeed have this intelligence, then what we ought to be about primarily is the pursuit of truth. This is what education should be about, although sadly, it seems not to be the Holy Grail it once was. Back in "my day" which was the nineteen-sixties, that's what a lot of us were interested in. Truth. We were into toppling institutions. Institutions we felt were based on lies. And, I guess that's why writers like Bukowski appeal to me so much. The one thing we weren't being in the sixties was *safe.* Although, that's not entirely true. There was a large contingent of folks that were concerned mainly with making sure they didn't go to Vietnam and get shot at. A lot of the hyperbole in that era was, in fact, centered around changing a system that could put one's physical unit in jeopardy. But for many of us, especially those of us who had been in the military at the time, the things we were involved in were anything but safe. That's what seems to be missing today. Most of the stuff I pick up and read, while quite good in many instances, is for the most part, *safe* writing. The mood has changed, as it always does, but the direction it has moved to is a dangerous one.

I'm speaking here of the phenomenon sweeping through this country referred to as being "politically correct." Like many grandiose ideas, there is a noble intent at the center of this outlook, but also like many other popular notions, it has been perverted until it is the antithesis of what it originated as. Being PC nowadays amounts to out and out censorship in my opinion. For every writer like Bukowski, William Vollmann, and David Sedaris who breaks through and becomes a cult hero, there are hundreds of writers who are being stifled, vilified, and destroyed, simply because they do not preach the party's message nor do they conform to the parameters set up by the PC folks who seem to be in charge. Too often they are stifling themselves by trying to placate society. What used to be considered simply bad taste nowadays takes on a more sinister connotation and that is dangerous if we value freedom of thought and value the time-honored tradition of the debate of ideas which is the only viable method for advancing knowledge and understanding.

Plato himself spoke about political correctness in *The Republic*, when he said: "Then the first thing will be to establish a censorship of the writers of fiction, and let the censors receive any tale of fiction which is good, and reject the bad; and we will desire mothers and nurses to tell their children the authorized ones only." How about that.

In another of Bukowski's stories, "3 Chickens," he continually beats his girlfriend. Definitely *not* a PC story. Here are some direct quotes from the story:

once she was screaming these insanities from the fold-down bed in our apartment. I begged her to stop, but she wouldn't. finally, I just walked over, lifted up the bed with her in it and folded everything into the wall.

then I went over and sat down and listened to her scream.

but she kept screaming so I walked over and pulled the bed out of the wall again there she lay, holding her arm, claiming it was broken.

and

now, another time she angered me and I slapped her but it was across the mouth and it broke her false teeth.

I was surprised that it broke her false teeth and I went out and got this super cement glue and I glued her teeth together for her. it worked for a while and then one night as she sat there drinking her wine she suddenly had a mouthful of broken teeth.

the wine was so strong it undid the glue. it was disgusting. we had to get her some new teeth, how we did it, I don't quite remember, but she claimed they made her look like a horse.

and

the bar was full, every seat taken. I lifted my hand. I swung. I backhanded her off that god damned stool. she fell to the floor and screamed.

There are more abusive incidents in the story. This is horrible stuff to anyone—and I imagine that's most of us—who is interested in consciousness-raising about spouse abuse and battering—but there is a value to being exposed to this kind of material. How else can we understand anything about violence unless we observe and portray it accurately? It exists, just as surely as serial killers exist, and how can one combat evil unless one understands its nature?

Gordon Weaver, who was on the faculty here at Vermont until a few years ago, told me in an interview, that, "If our special interest, as writers and/or editors, is the precise use of language toward the end of a viable perception of and effect on reality, we may argue there is some virtue implicit in *any* utterance (written or oral) that confronts the consensus of any gathering." He gives an example. "There is a cost that will be paid by all concerned if one tells a Polack joke in the presence of Poles, but I contend the cost is greater if one stifles or sanitizes the anecdote." Gordon has something here, I think. Weaver also told me that academicians are perhaps the newest bullies on the censorship block and perhaps the most dangerous of all. He stated that, "There is a greater danger, it seems to me, when the censors come from the ranks of the presumably 'enlightened.' It is not surprising that a number of college and university communities nurture factions who wish to control free speech; it is unsettling when more sophisticated citizens (faculty) add their clout to movements desiring to police our utterance in the interests of what minority or another deems politically incorrect."

Whether or not you agree with writers like Bukowski, or Weaver for that matter, is unimportant. What is important is that they and others of diverse opinions have a forum to be heard and read. That forum is disintegrating under the onslaught of those who wish to stifle speech that disagrees with theirs. Truth is in danger of being extinguished, and it may fall to us who write to be the last vanguard of free speech. That is why writers such as Bukowski need to be published and need to be read by establishment presses and before they're dead. There are some of us who feel we are plunging back into a Dark Age. History would confirm that to be so. After nearly every period of enlightenment, anarchy prevails again for a while, and this is what I see us heading toward, as a nation and as a world.

It is the nature of groups to want to stifle opposing viewpoints. In this country, supposedly the land of free speech, attempts at suppression have been with us since the adoption of the First Amendment, but the preponderance of that type of activity has been traditionally borne by extremists of the far right and far left political and societal spectrum. Those with the hot fire of righteousness in their bellies have been the usual standard-bearers for the termination of ideas contrary to their agenda and such should probably be expected.

Gordon Weaver told me that although he dislikes boorish and bigoted expressions, he sees a greater danger in disallowing their spokesmen an opportunity to be heard.

"The censors will always be with us," he said. "It is the nature of both institutions and individuals to desire the silence of those they wish to suppress. Institutions with political power or ambitions for same (government, churches, schools) can probably be fended off—as they have been in modern times at least—by organized responses. The American Civil Liberties Union has a pretty good record in this regard. Simple crackpots (racists, militant feminists, and other self-appointed arbiters of community morality) seem to wither away if studiously ignored."

Repression comes in many forms, not always overt. Kathleen M. Sullivan, a professor of law at Harvard Law School, in talking about the censorship issue as it affects funding for the NEA, says of the PC issue, "An artist who receives a check in the mail (from the NEA) with a 'hit list' of forbidden ideas attached will forego too much valuable and innovative expression for fear it will come too close to the line. As (U.S. Supreme Court) Justice Thurgood Marshall once put it, the problem with a 'sword of Damocles is that it *hangs*—not that it drops.'"

Fred Grandy, former actor on the *Love Boat* and now a Congressman from Iowa, says, "I am no artist and have ten years on TV to prove it. But I have spent enough of my life around creative minds to know that you cannot have art without risk. You cannot write language proscribing the human imagination that will not turn artists away in droves."

Speaking of Congress in terms that could be applied to college professors and publishers as well, Grandy said, "Trying to eliminate smut by allowing Congress to tell America what is and is not artistic is as misguided as attempting to legislate patriotism by amending the Constitution to prohibit flag burning."

And publishers. How do they, as deciders of what news is fit to print, view the censorship debate? Reactions range from the moderately perplexed to the horrified doomsayers.

Robert McDowell, who publishes the Story Line Press, wrote an opinion piece for the *Register-Guard* in Eugene, Oregon, which perhaps synopsizes the publisher's view. "The debate pits a democratic majority believing in our First Amendment rights of free speech against a well-financed and well-organized minority extolling the virtues of all that is wholesome and the government's right to control the subject matter of the books we read, the music we enjoy, the paintings and plays we experience." McDowell calls Senator Jesse Helms and other individuals and groups' efforts to censor materials funded by the NEA, "the most severe legalized censorship in this country since the McCarthy era," and labels such censorship efforts as being "shameful attacks on free speech and the artist's right to represent the truth as he or she perceives it."

Pulitzer-Prize-winning novelist, Larry McMurtry, in a *Washington Post* article, accused the Jesse Helms-led forces of attempting to "eliminate all sex from American art if they can. Rembrandt's sketch of a fully clothed hetero-sexual couple attempting the missionary position behind a bush would likely not be thought fund-worthy by Helms, whose stated preferences would limit us to snow scenes, pictures of bird dogs or romantic landscapes involving, if possible, humble tobacco farms." McMurtry goes on, "The narrative as these individuals see it, in their determination to tell Americans what they need and don't need in the way of publicly funded art, is rigidly chaste: no public money for anything with sex in it! (They may claim that (they) only want to withhold public money from art that depicts or describes 'wrong' sex—i.e., homoerotic (no grants to Leonardo or Proust!) sadomasochistic (no Westerns, no film noir), exploitive of children (no Lolita, no Lewis Carroll), but it's clear that they really mean to eliminate all sex from American art if they can."

Kathleen Sullivan puts it even more succinctly, when she says, "A free society can have no official orthodoxy in art any more than in religion or politics. And in a free society, such orthodoxy can no more be purchased by power of the purse than compelled by power of the sword."

Just a couple of years ago, Stanley Banks, Kansas City playwright and poet, offered the balance of such cost: "We will begin to see dull art which has no freshness of vision. Certain points of view will be silenced. When that happens our society will be seriously threatened without a bomb being blasted." He warns us not to "call for laws to censor artists who challenge our consciousness in ways that might be uncomfortable, irritating, risqué, etc. For those who don't want to see or hear or read about acts or points of view contrary to their own, he advises, "simply don't look, buy it or let the kids have access to it!"

Banks' "dull art which has no freshness of vision" is already upon us. It has always been with us, since censorship in one form or another has always been around—it has only increased mightily in the past few years. The result is art which is becoming blander and blander, much resembling the "art" that was allowed to surface in totalitarian governments such as the USSR of a few years past and in many other governments. America is not yet at that stage, but if current developments continue in publishing, in the university, and in government, we are not far from achieving total censorship, imposed by the group in control.

What scares me the most is that universities should be the bastion of free thought but the state of the matter is that free debate of ideas is rapidly disappearing from the college campus. As more and more writers come out of university settings and are being influenced by teachers with a decided political bent, the writing they produce becomes more and more insipid. These same writers take over the litmags and editor positions at publishing houses and impose their political beliefs on those who submit, publishing only those that can pass the PC test in the content of their creative material. As Kurt Vonnegut said in a quote cited earlier, "Literature should not disappear up its own asshole, so to speak." Well, it's in great danger of doing just that. It's about halfway up the anus.

In interviewing folks for an article I wrote on censorship for *Circle K Magazine*, I was referred to the brother-in-law of a friend of mine, an Australian, who was teaching physics and doing research at one of America's leading universities which I cannot name because I've promised him anonymity. This man says, "I think it's a myth that censorship doesn't exist on college campuses. I believe universities should be places where anybody can say whatever they want and everybody should be very tolerant, but it's just not true. Students are punished for saying certain things. You could say whatever you wanted at the University of Sydney (where he's from). They were much more tolerant there. In student publications there was much less concern about libel, for example. The litigation aspect puts a lot of pressure on what ideas you can express." This man only agreed to give me his views when I swore several times I wouldn't use his name or even tell what university he was at, for fear of losing his job. It's a sad day when a person from another country is allowed a greater freedom of expression there than in his adopted country which professes to be the freest nation on earth.

This professor went on to say, "I think there's more of a tradition in European-style universities for freedom of speech—that that's what universities are for. In America, the impression I get is that universities are for other purposes...for training professionals and for football games.

It's not about intellectual freedom. You pay us (educators) your money and you want something at the end. You want a guaranteed elite job in society, and it has nothing to do with expanding your mind. You're buying a product. It's more of a consumer orientation."

He adds, "The government is trying to censor more and more science that they are actually paying for. For example, on sensitive subjects as global warming, the government wants to see research results first, because of the possible political consequences."

Americans should be ashamed when they have prided themselves on theirs being the leading example of a free society, when others in the world community may be seeing us very differently, as evidenced by my anonymous critic and source.

Anita Manning, writing for *USA Today*, says that the issue is different in colleges than it is in the lower levels of education.

"In K through 12, there is a school board or some sort of governing body that chooses what books are included in the curriculum...whereas in the college setting, the individual professor or instructor chooses the books for that course and students choose whether or not to take the course, leading to entire different issues."

In June, 1992, Brenda Suderman, acting media relations officer for *The Bulletin*, the student newspaper at the University of Manitoba in Winnipeg, reported that the university deleted about one hundred seventy files containing material on sexual bondage and pornography from the Internet computer system the university subscribes to. Gerry Miller, Director of Computer Services, made the decision in consultation with Terry Falconer, Vice President (administration), saying the material was removed because "we felt they (the deleted files) didn't support the mission of the university and we felt they were objectionable."

Alisa Smith, co-editor of *The Marlet*, the student newspaper at the University of Victoria in British Columbia, published what university officials deemed objectionable material as exampled by a lesbian, gay, bisexual issue put out in 1991 which featured male and female genitalia on the cover. About two thousand copies were thrown into dumpsters by campus traffic and security functionaries upon administrative order. Even so, Smith feels the press is becoming a bit freer. (Yeah, well—go figure...)

She says, "The mainstream media is covering a lot of issues that only the alternative press used to cover. I suppose the backlash against political correctness is sort of an attempted censorship, like trying to silence people, but not by directly shutting down their newspapers. (Universities) are trying to shut down *thought,* rather than newspapers. All the articles that you see are about how PC's have sort of gotten a grip on society and how people can't say what they want anymore. I guess it's like a left-wing phenomenon."

Let money talk, though, and censorship takes on yet another clever form: the economic kind.

"Personally," says Smith, "I think the biggest form of censorship right now is the fact that the economy is so bad, making advertising really hard to come by. A lot of papers used to have a fairly idealistic boycott list for advertising that they wouldn't use because of things those advertisers were funding—like nuclear systems contracting or because they were pro-apartheid in South Africa. Editors are finding they can't make ideological choices anymore because of monetary pressure. If you're really dependent on advertising dollars, you have to basically write the kinds of things that won't offend your advertisers and don't disagree with their stances."

This latter statement seems to contrast with her earlier one that "the press is becoming a bit freer," and is perhaps a good example of why censorship is unnecessary. If you allow anyone to talk freely long enough, they may provide sufficient evidence by their own words that they should not be taken that seriously when giving us the benefit of their opinion.

Fearful of bad publicity during stressful economic times, it is not so surprising college and university administrations are increasingly acting to suppress anything that might bring adverse publicity to their campuses. What is surprising is that faculty members are increasingly joining in, even in the supercharged Politically Correct environment that has permeated most higher-education campuses in one way or another.

A 1992 incident at Nicholls State University in Thibodaux, Louisiana, exemplifies the debate and poses difficult and perplexing arguments for both sides of the issue.

A cartoon ran in the student newspaper, the *Nicholls Worth*, poking fun at three black singers in a rap group that had performed on campus. Black students who were offended, protested by burning about one hundred fifty copies of the paper publicly. Their complaint was that they were greatly upset by the exaggerated features of the cartoon figures and the stereotypes it reinforced. Eric Knott, president of a black fraternity denied that the protest had anything to do with being politically correct.

"I'm not one to hide behind racism and claim that everything in society is racist, (but) the cartoon clearly degraded the black race," Knott says.

Marty Authement, student editor of the paper, said that he "used poor judgment" in allowing the cartoon to be published, but was also concerned that "political correctness is limiting what journalists can do. These days you have to be more sensitive than you usually would be. If you live by the strict law of political correctness, there's not much left."

I had a very jarring and dismaying experience with PCism with my own novel *The Death of Tarpons*. A few years before it actually got published, a regional publisher in the Southwest wanted to buy it. A very few months before this offer, I was sleeping on a garage floor in California and eating out of a Bob's Big Boy dumpster, so the money he offered had the same value as a million dollars to me. I almost signed the contract until the publisher said, "Well, we have to change a lot of this. There's stuff in here that might make certain folks upset." He gave as an example a scene in which the boy's father whips him with a live king snake. This might offend the snake lovers, he said. That's got to be what?—seven or eight in the U.S.A.? Not counting, of course, the folks who use them in church services. He cited about twenty other scenes I'd have to change because they might offend this person or that. Reluctantly, I withdrew the book, not knowing if it would ever be published, and indeed, it was another five years before I found a publisher who wasn't as concerned about snake lovers' feelings and was more concerned with putting out a book that she felt had literary value.

Mind you, this was several years before the wholesale PC attitude took over the country. This asshole—and I *don't* excuse myself from the term—was merely the forerunner of what is a terrifying fact of life today.

If you believe this to be the ravings of a paranoid mind, consider these facts: A record three hundred forty-eight incidents of attempted censorship occurred in the 1991-92 school year, according to *The American Way*, a liberal watchdog group. That's an increase of twenty percent over the previous high, a figure they claim poses an alarming advance in assaults on a basic Constitutional right—a right almost universally assured in most of the free world.

The Literary Network, a project jointly administered by Poets&Writers, Inc. and the Council of Literary Magazines and Presses report over six thousand attempts to remove books from shelves in American libraries in the 1980s and "the number of incidents is noticeably on the rise."

Concerned Women for America, a conservative, pro-family group asserts all censorship attempts are not necessarily bad. Caia Mockaitis, speaking for the organization, says the issue is one of selection, not censorship, many times, in that "there are some materials that are appropriate for kids and some that are not," no matter what adults' political bias, liberal or conservative.

Mockaitis has plenty of like-minded supporters. Censorship attempts at banning outright or restricting access to books and magazines in secondary school libraries were successful in nearly one-half of instances between 1987 and 1990, reports a University of Wisconsin survey of sixty-six hundred schools. Challenged publications were removed twenty-six percent of the time, restricted by age or grade level twenty-two percent of the time, and more likely to occur at small schools.

The book challenged most? Judy Blume's *Forever*, a story of a teenage girl who loses her virginity. *Sports Illustrated*'s swimsuit issue and *Rolling Stone* were the most-challenged magazines at secondary schools, according to *USA Today*, Jan. 20, 1992.

Consider this item: "Pornography Victims Compensation Act" was a bill on the U.S. Senate floor that would enable victims of sex crimes to file civil suits in an effort to recover damages from producers and distributors of obscene materials (including publishers, wholesalers, and booksellers) if the victims can show that the materials "caused" the crimes. This "third-party liability" bill is a way of imposing censorship through a back door. This item was reported by the American Booksellers Association.

Here's another: In May, 1990, Ferris Alexander, operator of a chain of bookstores, theaters and video stores in the Minneapolis area, was found guilty of violating the Racketeer Influenced and Corrupt Organization Act (RICO) obscenity forfeiture law. His crime? Selling four magazines and three videotapes found to be obscene and valued at less than two hundred dollars. Alexander was sentenced to six years in prison, fined two hundred thousand dollars and forfeited a twenty-five million dollar business. This was reported by The Media Coalition.

Here's another. Three editors of the Ohio State University student newspaper, *The Lantern*, resign when members of the journalism faculty issue a policy statement that the faculty advisor had the authority to review articles for libel before they were published. This story from *The Chronicle of Higher Education,* March 4, 1992.

Censorship is everywhere and rising in attempts and more frightening, in successful attempts.

Free speech advocate Nat Hentoff, the author of *Free Speech for Me—But Not for Thee: How the American Left and Right Relentlessly Censor Each Other* from Harper Collins, feels that in too many cases, publishers, school boards and principals remove or change material for students rather than face the wrath of militant parent groups. Seeing authorities suppress ideas in some cases, and being in a school in which books keep disappearing, gives a graphic lesson to students, Hentoff feels, in that they may have doubts that theirs is a country of intellectual freedom.

And it appears it is special-interest groups that are

behind these efforts and that the majority of Americans are against censorship. A survey conducted by Louis Harris for the American Council for the Arts and sponsored by Phillip Morris Companies, Inc., in February, 1992, polled fifteen hundred adults over the age of eighteen by telephone. Part of the findings were that ninety-one percent felt it important for school children to be exposed to and participate in the arts; sixty-seven percent felt learning about the arts as important as learning about history and geography, sixty percent say as important as math and science, and fifty-three percent believe the arts are important as learning to read and write. It's evident that it's a small but vocal and politically-powerful group of minorities who are succeeding in censorship activities and these groups emerge from both ends of the political and societal spectrum.

Virtually every publisher in the country, from the smallest litmag to the largest publishing conglomerate, is terrified of antagonizing any reader whatsoever, unless the person offended is not part of a highly-organized, highly-vocal political group. This includes both right and left-wingers. It seems everybody in America has now organized, has a group with a slogan, a newsletter, a home page on the Internet, and a secret handshake. The battle is being waged over who gets ultimate control of the presses. And it doesn't matter who wins. We all lose. What we lose is freedom of expression. And once that happens, we are done as a free society. I go to Gordon Weaver once again, who said it as best as it can be said. "Censorship from without is bad for the language, bad for those who speak or write it; self-imposed censorship, *whatever* the motive is worse. If you won't say what you think, you run the risk of losing the powers of both speech and thought. I suspect we'll be safe just as long as we refuse to accept censorship for *anyone.*"

Again, I quote Gordon Weaver for perhaps the best take on the situation. "If the king is naked, we're all (including the king) better served if someone says so."

Well, the king is indeed, naked. The only problem is not enough of us are saying so, preferring to remain safe, keep our jobs, get our material published and so we go on, giving silent tacit agreement to what is happening. This is an understandable position for many in our society; it is unforgivable for writers, at least in my opinion. Writers should be like the canaries in coal mines, the warning system that things are not right and that danger looms. As a group, we have many of us become complacent, intent only on saving our professional selves at the expense of freedom of thought. Maybe we understand too well that although the canary in the coal mine provided a valuable service, in doing so he ended up room temperature.

I cannot count the numbers of instances acquaintances of mine have said to me, "I cannot say certain things I believe in, to my class, my teachers, my peers, or in my writing, because I would lose my job or be censured or not see my work in print, etc. What's wrong with us? What kinds of writers are we producing in this country that are fearful to take stands on issues they believe fervently about simply because they risk disapproval? What kind of chickenshit writer is it that the little squiggles he or she puts down on paper consist of half-truths and integrity that is compromised regularly? We are surrendering something precious more by what we don't do than what we do. Are we so enamored of safety and comfort that we are willing to give up the freedom to express ourselves honestly? It seems that we are. It is a growing malaise that is sweeping the country and I hold that the only ones that can stem the tide are the writers in our society. But where are they?

Some are out there. There are a few. William Vollmann.

Brian Everson. Michael Tolkin. Bukowski. There are others that we'll never know of because they can't find a forum. There need to be a lot more such voices. What is really needed is for establishment forums to begin looking more at the quality of the writing than the content. To give an ear to voices that refuse to be influenced by a job, a smile from an empty-headed bureaucrat, publication in a white-bread magazine or by a bottom-line mentality of a publishing conglomerate.

I think back to when I began writing as a grade school kid. One of the things I used to do was write humorous sketches of some of the more terrifying individuals I faced daily. Individuals like the bullies I and others faced, from the schoolyard rowdy to the teacher who thought her job was to intimidate her class into submission. I'd show these "pieces" to friends, they'd be passed around, and in some cases, public opinion ended those offenders' bullying careers. Nobody likes to push someone around if he's going to get laughed at by everyone else. It just plain takes all the power out of it, not to mention the fun.

The problem today is, the bullies have taken over not only the schoolyard, but the university, the Congress, the press, and the publishing house. Many of us in this room became writers because of a bully somewhere in their past. Maybe it was another kid, or a group of kids, or maybe it was a parent or a teacher. We found we could effectively combat these kinds of folks by the written word. If we were physically weaker we possessed a strength that was virtually indefensible against. The power of ideas, expressed upon the page and in open debate. Do we want to give up our only weapon against tyranny? I hope not.

And by the way—those writers I mentioned at the beginning of this lecture—Whitman, Steinbeck, Faulkner, Thackery, Milton, Shakespeare, Melville, Alcott—and that I described as "safe," were anything but that when they were being published. They were almost all rogues in their time and were, by turns, either censored, vilified, viewed with shock, attacked by those in power, or even unpublished in their lifetimes because of the content of their writing. It is only after many years had passed and the political climate had shifted, that the original perceptions of them and their work were considered nonthreatening enough to exist in our libraries and schools. Although many of them are still censored, even today. Steinbeck routinely makes his appearance at book-burnings and other censorship attempts, along with Faulkner, Whitman and even Shakespeare. They were "safe" to me when I read them, simply because I was reading them in a different, more removed era, but in fact, those writers who have become what we call "immortal" have largely been the risk-takers of their time, who wrote in line with their conscience, rather than the political and social mores of their period. Many of them endured great distress because what they were writing was politically incorrect at the time. The thing was, there were then and still are now, publishers who gave them a forum, often at great risk, and there were those who read them, and so the world has been enriched through those individuals' courage. Knowing this, it would be easy to say, "Well, hey, those folks got published and there are those today being published who don't parrot the party line, so what's the problem?" The problem is, once we as writers and future editors and educators begin to think like that, complacency sets in and we get the attitude to "let someone else worry about it" and that's when our freedom of expression becomes seriously eroded and in danger of disappearing. Freedom of expression is a value that must be continuously fought for, over and over. That war is never finished unless one side or the other lays down its arms. As part of this generation of writers, it is our duty to take up the battle.

There is another point of view that says that it's not the job of an artist to express a viewpoint or an opinion at all. While I respect the right of those who feel that way, I disagree. Indeed, is it possible to find a writer of note who hasn't expressed his point-of-view, politically, through his or her writings? What else was Steinbeck commenting on in *The Grapes of Wrath* if not a political system? Perhaps he didn't stand on a stump and proclaim to the world his political views but they sure are right there in his fiction. There are countless others I could give as examples and I'm sure you have your own list. Some artists feel it is their job to present a vision of the world, not a political opinion. I don't see a difference. It seems to be a matter of semantics. What is a "vision of the world" *except* a political opinion? Or you might call such a view a "philosophy" but again, philosophies (in my opinion) are nothing but political ideologies dressed up in a tuxedo. I believe it all comes down to politics and I mean politics in the purest sense, as in I want mine and you want yours and I'd kill you for yours if we hadn't agreed that we're civilized and have figured out a way for both of us to keep our stuff and not worry about the other taking it. And, for me, that's what censorship finally boils down to. It's refuting the principle that I can have mine and you can't take it and you can have yours and I can't have it either. You can just substitute the word "opinion" for a particular possession. What I object to is the closing down of forums for all but those who agree with the body politic, not in an overt way but by more subtle and insidious means.

Thank you for your time. I hope I've given you some food for thought. I hope you'll read some Charles Bukowski, some William Vollmann. I don't even care if you don't like or agree with them. In fact, the only way this little talk will be a success if people go out of here arguing with each other. Personally, I'm like Robert Duvall in *Apocalypse Now*—I love the smell of a good argument in the morning. I'd like to leave you with one of my favorite quotes. In the preface to the infamous *Story of O*, Jean Paulhan wrote, "Dangerous books are those that restore us to our natural state of danger."

Yes, they do.

Lecture delivered to MFA in Writing Students & Faculty at Vermont College, January 8, 1997. A version of this was published in *Circle K Magazine.*

I look out over the ball diamond at the Country Estates Mobile Home Park at the six boys lined up on the third-base line and another row of six along the first-to-second base path as they toss baseballs to their partners and I see another ballfield in my past. A diamond nestled in the corner of the recreation yard at Pendleton Reformatory, eighty-seven miles south of where I am today. And thirty years in the distance.

I'd been required to take a two-to-five year timeout from life for various crimes against society, mostly burglaries. Eighty-two of them, to be precise. Eighty-two second-degree burglaries were the "official" ones, the ones the authorities were aware of. There were possibly more...

There are no fourteen-foot-thick gray walls around this field. Just the mobile homes behind us, a community center to our right and a woods where left and center field end. Beyond right field is the access road to the park, which leads in from the highway.

The bubble-gum-chewing eleven and twelve year olds hurling the horsehide before me on this day are the members of my Wallen youth baseball team. I am their coach. We're an AABC team. This is my first year at Wallen. For the past five years I coached in Little League at St. Joe, over in the northeast part of town where I lived. None of these boys know my past, nor do their parents. If they did, I'd be their ex-coach, I think. I'm pretty sure at least some of the moms and dads would be demanding my resignation should they learn I served two years in prison once upon a time.

Although, *one* boy does know. My son, Mike. He's the tall one on the end, throwing lasers to the tough little guy who usually catches him in games, Steve Tipton, the son of my assistant coach, Steve, Sr. I know I can trust Mike not to divulge the information he has about his dad to his teammates. I can trust Mike with anything. We're best friends and we talked about his father's past a long time ago in one of our nightly "guy talks" we have each evening just before he shuts his eyes and drifts off to sleep. It's our secret. We have a couple-three secrets, us two guys.

Sometimes, after he falls asleep, I sit on the edge of his bed and simply stare at him. Sometimes, we hold hands as we talk and he falls asleep that way. I don't want to take my hand away, so I'll sit there until his unclenches and then I'll leave. Not before I bend over and kiss his slightly damp forehead, the sweet smell of his little-boy hair filling my nostrils. And my heart.

"Four-seam grips!" I shout at my team. "Remember. Always four-seam grips."

Our first drill at each practice begins the same. We warm up in these lines and work on our receiving and throwing mechanics. Once they're warmed up, we'll hold the competition they're all waiting for. Keep extending the distance between the lines until there's only one pair left who haven't dropped the ball or underthrown it.

They know to be in an athletic, "linebacker" position, glove extended, knees, waist and elbows bent, withdraw the glove slightly as the ball arrives. Use both hands to catch the ball. Get the ball out of the glove fast, get the four-seam grip and pivot, glove extended in front, throwing arm back, knees bent, fingers on top of the ball, hand slightly above the shoulder. The wrist is also bent. Every possible joint on the body is bent except the neck and the neck is turned toward the left if the thrower is right-handed, to the right if he's a southpaw. Bring the glove hand to your heart as you pivot toward your target and throw.

Give a good target, I say. I say this quite often. Hands up. Chest-high. Get the ball out quick.

Expect a bad throw, I repeat.

This is like life, I tell them, my attempt to weave a bit of philosophy into what we're doing. Give folks a good target and expect a bad throw. Be happy when you get a good throw and prepared if you don't.

How do you catch the ball? I ask.

With your feet, they yell out, in unison. *Move to the ball. Don't "arm" it.* They're well-rehearsed. Good kids, these. They pay attention.

Coach Steve and I stop the kids occasionally and walk up and down the lines, checking on their grips. I'm a preacher and the four-seam grip is my sermon topic.

I quiz 'em.

"Why do we always want to use a four-seam grip?" I want to know.

By this, the second week of practice, twelve hands shoot up. They all know by now.

"Because," says the other Mike on our team, diminutive Mike Rish, when I point to him. His dad sponsors the team. Rish Construction. "If you use another grip, the ball may sail or curve or sink." It's important Rish knows this. He's going to be our second baseman. I don't think "sail" was a word in his vocabulary before joining this team, but it is now. Probably "sink" wasn't either, at least not in this context. Mike Rish wants to be a pitcher—ten of the twelve players on this team do—so curve was a word familiar to him. They all want to throw curves but we don't let 'em. They throw 'em anyway.

You can only do so much and then you have to realize they have minds of their own.

I point to another boy who still waves his hand frantically. He has knowledge to share. They all have the same knowledge, but Ian Tipton is anxious to show his coach he's been paying attention. Coach Tipton and I have Ian slotted for third base and maybe do some catching. He's a hard-nosed kid, lives here in the trailer park. It's Jeff, his dad, who arranged for us to use their field for practice. Ian is Coach Steve's nephew. Jeff helps us coach.

"The ball may slip and you'll get a wild throw," Ian says, in a voice that's already changing, hitting those high and low tones during the same sentence, sometimes in the same word. "You gotta use the seams." Ian knows this now, but during the season, during a bang-bang play, he'll forget. I'll get ticked off for a second and then remember he's only twelve. I'm in my fifties and I forget lots more than that and most times my own memory lapses don't come during the pressure of bang-bang plays.

Bang-bang plays are kind of what got me into trouble all those years back. I was kind of a bang-bang guy. Guy with a million-dollar arm and a ten-cent head, kind of like the character Ebby Calvin (Nuke) LaLoosh in the movie *Bull Durham*...but with more serious consequences than Nuke suffered. Instead of nearly getting cut from a baseball team, I ended up close to getting cut by life. Like Nuke, I got lucky and was able to make a comeback.

To a large degree because of that kid out there.

"Four-seam grips!" I yell out at the boys.

It's my mantra.

(Excerpt from an as-yet unpublished memoir, titled *Mike and Me*.)

SNAKE FARM

*It starts with trouble. You don't
think it starts with peace, do you?*
—William Goyen,
in an interview with Reginald Gibbons

The guy in the cell next to mine confided in me once that his father abused him sexually. That isn't a news headline. What he told me later was. That his mother also assaulted him sexually. That's a story that goes above the fold. Either, by themselves goes on page eight if it goes at all. That both parents took him to bed is a headline. You know: *Man bites dog...*

His name was Jerome-something or other, I forget his last name, but I remember his prison number—#36693—since it told me right away how long he'd been there—before me at #49028. It's important to know how long your next-door neighbor has been inside—it tells you how you should probably conduct yourself around him. If he'd had a number newer than mine, that'd be different. That'd be someone I was over, you see?

He was a weight-lifter and a tall man. He took early parole by jumping off our third tier. The advantage in this kind of early parole is that you don't have to check in with a P.O. like a sixth-grader who's been grounded for not eating all of his supper.

The disadvantage is...It undoubtedly hurts when you stop, at least for a nanosecond.

The reason I mention James-something or other, Inmate #36693, is that he didn't make his swan dive because he was depressed over facing the rest of his life in prison. He didn't take an early out because he was being molested. Or because he'd been threatened.

He didn't even take it because he couldn't face one more meal of beans.

He took the flight to nowhere because of Thomas R. Melon.

Yeah. You read that right. Thomas R. Melon, the guy who writes those bestselling crime novels. Whose last novel was the sixth one of his twenty-two novels to be made into a movie, starring Mickey D'Angelo. Melon's the guy *People Magazine* does a feature on at least twice a year, the usual accompanying photo a shot of him staring soulfully out to sea, digging his toes into the sand, crinkly Photoshopped eyes. Who is regularly interviewed on PBS and MSNBC and even legitimate news organizations.

Ha! Got your attention now, don't I!

Thomas R. Melon who was known as a "franchise" to both the publishing and film worlds.

I'm sure you already have lots of questions at this point. "Story questions" as Thomas R. Melon referred to them in the few workshops he taught here at Pendleton Reformatory. One question answered, eh? Leading to even more questions. The biggest, of course, is how we came to partner up and create the justice system of human roach removal which you'll observe at the end of this.

I'll do my best to answer all of them. It's what Melon taught us in our workshops. To develop a tight plot, one that answers all the major story questions at the resolution.

To avoid those "godawful amateur epilogues" (as he referred to them).

Let's begin...

I was Melon's star pupil in those classes back in the joint. His "discovery." Like he was Columbus and I was the New World of writers. A Grandma Moses of convict writers. A thing like that plays great in *People Magazine* and on *The View* and other mindless venues.

We met a couple of years ago. He'd pulled some strings and got permission to spend the night inside our walls for some "research" he was doing for a prison novel he was planning to write. He thought if he spent a night in a cell in Pendleton he'd soak up the atmosphere and would have an inkling about what it was like to do time.

Yeah...

I'll give you a minute to get your head around that...

Anyway, he spent the night in the cell next to mine and kept me up all night yakking, asking dumb-ass questions. Guess he figured everybody was like him. In the morning, he'd leave, stop at a diner and have him a cup of coffee and a big breakfast, go over his notes, get him a motel room to catch some sleep-eye. Me, I'd drag myself over to the chow hall, try to keep my eyes open while I stuffed down some cold powdered eggs and a liquid that didn't resemble coffee in any form that a Starbucks barista would recognize, and then hoof it over to my job, where I'd stand on my feet all day, cutting other inmate's hair.

About six months later, his fucking book came out, where his main character was the warden in this prison and some kind of amateur detective on the side. He got just about everything wrong with the prison scenes and the story was lousy to boot. It was worse than any James

Patterson written-by-the-numbers crock of shit, if that tells you anything. I figured out who the bad guy was by page twenty-three and I don't think I'd ever encountered as many clichés in one single book as I had in that one. But, he mentioned me in the acknowledgements and I have to admit, that hit my ego bone. I mean, he was like a semi-big name and people on the bricks didn't know he was a complete phony, so it kind of made me a big deal for a while. I even got letters from those weirdos who like to write prisoners. I did what all of us do who get those letters—bled 'em for every blessed nickel I could, even tried to get one wasn't too awful fat to marry me so I could cop one of those conjugal visits. They all seemed to fall into one of two camps—either as big as a house and wearing a dress looked like a floral-patterned couch covering or a meth addict who was partial to tattoos and tooth decay. No bites on my proposals...Guess they were choosier than they looked.

As it happened, Melon got this idea he wanted to teach writing in the joint and got that arranged and that worked out well for me as he asked for me to be his assistant and that got me out of the barber shop once a month for all afternoon.

And that's where it began.

It got me out on early release and that's when the fun started. With Melon's help and connections, I got me a book published. Picture of me on the back, looking hard like the suckers expected and wanted. Did some TV interviews, stuff like that.

Whole bunch of phony hooraw. All the book was just some shit I'd done in the past. Burglarizing bars, holding up liquor stores, fucking a bunch of women. Stuff like that. Stuff I went to outlawing for that lots of guys wished they had the balls to do, but hadn't. So, instead of doing what

I'd done, they got some tattoos, hung out down at some strip club once a month, got a subscription to NetFlix. Lived the *Reader's Digest* condensed version of the wild life. The sanitized, safe version.

Like that.

But, that was my audience. Them and the bad girls. The bad girls recognized me. I was the guy they'd known when they were young. The guy their husbands didn't know about. That was some funny shit, all right. I seen 'em when I walked off whatever TV interview I was doing. Or, in the bookstore when they had me signing books. I seemed to almost always end up in the parking lot getting my weenie waxed with one of them old gals in the back seats of their Suburbans. I found out one thing. Fans of writers were nice, but most weren't lookers. Whole different crowd than rock star or athlete's groupies.

The one good thing Melon did for me was getting me to read other writers. And, not just the usual suspects. Melon really knew what good writing was, even if he didn't do much of it himself. I found there were some fucking fantastic writers out there. Harry Crews, Ken Bruen, Ray Banks, Tony Black, Paul D. Brazill, Tom Franklin, Larry Brown, Joe Lansdale, William Gay, Neil Smith, guys like that. Mostly Southern—although Banks, Bruen, Brazill and Black aren't Southern, but could be.

Even a blind hog can find acorns now and then.

Hi. It's me, your intrepid author, Thomas R. Melon. You can call me "Tom" or even "Tommy." All my friends do. I know I'm breaking all the rules by addressing my reader directly, but I do shit like that all the time—break the rules—and it hasn't seemed to hurt my sales much. Last time I checked—about two minutes before I sat down to write this, I had three books on different Amazon best-selling lists. Top ten for two of them and number nineteen for *Breaking Bad* on the Thriller/Heist/Novella/Noir/Experimental Fiction list. That ain't bad for a country boy! The meter just keeps goin' round and round!

All that crap about breaking rules is just that—crap. I use a million clichés, pretty much the same plot each time, and have a bunch of characters with names real parents never give their baby boys...and the readers eat it up. Hell, I'd even talk about my johnson like Elroy did and get away with it, except it maybe ain't that big. Ha-ha. Then, maybe it is...You'll never know...Unless you want to, that is. Only if you're a good-lookin' mama. Text me if you are and I'll sext you back...

Anyway, I've got this guy I'm teaching to write and got him hooked up with my agent and all, and Jim Twigs, our agent, told us he thinks a book we co-wrote could be a big seller. So, here we are. My co-writer is a guy named Jake Mayes. I know you don't know his name yet, but you will. His first book is just out and I hear it's doing okay. It's not number one or anything like that, but Twigs says it's holding its own and even got a mention in the *Times*. And, I don't want to brag, but I'm pretty sure he wouldn't have even written a book if it wasn't for me and for sure even if he had, it wouldn't have gotten published! So, there's that...

The book you're reading—which hasn't been written yet at this point in time—ha-ha—that's what I'm doing now—was laid out by our mutual agent (who I hooked Jake up with). There's two main characters—me and Jake—and it's kind of a memoir-kind of thing. Jim told us to just write our part of our time together—when and how we met, what happened in the last couple of years—stuff like that. Neither of us will see what the other is writing until Jim edits it and puts our two parts together. Which, since you're reading it, has been done. Obviously.

Anyway, that's how this thing came to be. I'm pretty sure Jake's going to be going on and on about how much I helped him and all that, but it might not show up in the final version you have in your mitts as I instructed Jim to tone down what I anticipate Jake is going to be saying. I want this book to help him, not me! I mean, like I need more publicity, right?!

Okay. Enough of the intro stuff. Let's get down to it.

I met Jake inside the walls of Pendleton Reformatory almost exactly two years ago. How that came about was I was planning my next novel—*Criminal Minds and Intents* was the original title, but if you bought it you know it as *Snake Farm*—it was number five on the bestseller's list after all, so chances are pretty good you've read it, right? And, if you haven't, now would be a good time to glom onto a copy. Just sayin'...

Anyway, I'd written a bunch of really good crime novels, but I wanted to write one from the criminal's point of view. I know a whole bunch of criminals from over the years from down at the Dirty Vixen, but for this one I wanted to do some really deep—some "down and dirty"— research. I wanted the experience a criminal has. So, I called my dad. Dad is a big-time contractor (as you know if you've read my bio), and knows all kinds of people in the state and even region. Lots of folks owe him favors, if you get my drift.

"Dad," I said. "I want to spend the night in a prison. Can you make that happen?"

Turns out he could. He just happened to know the governor of Indiana and half an hour after we talked, he was back on the phone to me to tell me it was all arranged. I would be spending the next Thursday night inside the gray, concrete walls of one of Indiana's two maximum security prisons. Pendleton.

Just like that.

The day began when I took the superintendent, H.W. (Henry) Clinton, out to lunch. He gave me the real low-down on what to expect.

"I'm going to put you in a regular cell, Tommy. Just like the prisoners have. I have to warn you—it's small. But, you'll have it to yourself. No cellmate."

Doesn't bother me a bit. I've spent many a night in a small space. After all, I regularly travel to Europe and if you think a prison cell is small, you obviously haven't spent a night in an Italian hotel! Bring it on!

"And," he said. "You'll eat the evening meal in the chow hall. Don't expect sirloin steak! Ha-ha!" (Which was what we were both having at that moment.) Again, that didn't bother me in the least. If it was really bad, well, I just wouldn't eat it. I can afford to miss a meal now and again! Least that's what my girlfriend says. She's a hoot.

All in all, nothing he warned me about was concerning. Yes, I said, I understand that sometimes it's difficult to sleep with inmates yelling and cursing all night. Again, I'd spent more than one night in Rome!

When we arrived at the prison, Henry took me into his office where he had a pair of dungarees, a blue denim shirt with a number stenciled above the left pocket—#90666—tidy whitey underpants and T-shirt and white socks, and a pair of black brogans. After I changed, he handed me a large soup spoon.

"What's this for?" I said.

"It's your eating utensil," he said.

"Then I just pick up a knife and fork in the chow line?" I said.

"Uh, no. It's your only eating utensil. You keep it with you all the time."

Well, that sucked! I wasn't expecting sirloin, but even if it was a poorer cut, how was I supposed to cut it? I asked him that and he laughed.

"You won't need anything to cut beans," he said.

"Thursday is Bean Night?"

Again, he snorted. "Pretty much every night is bean night," he said. "There might be some pork fat in it but you won't have to cut it."

I *had* been packing on a few pounds lately. As good a time as any to do a bit of fasting...

I entered the inside of the prison at five in the afternoon. Just in time for chow. First, Henry turned me over to a guard—one of the "bulls"—and he escorted me through at least four different sets of steel doors and then we were... *inside*! A truly exciting moment. I confess my heart was beating at a furious rate. I'd been allowed to take with me a ballpoint pen and tablet, and I tried to walk and scribble furiously as we went on our way to Cellhouse J. We kept passing various inmates and each time I looked 'em squarely in the eye and smiled.

Kind of a surly bunch. Not a single one smiled back. In fact, some of the looks I got were downright scary. I faked it well, though. I put on my "jailhouse swagger" and strode right along with the bull, a guy named Edwin Jones. A black guy. He looked like he could handle himself if we got into a tough spot. I stuck as close to him as I could without it looking...you know...*gay*.

And...just as we reached the steps of J, a big burly inmate walked by us and from barely two feet away...blew me a kiss. I almost wet my pants but I acted as if I hadn't seen him.

The cell they'd assigned me was on the ground floor. Directly across from the desk of the officer on duty. I guessed that was so he could keep an eye on me in case trouble went down. I truly wanted the "real" experience, but was secretly glad they'd put me there. After all, if I wasn't going to be in that cell, a real convict would have been, so it wasn't that big of a deal, right?

Mr. Jones saw me into my cell, shook my hand, wished me luck—luck?—smiled, and exited. Almost immediately, the door slid shut and locked with an evil *thunk*!

Shit.

Before I'd entered the cell, I saw that the cell on the left was unoccupied, but there was a guy in the cell on the other side. I'd smiled at him and nodded before I went into my cell, but he didn't return my greeting. Just stared at me.

I looked around. Two racks that were hooked to the wall by chains. A small shelf and a metal mirror, and a small sink. That was it. The lower bunk was already made up so I figured that's where I'd sleep. No chair or anything to sit on, so I sat on the bunk.

Besides my spoon, the superintendent had also given me a small cloth bag he called a "ditty bag." I meant to ask him where that name came from, but had forgotten. I opened it and dumped the contents out on my bunk. A pair of headphones, a washcloth and small towel, a toothbrush, toothpaste, a small bar of soap, and a small white gauze bag and a packet of cigarette rolling papers. A pack of matches. In the gauze bag was something weird. It was full of tiny brown flakes. It smelled like tobacco when I sniffed it, but it didn't look like any tobacco I'd ever seen. It was stamped with the word "Hoosier."

I knocked on the wall where the bunks were attached.

"Hey," I said. "My name's Thomas Melon. What's yours?"

At first, there was just silence. Then: "Mayes. My name's Mayes."

The bull who was sitting just across my cell at his desk, shook his head at something that seemed to disgust him, picked up a bunch of keys, and walked away down toward the other end of the cellblock.

I got up and moved down to the end of my bunk, close to the bars. "Mayes what? What's your last name?"

He must have been up toward the front of his cell too, as I heard him clearly. "That's my last name. Jake."

It took me a second to realize he was telling me his first name.

"Glad t'meetcha, Jake. What're you in for?"

"*Motherfucker!*" I jumped at the sudden vehemence in his voice.

"Hey—what's the—"

"Asshole, this your first time in the joint?"

My plan originally had been to act like I was an old con, but that story seemed to have collapsed. "Well, yeah. How'd you know?"

I could hear him sigh. "You never ask a guy what he's in for, punk-ass."

You don't? I didn't know that. Why on earth not? "Sorry," I said. "Why not?"

"You must be the writer," is what he said. Then: "Welcome to the snake farm."

"Yes," I answered. "Thomas Melon. You've probably read my books."

I heard a low chuckle. "Yeah, right. You seen the library in here?" He paused. "I guess not," he said. "They probably didn't give you the nickel tour, did they."

We continued talking and he gave me bits of advice. I

asked him what the "Hoosier" was and learned it was free tobacco the state gave the inmates in case they couldn't afford store-bought, or, as he called them, "tightrolls."

"Cigarettes are money in here," he said. "Why the state gives you all the free tobacco you want. Fewer fights that way. It's crap, but at least it smokes."

I tried to roll one. Three times the paper burst apart from too much spit. The fourth time, I didn't use enough, and that didn't work either. Finally, on the fifth try, I got one together, although it didn't look that hot. I got about three draws out of it before it too, fell apart. Fuck it.

"What's that about a snake farm?" I said.

"Just my name for here," he said. "It's pretty much like that. Boring, except when someone gets bit. Then it livens up some. You'll see."

A whistle blew.

"What's that," I asked my new friend. "A riot going down?"

He laughed. And laughed and laughed. Finally: "Naw, man. It's the chow whistle. They'll be rollin' the doors soon."

Sure enough, almost as soon as he'd told me that, I could hear doors sliding open all over the place, on all three tiers. Except mine. It stayed closed.

Jake walked over to the front of my cell. "Uh-oh," he said.

Uh-oh?

"Looks like you've been tagged."

"Whaddya mean, 'tagged?'"

"Somebody musta paid the hack. Why you're locked in. Bet while we're at chow, you get a visit. Somebody wants your brown eye."

My...Oh, fuck!

Then, he told me some other stuff. Something about a hammer...My blood sugar must have been low because I kind of blacked out for a minute. When I gathered my thoughts again, he was gone.

"Guard!" I yelled. "Again. "*Guard*!" It was more of a scream than a yell, but I couldn't help it.

"What?" It was the guard I'd seen earlier at the desk. He looked perturbed.

"Have I been tagged?"

"What the fuck? What's 'tagged?'"

"I dunno. It's what he—" Jake was gone.

"Look, Mr. Melon, we can't let you go to chow. You probably wouldn't make it back. Somebody will bring your supper to you."

A long single file of convicts paraded past my cell, exiting at the cellhouse door which was visible from where I stood. More than one looked my way and more than one smacked their lips and winked at me.

I wasn't that hungry anyway.

That first meeting with Melon was funny. They brought him in just before chow and stuck him in the cell next to mine. At the time, I was over in J Block, kind of the honor cellhouse. Had a first floor cell, smack dead across from where the hack's desk was. Which was why they put him there, I figured. Keep a better eye on him in case.

Right from the start he was a jerkoff. Asked me what I was doing time for. I just about lost it at that and then realized he wasn't a real con and just didn't know any better. So, I decided to fuck with him a bit. When they blew the chow whistle, he asked if that meant there was a riot going down. See? Fruitcake, all the way.

Then, when they rolled the cells, they kept his locked.

He freaked out at that and I got to have some fun. I told him it looked like somebody'd tagged him. I just made it up on the spot. Told him some queen musta seen him and paid the hack to keep him locked down when the rest of us went to chow. Told him some other stuff too. That when we left, whoever had the hots for him would come down and he'd know who it was because he'd be carrying a hammer.

"A hammer?" he said. "What's that for?"

"To bust out your front teeth," I said. "Lets you give better blow jobs."

I couldn't see him when I told him that, but there was a little noise from his cell, like he'd sat down hard. I guess I could understand that, I was him.

Then, we went out to chow and I had to dump half my supper in the garbage can as I'd been laughing too much to eat while I told my buddies what I'd done. That was okay. I still had two bags of Keebler's back in my cell and I always had my hotspot and a thing of hot chocolate powder. I wouldn't go hungry.

He appeared to be some kind of pissed off when we came back from chow. I stood outside his cell for the few minutes before we had to go back in for lockdown and tried to talk to him, but he pretty much ignored me. That was okay. I don't think he knew that in half an hour they'd be rolling the doors again. It was our night to have free time in the cellhouse. Half the cellhouses get to go out each night to the gym or the yard and the other ones got to have free roaming time in the cellhouse. We had a little black-and-white TV on the other side and some rows of benches. You could watch TV if you wanted, or just walk around, shoot the shit, play cards, checkers, shoot craps, play guitars, shit like that. All the cell doors stayed open and you could visit with your friends inside a cell. You could also get shanked, get raped, get your head busted open. All kinds of possibilities...

I figured I'd have some fun with him then...

Hooray! My new friend, Jake Mayes, talked the guard into letting me out of my cell during recreation period. Now I'll get the real low-down on what it's like being a real convict.

It turns out Mr. Mayes fancies himself a writer. That was a surprise—a pleasant surprise. It gives me an idea. Something I've mulled over at times. While he's giving me the cook's tour during rec hour, I'll pose it to him. My idea? To host a weekly writing class inside the walls! In fact, it's a done deal in my mind already. I'll make Jake my convict assistant. See if he does have any talent and if he does...who knows?

Ten minutes until they roll the doors!

Five minutes until we get out. I may have made a mistake. I talked the hack into letting Melon outside. He called up another hack so they could keep a better watch on him and Mr. Keyster (the hack) told me that if anything happened to the guy, it'd be my ass.

Just great...

Okay. They just cranked 'em open.

I met him on the walk.

"C'mon," I said. "Let's go 'round to the other side. They got a TV over there and it's where most of the guys go."

I had to chuckle at him. Out of his cell, walking down the range, every time I glanced around, his eyes were as big as soup bowls. You could feel the fear dripping from him.

We'd just turned the corner when a guy leaped down off the first tier in front of us.

A big-ass black dude.

Who I knew.

Jerome something. He was in for killing his Sunday school teacher or something. Plus his entire family. I thought he was over in safekeeping where they kept the really bad dudes.

Guess not.

He landed like a cat not five feet from us. Took a step toward us…something in his hand…

A bunch of papers.

His novel, turns out.

Turns out he found out Melon was here and he even knew who he was. Turns out he'd also been writing his life story and thought Melon would like it, get it published for him, get it on the bestseller list and make a pile of money. Turns out, he thought once all that happened, he'd be able to snag one of them pardons the governor gives out in honor of his cat's birthday once every ten years.

Turns out, all of that happened except: Melon didn't like it, didn't get it published for him, which meant it never got on any bestseller or even any worstseller list, didn't make even a small pile of money, and for sure never snagged one of them elusive pardons.

Pretty much no parts of Jerome's dreams turned out the way he'd envisioned them.

Why he took the early parole…

Seems Melon decided he didn't want any more of the inmate experience and ended up cancelling those writing classes after three or four of them. He did end up using the experience in a couple of his next books. He shoulda stayed a bit longer. He was still calling the hacks "bulls" in those books, which he woulda learned wasn't what we called 'em if he'd stuck around a bit longer. He still used words like "shiv" too. Our collaboration remained unpublished also. The only place it's appeared is in my cell. He left me his contribution and that's why I can let you see it here.

One thing he got out of it was the title to his next book. He called it *Snake Farm.* That came from me.

About a month after his last workshop, they moved me up to the third tier into the cell next to Jerome. You know, the guy who thought Melon was going to cream his jeans over his "novel" and make all kinds of exciting, magical things happen for him.

Melon didn't even read it. He told me that. He told Jerome he had but that it wasn't quite good enough and to keep at it. After that, Jerome sent him two-three rewrites and after the last one, he didn't even bother to send it back. Just ignored him. I passed on to Melon what Jerome said he was going to do to him next writer's workshop and that's when he cancelled the gig. Jerome had tried to get into the class but Melon wouldn't approve him. I guess he saw the writing on the wall—Jerome, that is. A week after the last class was cancelled, Jerome cancelled himself.

And, that's where we're at right now. I'm on my way up to Melon's apartment. He thinks I'm going to turn in my contribution to our memoir. I kind of am, but not exactly. What I am going to turn into him is the last chapter. Which I'm writing right now. Which I'm going to end with a shank.

Schmuck like that shouldn't ought to be allowed to fuck with guys inside. Guy gets fucked by both his mom and his pop shouldn't get more grief from a lame like that. Melon shoulda at least read his book.

Just purely irritates me.

First published in *Mama Tried* edited by James R. Tuck.

Long as the dude kept buying, I'd keep talking. Hot air for cool drinks. The trade made sense to me.

"Tell me that part again," he said. He was trying to take notes and I kind of talk fast. "What'd you say you called him."

"Six Bits," I said. "You know, seventy-five cents."

"Cool name," was his reaction. I leaned over, saw he'd written the name down.

"I guess," I said. "Six didn't like it much."

"Why's that?"

I squinted at the guy. "You kidding me? You'd like to be called *Six Bits*? Me, I'd rather be called *Million Bucks* I was named after cash."

"Yeah," he said. He scribbled something down in his little notebook. "I see what you mean."

I could see the bottom of the glass. I crooked my finger at the barkeep and he came down. "Keep the old ice," I said. "Just add new. Make it a good color this time."

He gave me a look, but didn't say anything. The dude was paying cash and after every drink and that made him king shit, this kind of bar. Been just me...

The dude watched me get the new drink and waited until I took a glug.

"So he tried to hold you up?"

I nodded. "Yeah. Tried to jack me with this punk-ass .22."

He wrote something and I looked over. He'd written ".38." I just shrugged. He was buying the drinks, made no never mind to me what he wrote.

"I mean, who jacks up a guy looks like me with a pissy-little .22?" I didn't expect an answer. "A guy who's named Six Bits, is who. Why he wasn't never named Million Bucks."

"What happened then?" the dude said.

"Nothing," I said. "I just laughed at him."

"And that's when he shot you?"

"Yeah. Little fucker shot me. In the arm. Here." I pointed to the spot on my shoulder, pulled the sleeve down so he could see the scar. "With that little pissy-ass cap gun."

"What'd you do then?"

I signed to the barkeep again. He came down—before I could say anything, he said, "Yeah, yeah. I know. Old ice."

"What'd I do then?" I looked at him like he was simple. "I already told you what I did. I took his little toy from him and shot him."

"In the head, right?"

"Well, shit, yes. Think we were gonna trade slugs like when you're hitting your homeboy in the shoulder, trying to see who can knock the other guy off his feet? Fuck, yes, I shot him in the head. That's a particularly bad place to shoot somebody with a .22."

The dude laughed. "I'd think the head would be a bad place to shoot a guy with any kind of gun."

I looked at him. Was this guy for real? "Well, a .22 works different on the noggin than say a .38. Works a lot different than a .45 or a .357."

"How so?"

"How so? Well, dude, it's a little bitty shell. Not a lot of powder behind it. See?"

He shook his head.

I sighed. Straights...

"Look, man, you shoot a guy in the head with a .38, with a .357, it's gonna come out the back with a lot bigger hole."

"Okay," he said. It was plain he was trying to figure out what I was saying, but just wasn't getting it. Looked like I needed a crayon to draw him a picture.

"The kid pissed me off, shooting me like that. So, I shot him in the melon. What happens when you shoot somebody in the melon with a .22 is it doesn't go through like a bigger shell will. It does all kinds of weird shit, but it almost never goes all the way through. I was teaching him a lesson."

"A lesson?"

I was getting tired of being patient with this dude. If he wasn't buying drinks as fast as I could put 'em down, I would've walked out. But...it was Jack Daniel's he was buying, not that Wild Turkey crap, so I told him what he wanted.

"Sometimes a .22 kills you dead. A lot of times it doesn't. A lot of times it just runs all around the inside of the skull, and next day, you're good as new—just got a headache. Sometimes, it runs around and then hits the right area and you end up in a coma and you're like that for the next ten years. And, sometimes, it kills you. But, it's never a for-sure with a .22 like it is with a .45. Way I looked at it, I was hoping he ended up in one of those coma things and had ten years to think about how he'd fucked up. Know why I'd laughed at him. Learned a lesson. You know."

I could tell looking at the guy he didn't know.

Fuck it. What did I care if he got it or not? The answer was, I didn't. All I cared was that he kept the drinks coming. And he did. He asked a bunch of other questions and I told him. Happened in New York, down in Times Square—the old Times Square, not the way they got it now. No, I didn't get nailed for it. Hiked on down to Miami, laid out on the beach for the winter, came back when the snow melted.

After a while, he folded up his notebook, held out his hand to shake, and then he was walking out the door. He'd left a twenty on the counter for me.

I looked down at the barkeep, crooked my finger at him.

"I know," he said. "You know who that was?"

"Yeah," I said. "A guy who has more money than sense. A guy who doesn't have a life, needs other people's lives to make his feel like it's interesting."

"No," he said. "You're wrong. That was Tom Waits."

Like I was supposed to know who the fuck that was.

I drank the twenty and then left. Took me ten minutes to make it to the door. My legs weren't working all that well. I went out the door and felt something and looked down. Looked like I'd pissed myself.

Fuck.

First published in *Off the Record* edited by Luca Veste.

I shot her.

Twice.

The first time so she'd feel it, get the picture.

I wanted to talk to her a bit before I finished.

I told you, you didn't know me, I said.

You kept giving me that stupid grin and saying—I lived with you for twenty-five years. I know you.

But you don't, I said. See?

Then, I shot her the second time. The first time it was a gutshot and the second I put a hole in her forehead.

I imagine she believed me now, I thought. For a few seconds anyway. Between the first bullet and the second.

She never said anything, either time. But then, she didn't need to. Her face said it all. She realized I was telling the truth after all.

After the second shot, the one that quieted her for good, I sat there awhile, waiting for the emotion to come, but it never did. Not even a general feeling. Nothing. Nada. That was what I was trying to tell her—had always been trying to tell her.

I sat there, in the chair across from her. From what wasn't her any more. Now it was just a body. I thought about what memories I'd carry with me of her after twenty-five years of marriage.

All I could come up with was our nightly routine. At

nine sharp, each evening, we'd turn off everything downstairs and come up to bed. I'd go in the bathroom first, and sit on the stool, lid down, and read something, usually a novel. I'd have my last cigarette of the day. Take my pills. Open the window so the smoke would go out. If it was summer, I'd close it before I left to keep the air conditioning in. Same thing in the winter, for the furnace. Those times when neither was on, I'd just leave it up.

I'd leave a cigarette for her on the sink counter. We kept a lighter there, all the time.

I'd go to bed, turn down my side and climb in. She'd usually have the TV on, the remote tossed on my side of the bed. That was because she'd go to sleep before me. I was a night owl. From my days in the joint. I couldn't go to sleep without TV or some kind of noise going on. Since our neighborhood was quiet, it was the TV's job to get me to sleep.

She'd go in the bathroom and smoke the cigarette I'd left for her.

You may wonder why she didn't have her own. Years ago, she'd quit. Only she hadn't. She just quit buying cigarettes. She just smoked mine.

Depending on the day of the week, she'd have whatever she liked that day on. On Thursdays, it was always *Cops*, either a rerun or a new episode. If *Cops* wasn't on, it would be Court TV for a long time and then ID. Both featured murder cases.

After she finished her cigarette, she'd come in, turn down her side, throw the covers off and lay there. For what seemed all of our married life, she had heat attacks as soon as she came to bed. Menopause, she said, but it was sure a long menopause. It lasted for at least the last fifteen years of our marriage.

Until I shot her. Twice.

It just irritated me, her saying she knew me.

Now she does.

I went and pulled the blanket up over her face. You see, I said to her. I really was the Iceman. You should have believed me. All I ever asked from you was respect.

I went into the bathroom and there was the cigarette I'd left her. I smoked it all the way down.

No sense in letting it go to waste.

First published in *Trouble in the Heartland: Crime Fiction Inspired by the Songs of Bruce Springsteen* edited by Joe Clifford.

For the longest time, I've been urging my twelve-year-old son Mike to quit that stupid middle school he goes to and get a good-paying job at the Woodvale Shopping Outlet 7-Eleven out on Highway 12.

"Look at all the advantages," I've said, feeling for the umpteenth time that my words were traveling through the space between his ears. "Most kids wait till they're sixteen and drop out of school to get their first position behind the counter. You'll have a four-year jump on those mug-wumps. Think ahead. I wish I had when I was your age! I'll help you, you know. I've got a source for fake I.D.'s, the whole schmear. My guy can even whip you up a gradua-tion certificate that you can't tell from the real ones, case The Man shows up." *The Man* being the truant officer who patrols this area, harassing decent, hard-working kids on behalf of something called the "system."

"You're big for your age, Mike," I said, in my conclude-ing argument. "You'll have no trouble at all, passing for sixteen."

Mike's got this whacky idea that if he stays in school and graduates he'll be able to go to college and become a doctor.

A doctor!

"Have you forgotten last summer when you fainted when you fell off the slide and broke your leg and saw a little blood? You think a doctor faints at the sight of a tiny little smear of red? That's a doctor that's not going to last long before he's driving a Yellow Cab on the graveyard shift!"

"It wasn't the blood," he said, in that irritating argumentative tone preteens seem to favor these days. "It was the bone sticking out."

Right. Like the sight of a dinky little white stick would make someone pass out!

"Whatever you say," I answered, more than a hint of sarcasm in my voice and probably a smirk on my lips, which I couldn't hold back. We both knew what it was that caused him to keel over and it wasn't some minuscule little bone fragment.

"Well, you better get more used to work than you are now," I said. "Doctors work twenty-two hour days, seven days a week. They don't even have time to brush their teeth before they have to stick somebody's heart back in their chest cavity or do mouth-to-mouth on some wino who's choked on their Boone's Farm. I can't even get you to make your bed on a consistent basis. And, when was the last time you picked up your underwear? I see a pair right now over in the corner that have been laying there at least a week."

That was a mistake. His eyes lighted up when he learned he wouldn't have to brush his teeth seven/fifty-two. That's all he picked up out of all I'd said. A major perk in his mind.

I tried to counter that with the many benefits of a convenience store career.

"Slurpees," I said. "All the Slurpees you can guzzle down. All day long. And magazines. Have you thought about all the magazines you can read? For *free*??? While your moron friends are studying calculus and logging time in detention popping their pimples, you'll be flipping September's Play-mate of the Month foldout open and reading informative and educational articles. Without having to even give up your allowance to buy it or having to hide it under your mattress! Not only that, but by the time you're sixteen, you'll be the assistant manager already. On the *day* shift! Do you realize people in the convenience business will kill to snag the day shift? And bossing around those slackers who waited too long and fell subsequently far behind you from the gitgo in their own shortsighted career paths."

None of my logic and arguments seem to work. He's bound and determined to stay in school. All I can do is hope he comes to his senses before it's too late and he arrives at the ripe old age of sixteen and finds out he's in line with twenty-nine other dropouts for the same job he could have had just for the asking four years earlier. Those four years will go by faster than he thinks.

I just don't want Mike to make the same mistakes I've made when I was his age. I think most dads can relate. Like Hitler said, "Youth is wasted on the young." Which is the real reason "Mein Adolf" founded the Hitler Youth. To help kids realize before it was too late they were throwing away their salad days along with the salad dressing. Hitler was lucky. He had a whole country at his disposal and didn't even have to do much to gain the people's support. Just make a few trains run on schedule and he becomes a regular god! Or was that that Italian guy that ended upside down and in a room temperature situation...No matter.

Would that I'd been so fortunate when I was a young lad!

But, no. I had the kind of father who was a miserable follower. A Merino sheep, trés-docile variety. Pappy looked around our neighborhood and saw that all the other dads made their kids go to school and sure enough, there I was, sitting on my butt in third-hour English with all the rest of the little lambs whose fathers bought into the Trilateral Commission's clever-but-insidious plan. That "not-so-secret" master plan to keep Americans wage slaves for the rest of our lives by wasting our formative days in studying utterly-useless information solely designed to keep us from thinking for ourselves.

George Orwell, you were sooooo right!!!!!!

There were no 7-Elevens when I was a boy—kids have it all today!!!—but there was a Conoco gas station on our corner and the owner told me he'd hire me in a minute to sweep his floors and do simple stuff like oil changes and tranny lubes. Think *my* father would let me quit school and take advantage of this man's generous offer to teach me a useful and high-paying trade?

Ha!

Oh, I've told Mike more than once about my own father and how I'm trying to provide better opportunities for him than my stinkin' old man gave me, but does it register?

Ha!

You'd think he'd open his eyes and unplug the wax in his ears around his own house, see what goes on.

I'm speaking of his mother. The woman I generously provided a home and marriage and many, many luxuries and other amenities to, at a time in her life when she was wasting away in college, misspending her valuable time pursuing such "useful" skills as training a mouse to run a maze. Yes, that's right. Training a rodent to go from here to there in a subdivided box. That's all she did in this one class, Psych 101, she was always yammering about. Three hundred sixty-four bucks she laid out at Rosedale Community College for Psych 101 and all you did was feed a rat a piece of Cheez-Whiz every time it made the so-called "correct" turn. For four months this went on. The hardest thing the prof had to do in his so-called "job" was stifle his giggling every time the suckers piled into his classroom and headed for the mouse housing projects in the back. P.T. Barnum was a piker compared to this slickster.

"Oh, yeah, *rat lab*," I remember mentioning to her at the time, with tongue-in-cheek. "There's a big demand for *that* out there. I was just looking at the want ads in Sunday's paper and there must have been six and a half columns of ads from big-shot mouse executives searching desperately for experts to train their rats to run mazes. And the pay! You'd be amazed at what these guys are offering for mouse professionals. And that's just with a bachelor's! Don't even ask what master degree holders are getting! If you've got a doctorate, you need to start looking at houses with enough land for a small landing strip for your own private Lear jet that'll be whisking you off to Bermuda and the South of France on your many generously-provided-for vacations."

Back then she used to laugh at stuff like that, say I was the funniest guy she'd ever known. That's all changed.

Boy, and how!

I wish Mike could have seen us together back then. When his mother was a kind, compassionate woman with a rich, warm sense of humor, instead of the shrew she's become and the kind of nagging, whining harpy he's always observed around the house.

Back then, she was more than happy to be married to an inventor-slash-idea man. In those early, halcyon days, she was more than anxious to give her full support, both emotionally and in a practical way—by working a couple of easy jobs—to help further her husband's career. Does she still grant that unconditional and loving succor?

Ha! I wish!

You wouldn't have even asked such a question if you'd

been by our house any weekday during the past six years at four-thirty p.m. when she arrived home...and just opened your ears a tiny bit as you were passing by!

You wouldn't believe some of the things she says to me. *Screams* in that fishwife's shrill, irritating screech she has, I should say. In front of our only child, Mike, the fruit of our collective loins. What she supposes that does to the integrity of our family unit, I can't imagine. She doesn't have a clue what massive, irreversible damage is being done to our son's *Id* and *Super Id* when she makes her crude, insensitive, hateful remarks.

Read some Freud, girlfriend!!!

I hate to think about what kind of family he'll create some day. Does the name "Son of Sam" ring a bell???

Just about every day, for instance, she'll come home from her first job, walk in the house and see me hard at work. Does she say, "Hi, sweetheart. Whatcha working on? Would you share with me? I love to hear about your work! Take a break, hon, and come sit by me and tell me about some of the many knotty problems I know you're facing. Maybe you'd like a nice backrub to iron out all those nasty tensions and relieve the mental stress. Can I fix you a tasty rum and Coke?"

No. She does not say that or anything resembling that. Not Miss Belinda nee Walker. Not Miss "I've Been Working-So Hard At The RV Factory And My Feet Hurt And Soon I Have To Go To My Telemarketing Job" Belinda. You kidding? You can't imagine a more selfish woman, who's totally into herself and no room for anything in that narrow world as inconsequential as a mere husband who's aged years beyond his chronological age from the never-ending tension she's created with her unreasonable attitude.

No. What she says, almost every time is, "On the couch

again, eh? You know, when you get up, there's an imprint on the cover looks exactly like your body? I catch myself thinking it's the pattern they sewed in at the factory and wonder why they chose that. I wonder more why we bought it."

Funny lady!

She knows my work is 99.9% in my mind. Maybe a stranger or layman not familiar with the processes that are crucial to inventing the new products and ideas society desperately wants and needs would imagine I was just lying there daydreaming instead of what I'm actually doing—*working my butt off to the bone*!!! But, Belinda knows better and yet she elects to lash out at *moi* (yours truly) with these infantile, hurtful remarks. She also knows that the TV helps me immensely in the thinking process. I'm not really watching *Days of Our Lives* even though to an uninformed eye, it may appear that's what's going on. That's merely a form of white noise that helps me attain the proper frame of mind which only happens to be *absolutely necessary* for the tough mental drudgery required. I work much the same as a writer does. If I was a famous novelist and had sixty-eight bestsellers out and was lauded on *The Larry King Show* and *Oprah* and *Nick at Nite* would she make such asinine comments?

Ha!

I'd like to talk to Mrs. Stephen King and see what she has to say. What I'd really like to do is get Mrs. Stephen King over to the house, get her in the kitchen with Belinda and say to her, "Hey. Educate this woman, will ya? Tell her what *you* say when *you* walk in on Steve in the Barcolounger and he's staring at the ceiling. Bet what you *don't* say is, 'Hey, Stevie, you on the Barco again? You know when you get up there's an exact imprint of your body on the leather. Ha, ha.'"

We both know the answer to that, don't we?

Unfortunately, not only am I not Hitler nor do I have his historical luck to be in the right place at the right time with the trains and all—I'm not Stephen King either and that puts me at the mercy of a short-sighted and sadly-ignorant woman who doesn't deserve to have the genius of a husband she was fortunate enough to have trapped into that blissful state of matrimony she enjoys.

Moi.

Mike doesn't take notice of other things, either, that might have a positive influence on his career decisions. Like the times I've put on hold the important work I'm doing to go out and get a job in what usually turns out to be a vain attempt to keep Belinda from her constant yammering. More than once, I've sacrificed my call to the inventing/ idea profession to simply shut her up and gain a bit of peace in the household.

Pacify the witch!!! is a crude, but accurate way of describing the sacrifices I make many times!!!

A good example was the time I became a genealogist. It wasn't my first choice, but after poring over the help wanted ads for several weeks and not finding anything I could put my unique abilities and talents to use in, I spotted what seemed at the time to be an interesting offer. It even seemed to be intellectually-challenging and that's what I was after more than anything else. Some kind of work that would stimulate the ol' gray matter, get the lead out, so-to-speak, to coin a phrase.

What the ad wanted was a person who could assist this guy in researching his family's history.

Detective work.

Oh, sure—I figured some of the work would involve boring computers and probably even being stuck in some musty library poring over faded marriage certificates illegibly-written in Olde English and such—but I sensed there might be some travel involved too, and probing interviews with all kinds of interesting people, some of whom might even be famous. If I was lucky, maybe the guy (his name was Aaron B. Rodthistle, according to the ad), would discover he had some one hundred and two-year-old great-aunt or a fifth-cousin living in Bimini and I'd be dispatched to gather vital information from her before she shuffled off her mortal coil (whatever that is!!!) and the critical info was lost forever.

Would I bring my swimsuit to *that* interview? You decide!

Yeah, well, was I fooled...

As it turned out, my first hunch was correct. I spent days and days at the downtown library—the main branch where all the genealogy stuff was kept—and mostly what I did was walk around asking dumb questions of people in the genealogy department who didn't know squat about genealogy. "Look over there," was their most common answer, pointing to some bookshelf way in the back, looked like you should take a cab to get to. "Look under R."

I'd hike my way down to the spot indicated, weaving around the winos who used the library for their naps, only to find sixteen books of Rodthistles alone. I'm supposed to wade through all that, I thought? Yeah, right.

Realizing it was a hopeless cause, I decided to use my time more constructively than in some useless rummaging around in a bunch of moldy books that were hopelessly out-of-date and probably about a different branch of the Rodthistle family than the one I was supposed to research. I'd been working on a process to keep unsightly dandruff off of executives' suit shoulders and was close to a breakthrough. My inventor's instincts told me the solution was hidden somewhere within the magical and fascinating worlds of electro-magneticism and molecular chemistry. Some compound that would repel the nasty flakes away from the material in suit jackets. I knew the answer lay in something simple that no one had thought of. A combination of two common household elements that, if the suit was simply and easily treated with the formula, would cause the offending particles to fly off in the opposite direction like steel shavings do when they come into close proximity with a negative magnet. Something like that. A solution, so simple in hindsight, that I'd smack my forehead in rueful, self-deprecating humor, exclaiming something out loud like, "Boy-o-boy! Doesn't that beat all! This was right in front of my very nose all the time!" A humorous anecdote I could use in my speech should I find myself in Stockholm, accepting a certain very well-known prize...I can see my idea culminated symbolically and expressively in my imaginative mind. It appears to me as a cartoon, in which a delighted Armani-clad CEO is watching tiny flakes whiz away from him, disappearing in a mist of white and falling harmlessly to the floor as he stands outside his firm's board room, a sign informing, "IMPORTANT MEETING TODAY!!! BE THERE OR BE SQUARE!!! I find it hard sometimes to articulate exactly what I see in my head, but it doesn't matter, as I know exactly what I'm seeing and that's all that really matters for the inventing process. If I can see it, I can do it. Gandhi or Vince Lombardi or someone like that said that and it's true. I've even got that posted above my workspace in the garage. I typed it out and framed it and I look at it every time I go out there to work, taking a silent moment to let the words make their impact. It doesn't say, "If *I* can see it, *I* can do it"—substitute "you's" for the "I's" and that's what it says, literally, but you get the idea.

Anyway, instead of frittering away precious research hours on Mr. Aaron B. Rodthistle's stupid family crap—the bit of investigating I did complete revealed a family tree more boring than you could possibly imagine—I invested my time instead perusing the many informative volumes in the hard science section. Once or twice, I was *this close* to a breakthrough, but even though I came tantalizingly near to the elusive answer I sought, I was unable to unlock the formula (that was probably right in front of that aforementioned nose!) during my time there. It wasn't wasted time, though. Not in my estimation. In my mind, every dead end you encounter leads you closer and closer to the right cul-de-sac! Take that for some constructive criticism, you "the glass is half-empty" negatoids!!!

I may still have been employed in that useless and (in my opinion) vain work on behalf of Mr. Aaron B. Rodthistle, when one day, whilst poring over a college-level chemical text, one of the librarians who'd gotten to recognize me and knew my mission, came over and asked if I was still doing research for Aaron B. Rodthistle.

"Why, yes," I replied. "I'm taking a brief sabbatical from my investigation at the moment, but shortly I'll be cracking those hundred-year-old death certificates, you bet!"

She snorted. "You know, we all think he's a 'lune,' don't you? It's why he hired you. He won't come around here anymore because we all fall down laughing every time he comes in the door."

"What's so funny?"

"HE'S AN ORPHAN!" She hooted that out and over behind the counter by the autobiographies and biographies of the famous and near-famous, I saw two librarians collapse behind the desk in paroxysms of laugher when they heard her say that.

"Why does that make him a nut?"

"Why?" she said. "*Why???* Why is because he isn't researching his *birth* parents. Couldn't care a fig about his *birth* parents. He's researching his *adopted* family." She pulled out a hanky and swiped at the corner of her eye. "Father's side mostly."

"You're kidding," I said, trying to sort out what this information meant. "Why?"

She sniggered. "We all asked him the same thing. Know what he said?"

I didn't and admitted as much.

"He said...get this...he said his adoptive parents were his only *real* parents and his biological mother and father didn't count. They'd abandoned him so they didn't matter in his eyes. He only wanted to learn about his heritage...*on the adopted parents' side*!" She burst into uncontrollable giggles at this last and walked away, shaking her head from side to side.

Well, what could I do? I mean, the guy was an obvious Fruit Loop of the mixed nut variety. While the money was good and the work easy—if you didn't mind being bored into an early grave called "Ennui"!!!—in good conscience, I couldn't keep on backing up to take my check from this fool. Not to mention the harm this might do to my professional reputation should it ever leak out the inane pursuit I'd been involved in!

So I quit.

Do you think Belinda would have empathy for my situation?

Ha!

Double-ha!!

I won't repeat the tirade she launched into the day she came home, expecting me to be down at the library as I had been those many long weeks (three) on behalf of Rodthistle's insane pursuit, and found me toiling furiously on the couch. Imagine that for yourself!!! It shouldn't be hard, with what you now know about the woman!

And guess who had just arrived home from school in time to witness her vitriolic harangue? To behold his mom, spittle flying from her mouth as she loosed her invective on her poor, hapless, and bewildered husband?

That's right. My poor, misguided, foolish, *overeducated* son.

A front-row spectator at this unseemly, savage scene.

"You see?" I said to him, once Belinda had left for that cushy gig she has the nerve to call "work" down at the Speedy Vacuum Cleaner Telemarketing Center. How one can have the balls to call a well-paid and highly-pleasurable activity "work" when it involves chatting for four hours with other housewives, is something I'll never understand. Getting paid good money to gossip over Ma Bell's and Glen Campbell's lines would represent a dream come true for most women of my acquaintance!!!

"You see, Mikey?" I began, the second she slammed the door on her way to that dream job. Loosened it right off the hinges. Just another chore created for the ol' job jar for yours truly by you-know-who...It just never ends...But, I digress!!!

I went on. "Son, your daddy's plight may well become *your* fate, if you persist in that ill-advised course you've set sail on. You may wake up one day, forty-one and a half years old, at a time when you should be anticipating the golden years of retirement, and find yourself chained to a woman like your mother—a woman whose only aim in life is to cut her husband's balls off at the knees! That what you want? Well, Mister...that's precisely where you're headed if you stubbornly cling to this foolish school thing."

Sensing he didn't quite grasp the same picture of his

future I saw oh-so-clearly, I went on. "It's the same old historically-proven domino effect," I said. "You keep going to school, let's say. Let's suppose you even graduate from middle school. You with me so far?"

He nodded.

"The next thing you'll want to do is go to high school. Is that a fair assumption? Can you see where that might happen?"

Again, he nodded. Maybe I was getting through to him after all!!!

"Okay, then. Put yourself in the future. You're standing in a big mob of people with teal-blue robes on and mortarboards on their heads. You've all just been praised to the rooftops by a bunch of middle-aged geezers who've spent the past two hours telling you you're the "hope of the future" and "the brightest of the bright" and other such pablum and ludicrous drivel. You're human—you like praise like all of us do—and you buy into this crapola they've been dishing out. Follow?"

He claimed he did by yet another nod.

"Right after this graduation charade, you'll probably go to some classmate's house for a big party, where you'll get drunk on three-point-two beer and wind up in a bedroom with Easy Sally, getting some honey on your stinger. I know what I'm talking about here, son. Don't ask how I know."

Again he nodded, more vigorously than the other times and I noted he had that same gleam in his eye that he did when he found out doctors don't have time to brush their teeth.

I cut to the chase.

"What'll happen after that, is that you'll get this bright idea to go on to college and what do you suppose will happen there?"

He shrugged his shoulders. I could tell from the distant look in his gaze that he was still back there with Easy Sally at the graduation party. Kids...

"I'll tell you what will happen." I grabbed him by his shoulders, pulled him sharply toward me until our noses were inches apart. I had his attention now!

"You'll be going to rat lab and buying into the same propaganda your mother did and your brain will atrophy away until it's the size of a diseased black walnut. What little of it you've still got, that is! You'll end up conning people on fixed incomes to purchase life insurance or maybe find yourself back at your old middle school, leading little morons down the same dead end path you just traveled on, but now on the other side of the desk as a 'teacher' —" I spat out the last word, "—You know what else will happen, Mike? You'll think you have to marry a girl who also has a college education. Don't smile. You will. You'll look down at those girls who had the smarts to quit school early and make something of themselves. You won't even look at the girls who could do you some good, stand by you in your climb up the 7-Eleven ladder of success. You'll want one of those silly college girls instead. Someone like—" I hesitated and took a deep breath, "—*your mother*. You want that?"

He didn't know what to say. He was obviously stricken by the horrible Polaroid of the fate that loomed before him that I'd just shared with him. Dazed and downhearted and woebegone. It was all over his forlorn little kisser. At that moment, I so desperately wanted to take pity on him. After all, he was my only son and I loved him to pieces! I detested having to do this to him, but the sooner he learned about the real world, the better off he'd be. The truth may hurt, but it's the truth that shall set ye free as it wisely says in Joshua or Deuteronomy or Acts 3:11, somewhere like that.

"Okay," I said, more gently now. "That's one scenario. The certain fate that awaits you if you keep hopping on that yellow bus every morning."

I waited to let that sink in before going on.

"But then..."

Once more, I outlined what could be clearly a more glorious and rewarding future in the convenience store business. When I finished, I reached behind me to the object I'd been waiting to give him. The "deal-clincher" as an aluminum-siding salesman would say.

Without a word, I handed it to him. This was an event that needed no explanation. One of those ageless father-son ritual moments.

The December issue of *Playboy Magazine.*

The year-end, wrap-up issue, the one with the photos of all the previous year's Playmate's of the Month.

"Here, Mikey," I said, after giving him a moment to comprehend what he held in his hands. "This is a glimpse at your future should you choose the right road. While other kids your age will have to sneak around to get their hands on these, you'll have free and easy access to as many as you want. While they're hiding their purloined copies under their mattresses—not knowing that's the first place parents look!—you'll be able to just casually stroll over to aisle six and pick up your own copy...*whenever you want!*"

I waited until he looked up, my heart gladdened at the emotion I saw expressed there.

"And, best of all—you'll be getting paid serious money to read these!!! You'll also be getting paid to eat all the Slim Jims you want. I've already mentioned Slurpees—you know how much you like Slurpees!!! Hostess Ho Hos! At the same time you're knocking down a regular, man-sized paycheck for all this fun you'll be having, picture your former schoolmates. Hunkered down over their six-pound math books, struggling to understand something called 'quantum physics.' How many times do you suppose anyone uses quantum physics in their jobs? That should tell you something right there about the value of your so-called 'education!' Think about it. How many times do you suppose someone's boss comes up to them and says, 'Well, Ralph, you know it's time for your year-end review. If you can tell me what year Columbus sailed the ocean blue, you'll get a nice raise and that promotion you've been wanting!' Can you guess how many times that happens in the workplace, Mister Student?"

We talked some more and while I'd like to report Mike saw the wisdom of what I was telling him and quit school on the spot and went down and filled out a 7-Eleven app, I'd be lying. A victory of sorts was achieved, however.

At the end of our talk, he agreed to at least go down and see if he could snag a part-time job after school. While this isn't the complete triumph I'd hoped for, it represents at least a partial one. I feel confident that once he's on the job and experiences the many benefits therein, he'll take that next step and apply for full-time hours.

I praised him for his mature decision, and in the true nature of the born salesman which I could have been if I'd so desired, ended our talk by letting him in on yet another of the many benefits of the career he was embarking on.

"I haven't even mentioned the uniform," I confided. "Women go bananas over uniforms. Picture yourself in your white shirt with the company logo stitched over the pocket and that snappy azure-blue bow tie! Think that doesn't attract the babes???!!!"

I can't wait to see his mother's face when she learns about the decision he's made.

We'll soon learn who's captain of this ship! I don't think it will prove to be a certain telemarketer!!!

Scams just keep popping up in my life. Uninvited. It's like I've got this big sign on my back somebody's stuck there, with big neon letters flashing, "I'm an idiot. I'm a big, *dumb* idiot. Sell me all your lame-brain ideas."

You'da thought a sharp guy such as myself would have called it quits after the last fiasco, the one in which Tommy LeClerc conned me into whacking off the right hand of Charles Lacy Deneuve, the Cajun Mafia King, and holding it for ransom. Well, that actually didn't turn out too bad, except now I look like an impersonation of an Elvis impersonator—kind of a "Third-Hand El"—and Tommy is sleeping with a couple of sled dogs up in Alaska and not about to return to the family digs any time soon. His family digs being here in New Orleans, same as mine, where I'm putting this down, looking out my apartment window at the Roman Candy wagon parked just up the street where Burthe deadends into Carrollton by the Little Professor Bookshop.

But, that's another story.

Yessir, I'm back in the Big Easy, Cat and me have done the Splitsville thing and she's still back in Lost Wages, running the po-boy sandwich shop and getting her nails done three times a week, trying to break into the chorus line at the Stardust, which will be quite a feat if she does, considering one of her legs (the left) is an inch and a half shorter than the other. Not to mention the same plastic surgeon who worked his miracle on me has rendered her into sort of a Bette Midler look-alike. Not bad...except she wanted to look like Cher.

Deneuve finally passed on to his sorry reward, making it safe for me to come back to the land of crawfish etoufee and the hottest-looking female impersonators in the U.S. of A.

I left all of the loot with Cat when we split. I found out something about myself. I like the action part of getting rich, but once I've got more green than I can ever spend, life gets sleepy-time. I guess I'm one of those guys what likes climbing the mountain rather than sitting at the top getting eagle shit dropped on his head. It's just like that professor Willie Sutton once said, "Money's just a way of figuring your handicap on the championship courses."

Anyway, all that trouble is in the past now and I'm scrambling around doing what I do best. Hustling off-shore riggers and tourists at the pool tables, keeping my eye open for opportunity. America's for sure the land of opportunity, just like they told us back in junior high and New Orleans seems to have more than its fair share of new and ingenious ways to turn a buck, some of which work out and some which leave you with a short and perilous future.

I was getting along though, no more than a month or two behind in my rent, and seeing a couple of ladies that definitely don't fall into the pooch category, when somebody seen that sign on my back and laid out this master plan that was going to make the both of us richer than ex-Presidents. I'm speaking of Mister Dooley Thibidoux who most folks usually call Spitball on account of his face kinda looks like one of those little glops we usta fling at the teacher back in H.S. His features are all sort of scrunched around in this ball that's his face. He's also bald as a three-minute egg and has all these folds of skin where his hair usta be which at a distance looks like a Dudley Do-Right pompadour. It's not a common name—the only other time I seen it was in that great novel, *The Bitch*, which was written by my favorite writer and ain't about what you think it is…maybe. Except his "Spitball" was a crud and my Spitball…well, I guess he's kind of a crud, too.

Must be the name.

I'm out matching quarters for tenspots out at The Speakeasy in Metry, when Spitball walks in and right over to me. "Pete," he says—that's me, Pete is short for Peter which is my middle name, my whole handle being Evan Peter Palmer, but where I run you don't want to let folks get wind of the fact your parents named you something like Evan—"Pete, I got something in my pocket you're gonna be very interested in."

The guy I was hustling gives me this look and says right then he's got to go and won't listen to none of my explanations that what Spitball has got in his pocket probably ain't what he thinks at all—it better not be, I say, ha ha—but I can't convince him to hang around now that he thinks he's the potential third party in a lavender triangle, not the place for a straight-shooter such as he is, to be circumstanced. "How 'bout them Saints," I say, in a last-ditch attempt to keep the mark there and show him I am a regular stud type of guy, but he's out the door and I see my rent money is aways down some other road.

"Fuck you want, Spitball?" I growl and throw down the last of my Jack and water. "I was working here."

"Screw that shit," he says. "I got something here will make you throw the word work right out of your dictionary." He pulls out this piece of paper I see is a list of names.

"What's that?" I come back with. "All your relatives

you ain't borrowed past your limit from?"

You got to know something about Spitball. He means well and is sort of a hustler his own self, but things just never seem to work out the way he intends them to. I recall one time when he had this great scheme to steal this cow he kept seeing standing in a field just outside town. He passed this cow every few days or so and got to thinking that what with the cost of hamburgers and T-bones a whole cow might fetch a lot of money. In the dead of night, he gets him a truck and goes out to the pasture where this cow— which turned out to be a Brahma bull that had starred in rodeos, only Spitball didn't know squat about farm animals and that you can't eat Brahma bulls unless you plan on chewing for about an hour per bite—and he sneaks up on the cow and busts him in the melon with a ten-pound sledge hammer. He knew enough to do that, having seen some PBS thing on slaughterhouses one night when he misdialed the channel looking for *Baywatch* reruns. He was also smart enough to know that he couldn't lift a big lunk of an animal like that up into his truck by himself without chancing a serious hernia, so he borrowed Dewey Thornton's rig which has a winch on it, Dewey being into the stolen car racket himself.

After he creams the bull, it goes down as planned, and Spitball drives the truck right through the fence and hooks the cable around its feet and hoists it up and into the truck bed. He drives into town and starts calling on restaurants in the French Quarter, figuring they only had to feed tourists which wouldn't know any better anyhow, never having chowed down on good food back where they were from and so the cooks there would know a good deal when they saw one. He had it figured out that the cow weighed about a ton, give or take a few ounces, and he was going to sell it for about half what ground round went for at

Schweiggman's. A good deal all around.

The first guy he approached was the swamper at Arnaud's who was out back copping a doobie when Spitball pulled up with this poleaxed bull in his truck. Spitball laid down the deal to him and I guess this guy just about popped a vein hooting at him. First place, the guy said, it don't work like that. This here's a Brahma bull which you don't eat and second, when you sell by weight you don't include the head, horns, feet, hide and guts and some other odds and ends like the penis except maybe to some depraved Chinamen who are always looking for things like that to get the old trouser worm up with, and when you take those away you got about half what you're figuring. He was telling him some of the other fine points of selling stolen beef when the bull, who Spitball had figured to be expired, all of a sudden lurched to his feet and began bellowing like he was the kick-off act to Armageddon. This gets the swamper agitated and also pulls outside some of the other boys what worked at Arnaud's and they're going nuts, yelling coonass French and what-not at poor Spitball who hadn't covered this contingency in his original planning.

The upshot of it was, the bull busted loose and sprang off the truck and started right for Spitball and the gang that was gathered there in debate and he missed all the people but got a corner of the restaurant building and part of the roof came down. Then, it got interesting.

Everybody out back had pistolas and such in violation of their parole agreements and started pulling them out and firing at the bull which didn't have the desired effect but only made him madder. Most of the bullets hit upstairs windows where guys were busy doing stuff with women who probably weren't their lawful wedded wives. The bull lit out after the dumber ones who hadn't gone back inside like anyone with any sense would have and they scattered in every direction. There must have been four or five of them had stuck around outside when the bull started playing tag. Spitball himself would have split along with the rest of the gang, but he couldn't leave Dewey's truck. That was another thing. Dewey's truck was painted red and when the bull seen he wasn't going to catch any of the guys as they had left the premises, he went after the truck. Caught it a good one, smack dab in the middle of the grill which didn't do the radiator and some other parts any good. When we heard the story, we could all picture Spitball standing there with this fuck-me look on his face, steam coming out what was left of the radiator and this pissed-off bull stamping his feet and snorting fire and eyeballing Spitball who decided at that point he'd had enough and left the scene himself, went down and had a few cold ones at the Dungeon over by Pat O'Brien's.

"Spitball," I told him, "cows are colorblind, I think. That stuff about them going after red is one'a them urban myths, I believe."

No matter, he said; that might be the case, but something about Dewey's truck got this particular bull mad. Maybe he was nearsighted and it looked like one of his ex-girlfriends or something. I think it was about the same size.

Spitball told us later that was the toughest phone call he'd ever had to make when he give Dewey the news. Far as I know, he's still paying off the damages. At first, the cops wanted to arrest Dewey for stealing the bull since it was his truck, but Dewey had an ironclad alibi for where he was during the heist, which is another story since it led to two divorces, his and the lady he was bedded and alibied down with at the time. Dewey told the police that his truck must have been stolen and they had no choice but to believe him. That must have been a tense moment when

Spitball and Dewey finally had their tete-a-tete. I would have liked to have been a fly speck on *that* wall.

Anyway, that's Dooley "Spitball" Thibidoux in a nutshell and here he comes with this scheme that I could see right off after he explained it was your basic short cut to a closed casket funeral. For him *and* me, should I take French leave of my senses and join up with his madcap scam.

It had *potential* though…Lots of high-octane potential.

What he had, what was nestled in his hip pocket, right next to his rosy-red lard ass, was a list. It was some doozy of a list. What Spitball also had was the gift of charm. He could sell a Santa Claus suit to a rabbi and get him on the Ham of the Month Club as a bonus.

He had the Fixer's list.

Excerpt from a new novel in progress, working title, *Kidnapping's an Ugly Word*, the second novel in a trilogy.

Claude's was the best place we could go, if we were gonna go out in public, Tommy explained, on the way over. "No honkies go in there hardly ever. Anybody recognizes us from the TV ain't gonna give us up. They got that black code. Plus, we all look alike to the brothers."

I wasn't too sure about any black code, but what the hell.

When we went in, sure enough—there's about twenty-five black brothers and the noise level went down appreciably the second we walked in. Tommy fetched us a couple of brewskies from the bartender while I used the coin phone in the back to call Cat and tell her where we were and invite her to join us, which she said she might, and we went on back to a booth. After a couple of minutes and some looks from the brothers I wasn't crazy about, things seemed to go back to normal. Somebody played the juke box and B.B. King began to sing.

"Tommy," I said. "I guess I'm with you on this deal—way I see it, I got no choice. But, I have to wonder if you've covered all the bases here. If you've told me everything, for instance."

"What else would there be?" he said. "Have I ever held anything out on you in our partnership, Pete?"

"Well," I said. "I wasn't aware we had a partnership, but yeah, you have held stuff out on me before." I leaned forward until my face was a foot from his. "Why the fuck didn't you tell me ol' Fred ran a Mafia laundering operation?"

"You think I knew that? I look stupid?"

I leaned back, turned my head like I was talking to the imaginary person sitting to my right. "This is too easy," I said. "I'll leave this one for an amateur."

Tommy looked contrite. "Look," he said. "I know I fucked up. But now I got the solution. Deneuvé."

I was having second thoughts about that. No, make that third and fourth thoughts.

"Oh, that's swell, Tommy. Now my mind is at ease. For a minute there, I thought I was a dead man."

He flashed me a smile. "Only one thing is gonna get us out of this alive. My plan."

"Yeah," I said. "Or the Second Coming."

We had us a second beer each—Tommy had to go up to the bar as it looked like the waitress was on break—and he laid out some of the other details. He was just finishing up with all that and the door opened and in sashayed Cat, hips swinging.

That got a reaction from the crowd. There was a hitch in the noise level and I could see the brothers stare and the sisters dig elbows into their dates. Looked like we were really on the radar now.

"Hey, Cat," Tommy said.

"Hey, Tommy. Hey, Pete." She slid in beside Tommy. So that's the way it was going to be.

"What's your pleasure, miss?" It was the bartender. Come to wait on us.

She shined him all of her teeth. "You wouldn't have Parfait Amore, would you, sugar?" she said. The only thing left off of her Scarlett O'Hara impression was batting her eyelashes. Pulling down her top a couple extra inches to show off her twins probably made up for that.

"Ah," the barkeep said. "The Drink of Love. I'm sorry, no."

"That's all right," Cat said. "I'll have Black and White, neat, water back."

"From my bottle to your glass," said the bartender and whirled around like a matador and quickstepped back to behind the bar and began pouring.

I looked down at mine and Pete's beers, both empty.

The bartender returned with Cat's two glasses.

Tommy looked up at him and tried to match Cat's smile. "Uh," he said. "You suppose my friend and I could get a refill?"

The best way I could describe how the bartender looked at him was "frosty." "I'm a bartender, not a waiter, Slick," he said, and stalked away.

Tommy shot me a "fuck me" look and shook it off. "Look," he said to me. "I've got some more stuff to do before tonight—"here he narrowed his eyes and furrowed his brow at me like I was supposed to pay special attention to what he was saying, "—and I'll see you back at 'the place' at six, Pete. Six. O'clock. Got it?"

He stood there waiting until I repeated his instructions.

"Yeah, Tommy. Six o'clock. I'll set my alarm."

He nodded, gave Cat a little salute, and walked to the door and out.

Cat smiled. "When Tommy told me about you, he said you used to play baseball, Pete. Did you ever meet Mickey Mantle or Babe Ruth?"

I guess this was her version of chit-chat and socializing.

I leaned forward, put my head in my hands. "Mantle and Ruth? Oh, yeah. We was all teammates. Back when baseball was fun." With Tommy gone, I was starting to have buyer's remorse about this kidnap plan. "Right now,"

I went on, more to me than to her, "I'm in a rundown between third and home. You got any idea what Tommy's brilliant scheme is that we're supposed to do?"

She gave me a coy little smile and stirred her drink. "I think so," she said. "He's grabbed some rich dude. Tommy's a smart guy. We're all gonna be rich."

We? Tommy had neglected to fill me in on the part where Cat was involved in his plan. I was just about to quiz her on that, in a particularly witty and cutting way, when the front door of the bar opened, letting in a shaft of brilliant New Orleans' afternoon sun.

And Sam Capelli.

At first, I didn't realize it was him, not paying strict attention like I shoulda been. He was halfway back before it dawned on me who it was. I flopped down below the table, like I had dropped my change, going down quicker'n vanilla ice cream off a sugar cone in August.

"What?" said Cat, and I yanked on her Capris, and whispered, "It's Sam. Capelli. You know him, you said. He sees me, the only thing left to do is make the funeral arrangements. What the hell's he doin' here? They don't serve no pasta here. God! Let me know what he does."

What he does is plunk his large ass in the booth right next to ours. Cat don't hafta tell me. When he plopped his butt on the seat, he did it with such force the edge of my seat smacked me on the head so hard I saw stars. I almost yelped, but kept it in by biting my lip in half. I sat there with blood running down my chin and tears in my eyes from the pain.

Now I was in it but good. I'm sitting on the floor under the table in a booth in a black bar with a hooker the only thing between me and Doctor Death. There was other places I would rather be at, just then. I couldn't stay down there for the rest of my life; somebody was sure to take note of the honky on the floor, that is, if Cat didn't blow the whistle first, to save her own ass.

Just then, she leaned over with an evil leer and whisper, "I shouldn't do this, asswipe, but I feel sorry for you. I'll get you out of here."

"How?" I whispered back. If she had an idea could spring me out of this jam, I'd go pick out the ring tomorrow, order the tux.

"I'll create a diversion. When I do, you slip out the back, get my car and park up the block. I'll be along presently." She reached into her purse and took something out and handed it to me. Car keys. "It's the red Buick convertible."

What was she going to do, I wondered. Take her clothes off? I couldn't think of much else she could do to not only get Sam but the other twenty-five black guys not to notice me go out the back.

What she did do, I wouldn't have guessed in a thousand years.

She didn't take her clothes off.

She stood up and she threw a fit.

I mean, *she threw a fit.*

She starts yelling and screeching and wandering around the bar, and screaming out all kinds of derogatory things about our black brethren. Like, she said the N word. A bunch of times. "Cocksucker!" she yelled. "Mufucker! N-nigger! F-Fuck. Mutha, mutha, mutha...fuck! Nigger! Whoop!"

You coulda drove a fork lift into my mouth, it was that far open.

"Pussy, pussy, pussy! Whoop! Whoop, whoop, whoop! N-nigger! Shit! Fuck!"

She was in high gear now. All I could see from the floor was black guys moving toward her from all corners.

She kind of staggers up toward the front door, giving out with the insults, and it ain't two seconds before she's drawn a major crowd around her. From under the booth I see a dozen or more black dudes, most of whom have things flashing in their hands, like razors and knives and other sharp and dangerous objects. It appears as if we're about to have a honky woman massacre. The booth shoots back again as Sam gets up and catches me up alongside the head again, and I chomp half my tongue off this time, but keep the sound effects down, just barely. It probably don't matter; there is so much noise and babble up at the front of the bar by now nobody woulda heard me anyway, everybody present with the same fierce desire to be the first to smack Cat, separate her from her gizzard.

Then, I caught on, almost too late. This was the diversion she was talking about, giving me a chance to slip away out the back door. I couldn't figure out how she planned to walk away from this, being as how she was using every racial epithet any cracker had ever thought up. I hoped she knew what she was doing, but it sure looked like a suicide mission from where I was. Might as well one of us get out alive, I thought, and crawled out fast. Nobody paid me any attention, they was all up front, trying t'get at Cat and rip her apart, I figured, and I silently wished her luck and made for the back door. As I was going out, I heard her voice above the murmur of the men, and she was screeching, "Tourette's; I got Tourette's. It's a disease." I shoulda split, soon as I was clear of that door, but I hung around a minute and listened.

"Man, I hearda that," a man's voice said. "It was on TV," said another. "*Oprah*, I think." "Yeah, poor bitch can't help herself," said still another, and another voice, I could swear it was Sam, said, "My brother-in-law has that, always yelling cusswords and stuff when he gets an attack," and then I was gone, whipping out through the back parking lot, knocking over a couple of garbage cans I didn't stay around to pick up. I ran the whole way till I got to the car, grabbed the keys out of my pocket, jumped in, and started it up.

I did like she said, pulled past the bar and parked about half a block up.

The door of Claude's burst open and a wave of black humanity poured out. Black except for the white hooker and Sam The Bam, who were way in the back taking up the rear of the mob.

Then, the damnedest thing happened. Three or four black dudes were around Cat, and it looked like they were slapping her on the back and hugging her. No, they must be stabbing her. No; by golly, they were patting her on the back and hugging her! I put the car in reverse and rolled toward her. When I got close, I leaned over and opened her door and pushed it out, trying to keep the car in the middle of the street, and just as I came abreast of her, I honked the horn and yelled, "Hit it, Cat! Jump in!"

She waved at me and took a bottle of beer a smiling brother handed her and just sauntered over to me. She climbed in the car and just as she gets in, I hear a voice I don't wanna never hear again in my life, yelling. It was Sam. He was trying to knock guys down and they were turning when he elbowed them but then got polite and got out of his way when they saw his gun.

"Better kick it, slick," Cat said.

I was half a beat ahead of her, the car already leaving rubber and fishtailing as I floored it.

Bam! Bam! Bam!

I look in the rearview mirror and see Sam standing in the street, a two-handed grip on his piece just like Dirty Harry.

A slug hit the rear window and it shattered just before I turned the corner on two wheels. I flew through a stop sign and we almost got broadsided by a huge, oncoming garbage truck, but I drove around him and got clear.

"How...how the hell..." I couldn't get the words together.

Cat was laughing so hard she started to choke. She wiped tears from her eyes. "I always wanted to try that!" she said.

"Try what?" I said. "What in holy hell was all that back there?"

I went up Terpsichore, went under the Ponchartrain Express and turned left on Thalia, taking that on up to Magazine. I turned left onto the Street of Dreams.

I looked over at Cat, trying to spot bruises, contusions, slash marks, but she's clean as a newborn, not a scratch on her.

"What happened, Cat?" I said, and she starts laughing so hard I thought she'd bust her bra.

"I saw Digger O'Henry do that one time in a bar over on Camp Street," she said. "He bet a bunch of other hillbillies he could go into this black bar and call 'em all niggers and they'd end up buying him a drink. He done just what I did; went in this joint and starts yelling out all kinda names that black folks don't normally go for, and then goes into this 'Tourette's' thing. I'll be damned if don't everybody believe him and they end up buying him drinks and wanting to know where they can send money for the Tourette's fund."

"I'll be damned," I said. "They went for that lame shit?"

"Well...not really," she said. "I think they was just playing along with a good-looking woman. I figure they just played along 'cause I showed some balls."

"Fuck me," I said. "Just, fuck me. I am a dead man no matter what I do."

"You're the 'glass is half-empty' type, aren't you?" she said, her smile fading. "Your song is already getting old. Turn left here."

Excerpt from *The Genuine, Imitation, Plastic Kidnapping* and published as a short story in *Down, Out and Dead.*

Well, here it is—my annual Mother's Day post. In reality, this won't be an "annual" post unless I do one next year since this is the very first one. I plan to do one next year, though. If I remember…

And…I'm aware that it's late, but I thought that appropriate, since I always forget it until about a week later, despite a loving wife (Mary) who considers it her mission in life to let me know about things like this. The only problem is, she always lets me know the day before. Like I'm expected to remember it that long!

To make up for not sending a card on time, I decided to send Mom more than just one of those syrupy Hallmark cards. This year, I sent her a cassette tape of the movie *It's a Wonderful Life* starring that irrepressible boyish Jimmy Stewart from my private collection. (This is the movie where he isn't dressed up like a giant rabbit, in which he's also irrepressible and boyish.)

Then, the second I got home from mailing it to her, I realized I'd made a grievous mistake. I hadn't sent her the movie I thought I had. It dawned on me that I'd sent her an entirely different movie. To be exact, my copy of the classic film noir, *College Girls Having Monkey Sex, Part XIV*. If you haven't seen it, it's the one where the coed from Vassar has her boobs pointed in opposite directions and her co-star ends up with whiplash trying to treat them equally and stay on his mark. ("Mark" for you non-theater majors is the piece of tape the director places on the floor to show the actor where to stand.)

Oops.

The reason I realized my faux pas, was that when I got home I thought I might want to watch a few minutes of it and couldn't locate it and then remembered I'd labeled it...you guessed it...*It's a Wonderful Life*...in the unlikely event Mary went through my collection looking for a something to watch.

I ran all the way back to the post office in hopes I could talk the mail guy into letting me have my package back, but it seems they have rules against that kind of thing. You can guess how that turned out, if you've ever had to deal with the United Nazi States of Mail Carriers. Guy treated me like I was the Unabomber. I called him "Cliff" and "Newman" but he didn't get it.

I was in a sweat when I found it had already been shipped, but then I remembered Mom didn't have a cassette player. Or a VCR. Or, even a TV. She'd sold her TV when *The Ed Sullivan Show* went off the air a few years ago.

The luck of the Irish!

Realizing I better do something more than send her a tape she couldn't watch, I asked Mary if we could take her out to dinner.

"When?" she said. "On Father's Day? That's the next holiday."

I laughed. (That's it. I just laughed) Then, I said, "Of course not, silly. This weekend."

"Only if you don't use that name in the restaurant that you always do," she said.

I agreed and called Mom to give her the good news. "We'd like to take you out to dinner for your big day," I said. "Where would you like to go?"

"Would this be an early Mother's Day for 2011 or the late one for 2010?"

I laughed. (That's it. I just laughed. I've been trained by Mary.) Then I said, "Of course not, silly. The second one. 2010. The battery in my calendar died."

Golden Corral was her first choice, but I talked her out of that. "They're closed," I lied. "There was a big pileup of people on walkers and the health department closed them until they widen the ramp. Thirty-six people suffered aluminum whiplash. There are herds of lawyers everywhere and you couldn't get in even if it was open."

She sounded skeptical, but then said her second choice was Red Lobster. This, to a guy who's lived in New Orleans half his life and has actually eaten real seafood was like the chef at Ruth's Chris Steak House grabbing a square hamburger down at Wendy's on his day off, but, hey, it was my mom and it was her day. I looked forward to gazing at their menu with pictures of the nine-pound lobsters on the menu and them seeing the actual three-ounce one they served. To be fair, the actual meal *is* the same size as the picture when you put them up next to each other.

She decided to drive down from where she lived in South Bend to our home in Ft. Wayne, a true adventure for the other drivers on the highway since she's eighty-eight and drives older than her actual age. You've heard that saying? "(Blank) drives like old people fuck? Slow and jerky." That's Mom. If you ever see those long lines on winding country roads where there are one hundred seventeen cars trailing behind the John Deere tractor, it was Mom who taught that tractor driver how to navigate our rural byways. I suggested she might want to start out the night before to get to our place on time, but she didn't think that was all that funny.

"You're not too old to get a spanking, Mr. Smart-mouth," she said. Well, yes, I am, Mom. I have gray hair and arthritis and can remember when phones had dials. Besides, how are you going to catch me? I can crawl faster than you can walk. I didn't say anything like that to her, of course. After all, she's my mom and deserves respect. Besides, as long as I knew I could outrun her that was enough. I didn't have to rub it in.

Before she hung up, she said, "You're not going to use that name you always do in restaurants, are you? Because if you do, I'm not coming."

"No, Mom, I'm not. I'm grown up, now." Jesus! What do she and Mary do? Get together and compare notes?

She gets here, only two and a half hours past her ETA, and we all climb in the car and head for the gastronomical delights only available at national chains.

We get to the Red Lobster and I'm anticipating something on my plate that looks like a medium jumbo shrimp that they're going to try to pawn off as a Maine lobster and we all go in. This takes a while as we're proceeding at Mom's pace which is about as fast as the last day of school.

"We should hurry, Mom," I said. "They close in only six hours."

Mary gives me a dirty look. So does Mom, who says, "You're not too big to get a spanking." I consider showing her my driver's license to show her my age as she's obviously forgotten, but I don't. It's Mother's Day. Well, not really—that was last week, but we're operating on the theme of Mother's Day and I want to remain true to the spirit.

I hustle ahead of them and give our name to the hostess.

When I come back, Mom says, "How long?" and Mary says, "You didn't give them that name, did you?"

"Twenty minutes," I say to Mom, and to Mary I just

give a pained look, as if to say, "How could you even think I'd do that?"

We pass the time listening to Mom complain about the present government and ask to see a menu so she can make her choice, which is always the same. The lobster/shrimp combo. I think she just wants to check to make sure they haven't taken either off the menu. Although, if they ran out of one, they could just serve the one that was left and tell the diner it was the missing one. Who would know?

Then, she lays a bomb on me. "I love that movie, you sent me," she said. "I'm going over to your sister Ann's house to watch it when I get back home."

And then, our table is announced over the loudspeaker.

"Donner, party of three."

I get two dirty looks from the women I'm with.

"That's us," I say.

I love Mother's Day!

First published in *Last Word edited by* Liam Sweeny.

I'm afraid I have some bad news. Let me take that back. I have some *terrible* news. *Bad* news is when your wife says she's leaving you for the water softener man. This is far worse than that. This is on the level of news that she's leaving you for the guy who lives down by the river in his refrigerator carton...and *not* taking the kids with her...

Okay. Ready? Sitting down? Here goes...

It's official. Once again, I didn't win the Pulitzer Prize for Literature. How many times must I taste the bitter truth that time is running out? Once a year, I guess, until *I* run out...

And, what beat me out this year? *The Orphan Master's Son* by Adam Johnson. You're kidding, right? Here's the description: An exquisitely crafted novel that carries the reader on an adventuresome journey into the depths of totalitarian North Korea and into the most intimate spaces of the human heart.

It's a book set in *North Korea?* Who the hell nominated this? Dennis Rodman? Who even reads books set in North Korea? Even North Koreans don't read books set in North Korea. Well, that's not exactly their fault—they aren't allowed to by that sweet little cherub, Dear Leader. Speaking of cherubs, I woke up this morning with a sweet little cherub in my skivvies...Or was that a chub? Whatever. They both look the same.

I suspect it won because of the author's name. He's named after two American presidents. Jingoism at its worst.

I should have known I wouldn't win once again after last year when they couldn't find a single book to give the award to. There were only five million books published last year (even taking out the four million self-published auto-biographies that really suck swamp water, that still leaves a million books, give or take a few hundred thousand.).

How can you not give one single book the award? Even the year the Miss America contestants were all dogs, they still gave the award to someone. Bert Parks took it himself one year. That was the year there weren't any brunettes from Mississippi and Georgia. But, hey—they still awarded it to somebody.

I've had it. I'm taking serious action. I've just composed a strongly-worded letter to all the judges of next year's Pulitzer committee, notifying them that I'm officially with-drawing any and all of my books from consideration. I'm sending it via overnight delivery, certified mail. That means it won't arrive in their mail boxes until August, 2020 but I have no control over that. They'll at least be aware of my sentiments.

And, as it happens, I'm outlining a new novel that fits all of their crappy requirements. It's set in (some obscure country which I haven't decided yet, but one with lots of consonants and only one vowel) and it's about the Mayor of Cracktown. It's about this guy who lives in a village with the *Entering* and *Leaving* signs on the same pole, and in this little shack with a bunch of farm animals of various religious persuasions living inside with him. He has no money (always a requirement of these kinds of books and which immediately makes him a genius). He has a major fight with the *garda* who have discovered he's far exceeded the legal quota of farm animals allowed in a domicile, one of which he claims shouldn't count as it's a very pretty Merino ewe to whom he's pledged his troth. He's not sure what a "troth" is but it's in a lot of Dickens' books he read as a kid so he knows it's important to pledge his.

In this book, I devote a lot of pages to his internalizing, which seems to be high on the list of stuff these Pulitzer folks look for. There's one really dazzling scene where he ponders how clichés came about and fantasizes about their origins. Like that delightful phrase "blind alley" (which, I, for one can never hear too many times.). He ruminates and ponders and rumes some more and comes to the conclusion that it originally denoted a place where German shepherds congregated en masse, waiting to be hired by the seeing-challenged (PC term for blind people) and veterans with PTSD. This riveting scene takes up twenty-six pages, which is guaranteed to manipulate them even more than a teen-aged boy's chub during bathroom time. And, in much the same way.

One of the indoor farm animals will be a dog. His only function is to be in the book so I can use his picture on the cover and on the Intergnat. You and I know it's just a frickin' mutt, but people on the Intergnat have assigned a mystical aura to dogs and cats. You know, those critters that eat their own poop, cough up furballs and lick themselves all day long. We know that mostly they're glorified door mats, but people get all weepy about them and giggly and attribute them with the same wisdom they do old Indian guys crying over some trash on Highway 10. THEY SELL BOOKS. And influence Pulitzer judges...

The protagonist will be a creepy loner who, in real life, people would take a wide berth around when they see him with his sign begging for work outside Target, but instantly make into a wise man simply because there's a whole book centered around him and we see he thinks about pithy stuff like *blind alleys.* If he was so frickin' wise why ain't he a plumber's assistant or a governor or something?

My protagonist is also an orphan. And a master. And the son of a dog. This makes it a sure winner.

Yes, I could easily win next year, which makes my protest even more meaningful. I know what it takes after studying these things for ~~hours days~~ weeks. It's important to know who's handing out the hardware. The judges are elderly folks who braid the hair in their noses (the women) and meet at Golden Corral to discuss the nominated books. The men on the committee treat the books nominated the same way they do the fine wines they own. They don't open them. That would destroy their value and besides, who has to actually read the nominated book? They can learn all they want to from the glorious Intergnat. The men also have lush bushes in their noses, but they use them differently than the women (most of the women...). They weave them cleverly around their noggins kind of like the comb-overs aging sportscasters do. Along with a few well-placed strands from the ear hairs.

This is the real secret as to why my book never gets nominated. I labored for years thinking they actually read the books. Don't laugh—I bet you know at least one person in your own circle who thought the same thing. So maybe *you* knew, but are you willing to say that all of your friends wear those helmets and rode the short bus to H.S. and took all A.P. classes? So—cut me a break here.

The trick to getting on these judges' radar is to effectively utilize the Intergnat. Most of us writers have been sold a bill of goods about what the 'Gnat does. Social media doesn't sell books. It doesn't sell squat. It doesn't sell books—it sells social media. No one cares about your stupid book on social media. They pretend to...so you'll buy their stupid book. Writers who can't sell books have one problem—they write crappy books. Yakking about them all day long on social media sells three books total. That's it. And that's to trolls who are burning to write one-star reviews on it. When social media sells books, let me know. Otherwise, lay down by your dish with your butt-licking dog.

But, Pulitzer Prize judges do look at the Intergnat. All day long. It's why they don't have time to actually read the books themselves. Too busy Facebooking each other or Twittering about "that wonderful book about North Korea Dennis Rodman likes so well." Think about this. 1. Dennis Rodman picture with Dear Leader was on the "Gnat" one million, three hundred thousand and sixty-nine times last year. 2. A book set in North Korea won the Pulitzer. Make the connection, dummy! This ain't nuclear physics!

So, if I weren't about to withdraw from consideration, here's what I'd do. Get me a babe to do my networking for me. As my pretend girlfriend, Lo Hai Qu so eloquently pointed out—"Blogbitches rule, blogdicks drool." Okay. I accept that. If I was going to remain involved in the competition, I'd be on my knees beseeching my pal, Anonymous-9 (Blogbitch Supreme) if she'd please help this lowly Blogdick (me) out.

But I won't. You can relax, 9. I'm out of all this. I just hope you nice folks "twit" and "face" my new book all over the Intergnat. I have but one goal for next year. That all the UPS drivers who deliver my books are forced to buy trusses.

(I hope you know this was all in fun, folks. Although, if I have to say this, it takes all the force away...) I do love the Intergnat and I truly do love the folks on here. True dat. And they do sell books. Books on how to use the Intergnat to sell books...)

As John Goodman once said, "See ya in the funny papers."

Blue skies,
Les

LURLEEN

For Mucho Mojo

So here I am, sitting at a table with Mauro Falciani in his fine bookstore, the Libreria Mucho Mojo inside the nightclub Speakeasy 23, drinking grappa and swapping stories. I ask him about the club I hear whispered about.

"So, Mauro, what about this 'Mucho Mojo' club Joe Lansdale and Neil Smith tell me about? How does one become a member?"

Mauro smiles. "You are already in that club, Les. You have been Mojo, real Mojo all your life, I think, with the breath of the big American stories. For you to become a member, I ask what I asked of Neil of Joe of others…and ask you for a story celebrating the club, a story that will help build a cultural association to support us. One story that mentions the club and something bad, crazy or funny that happened inside."

I thought about his request for a moment.

"What if I tell you a story that I've never told anyone? One that I've held close to my vest for more than sixty years? For reasons that will be obvious once you hear it. A true story? A story that has only been told here. Will that get me in?"

Mauro looked at me intently. "I think yes. Tell me the story and I will judge."

I took another drink of the grappa. How to tell Mauro this story? Then, I knew how I'd tell it. By beginning with the town in East Texas where it took place.

"Okay, Mauro. Better get a new bottle of wine. This may take a while. I'll begin with the town I grew up in."

And so it begins...

Entering the town of Freeport, Texas in the year 1954, you drive to the town square. At one end is the Dow Hotel. On the opposite end is a vacant lot. In the middle is a grassy park with a tall palm tree. If you walk across the park, a huge crow who makes his nest thirty feet high in the tree, will swoop down on you and try to peck your head. Maybe it's your eyes he's after, who knows? On the two sides are stores and businesses. On the left (looking toward the Dow Hotel) is a café, owned by Mrs. Stringfellow. I forget the name. The Stringfellow Café? Maybe...Down that side of the block is the Lack's Sporting Goods. I once broke into it with my friend Richard Barnes and we stole fishing reels, hooks, lures and other things ten-year-old boys found valuable. And a snub-nosed .38 Police Special and a box of shells for it.

On the opposite side of the street, stands my grandma's bar, the Sweet Shop. Next to it on the right is another honky tonk, for which I forget the name also. I remember it was owned and run by Red, a one-armed drunk. Sometimes, I set up my shoeshine box in front of Red's and shined the shoes of the drunks coming and going. The drunker they were, the more they tipped.

On the other side, was a vacant lot and a small shack which served as the dispatch office of the Star Taxi, which my grandma also owned. Next to it was the town movie theater. When I was ten I had a job there, hauling up the movie reels in exchange for free passes to the movies. Further down the block was Thom McAnn shoe store. Some other businesses and shops I've forgotten. A flower shop, I think, on the far corner by the hotel.

Grew up in the bar, listening to Norwegian sailors singing along with Hank Snow in accented English. Lapsing into their native German or whatever it was when they got liquored up and mixed up in a fight over Lurleen, the retarded white girl who cleaned tables for my grandma.

The first guy who bought a beer for Lurleen earned her love. For the moment, that is. If another man came over to the table with a new beer, her loyalty was instantly transferred, along with her ready smile. That's when the fight usually started. Her problem was her disability to focus. New man—new beer—new boyfriend. Neither man—the first one or the second—were aware of her fidelity issues. The kinds of men my grandma's honky tonk attracted weren't men of deep thinking or great insights or in empathy in general. Mostly, they just wanted to get drunk and get laid.

Lurleen was my friend. My second-best friend. Richard Barnes was my very best friend. We did everything together. Fished, hunted for ducks sitting on ponds on the Dow Chemical ponds with our air rifles and .22 rifles, went floundering in the Bryan Beach shallows at dusk with gigs, hunted gators in the bayous with .22s. Broke into the Lack's Sporting Goods store. Shit like that.

Sat in my next-door neighbor's house one afternoon with Bobbie Ann my next-door neighbor who was fifteen when she showed us her boobies and let us touch 'em.

I had a job washing dishes in the Sweet Shop and when I got snowed under, it was always Lurleen who came back and gave me a hand, catching up. She also showed Richard and me how to do a couple of neat tricks. She could pop off the cap to a Dr. Pepper with her teeth. She could also eat glass and showed us how to do that. The trick is, you get a piece of thin glass, kind of like on those beer glasses. It has to be thin or it won't work. The trick is, you break off a piece about an inch and a half in diameter and then put it back on your back teeth. You start applying pressure and grinding the glass back and forth between your teeth slightly and if you have faith and don't chicken out, pretty soon it starts to break and not into pieces but into sand. It's a pretty cool trick and years later I made a lot of money doing it in bars on bets. Had to quit eventually, when I got cavities, 'cause the glass didn't cut me but it flat-out chewed up the fillings and whatever I made on the bar bets I had to use to pay the dentist to fix the fillings.

Anyway.

Lurleen was what we called "simple" in those days, which later changed to "retarded" and now is called "mentally-challenged" or some other stupid thing. She was pure-hearted and never had a bad thought about a single human being in her life. Sometimes other kids teased her and then we'd fight.

My grandma—Miz Vincent is what folks called her—had Lurleen a house trailer she gave her that perched in the weedy lot behind the bar. She paid Lurleen to bus tables. In those days, that had to be a white person. We had blacks working for us, but they couldn't be out in the front. They had to be cooks and dishwashers and stay back in the kitchen.

We had lots and lots of sailors that came in the bar. My grandma was a smart cookie. Freeport is in Brazosport County which happens to be a dry county. In Texas, in those days, your county was either wet or dry. The Baptists had voted Brazosport to be a dry one. That meant you could get beer and wine in the local bars, but not whiskey or vodka or rum or anything hard. For that, you had to go to Houston or Galveston, both about a fifty-mile trip, one-way.

Grandma created the cab company, which ended up making her a millionaire. Freeport was a major port for off-loading sulphur, gas, oil and other chemicals into tankers bound for other parts of the world. Sailors would be in port while their ships were being loaded up and naturally, head for the nearest bar. Grandma's own Star Taxis would pick them up at the docks and deliver them to her own bar. There was one other cab company in town—the 411—but they sucked hind tit to the Star Taxis. The 411 didn't have a bar to go to. Mostly, they delivered to our bar and Red's next door. There were a few other bars in town, but these two were the heart of the honky tonk district. And, then, when they got drunk on beer and wanted something harder, voila! There were our taxis standing just outside the bar doors to take 'em to Galveston or Houston, a fifty-dollar bill the one-way toll in those days. She was just minting money.

For some reason, Lurleen was partial to Norwegian sailors. I think it was something to do with the fact that they were mostly all blond, tall, and good-looking. I'm not a girl so I'm not sure what the attraction was, but I think that's a pretty good guess.

And, it seemed like there was always a fight whenever Lurleen befriended one of them.

And, that's what happened the night of February 13, 1954, which happened to be my birthday. My eleventh.

I was washing dishes that night, back in the kitchen, and even though it was February, it was a hot one. No air conditioning in the kitchen. There was in the bar itself, but not back in the kitchen. Just a big ol' fan that barely turned and mostly just stirred the air around. Richard was there with me, sitting on a stool and drinking a Dr. Pepper. Richard was my best friend, but not the kind of guy who'd give me a hand. He preferred to sit around and razz me instead. Tease me about my "dishpan hands" and whatnot. Yuk it up.

After a bit, I took a break and went and got me a Coke-Cola out of the cooler up front in the bar. I couldn't drink Dr. Pepper. My mother told me a long time before that it was made out of prune juice, so there's no way I would drink it.

I saw Lurleen sitting at a table with a sailor and gave her a little wave and she caught my eye, grinned back and give me one back. I went on back and finished up my job and me and Richard were about to go home and get our gigs and go after some frogs, when Lurleen came through the French doors, with her sailor in hand. They were headed on back to her trailer, looked like.

"Hey, Butchie," she said, and tousled my hair. "This here's my friend Hans."

It looked like Hans wasn't a big kid fan and he barely acknowledged me and then they were gone, out the back door. I turned off the light and Richard and I exited the same way. Lurleen and her friend Hans were already in her trailer and we heard her squealing like girls do when they're being tickled or just being girls and Richard and I just looked at each other and shook our heads and walked on past, out to the alley. Just as we hit the alley, we heard her scream, which made us stop dead in our tracks.

"C'mon," I said to Richard. He didn't say anything, just followed me back to her trailer. I got a wooden milk box from behind her trailer and hauled it over in front of the one window that looked into her bedroom, and perched it there and climbed up on it so I could see in.

God. The Norwegian guy was smacking her as hard as

he could. Hard, Jack. So hard it looked like she was already unconscious. Her eyes were closed and blood was everywhere.

"Lemme see! It was Richard. He grabbed my arm, pulled me down, and climbed up on the milk box.

"Jesus, lordy!" he said, climbing back down. "He's killed her, Butch!"

I climbed back up and it looked like he was right. The Norwegian guy wasn't hitting her any more. In fact, he was just sitting there on the bed with her, his head down and it looked like he was panting, out of breath. Then, he just kind of fell over beside her and closed his eyes. Looked like maybe he passed out.

"We gotta tell somebody," Richard hissed.

"Naw," I said. "They'll just let him go. He's a foreigner and they got lots of money. Lurleen's just a retard and they won't nobody do anything about it. Naw. I got another idea."

I told him what I was thinking and Richard just nodded. He was a true friend. He'd do just about anything I suggested.

We busted ass, got to my house just three blocks over and went out to the shed in back where we kept our fishing and hunting gear, stuff like that. Up along the eaves, I'd hid the gun I'd stole at Lack's Sporting Goods, the .38 Police Special. Snubnose.

It was loaded and ready to go.

I grabbed it and we ran back to the Sweet Shop and Lurleen's trailer.

The lights inside were still on and the milk box was still there. I climbed up and looked inside. The Norwegian sailor was still there. Still asleep or passed out. There was more blood.

We crept up to the door and eased it open. In a second,

we were inside. We went back to her bedroom, and it was worse, up close and personal. There was blood everywhere.

The guy was snoring. Lurleen wasn't. It was clear she'd never be snoring again on this planet.

'Whaddya want to do?" It was Richard, whispering.

"Kill the fucker," I said.

"Oh, no," he said. "We can't do that, Butch."

"I can," I said. "She's my friend, Richard. You saw what he did to her. We don't do this, he gets off."

"Yeah, but..." He didn't have an argument to offer.

"Go home," I said to him.

"What?"

"Just go on home, Richard," I said.

He stood there a minute, not saying anything. Then: "You sure?"

I nodded. He stood there another minute and then didn't say anything, just turned around and walked back out of the trailer.

I sat down on the bed with Lurleen and the Norwegian sailor.

I sat there for over two hours.

Then, the Norwegian sailor groaned and sat up. He looked around. Saw me and the gun I held. Saw Lurleen and all the blood.

"Wha?" he said. And then some stuff in German or whatever. I figured it was German. Sounded like a bunch of barnyard animals. Muck, yuck, actch, whatever.

"You killed my friend," I said.

He was silent for a second or two, and then he grinned. "You can't prove anything," he said. "I'm protected. I'm a Norwegian national. She's just a common whore. Call your police," he said. He grinned the whole time.

"Yes," I said and I shot him. In the stomach the first time and then in the chest. With the second shot, he just kind of wheezed and all the air went out of him and he bent over onto his knees. He didn't fall over, but I knew he was dead.

I was only eleven but I wasn't stupid. I knew some shit. I wiped the gun free of my fingerprints with my shirttail and then I put it in Lurleen's hand. I aimed it up at the roof and used her own finger to pull the trigger again. I sat there for a few minutes looking at my friend Lurleen and then I left.

Later the next day, Richard and I met and went fishing for piggies and croakers on the wharf across the street from our house on the Brazos. He never asked me about the night before and I didn't say anything about it. A couple of years later, my parents and my sisters moved north to Indiana and I never saw Richard again.

I don't know what happened. I'm sure there was something in the newspaper, but I didn't read the papers in those days. We didn't have TV so I never saw anything about it there. There was talk around the bar, but mostly bullshit, people talking like they do. I just kept my head down and went to Lurleen's funeral like everybody else in my family. After the funeral, we went back home to Grandma's house where we all lived, and she changed out of her black dress to her white uniform and went back to work.

Until this very minute, Mauro, I've never thought about that time until now. You asked me for a story and here it is. It just came up back in my memory like it was yesterday.

Isn't that some shit?

Is it good enough? It's got some mojo, doesn't it? And I told it here for the first time so that meets your qualification, right?

Say, Mauro, do you have a bottle of Jack anywhere? This grappa's good, but what I really want is some whiskey.

Mayonaise. (Richard Brautigan fans will understand.)

ACKNOWLEDGMENTS

Kudos to Eric Campbell, the best publisher running around out there. To Lance Wright who does the heavy lifting. To JT Lindroos for an amazing cover. To my amazing agent, Svetlana Pironko, Author Rights Agency, who never sleeps.

ABOUT THE AUTHOR

Les Edgerton is an ex-con, matriculating at Pendleton Reformatory in the sixties for burglary (plea-bargained down from multiple counts of burglary, armed robbery, strong-armed robbery and possession with intent). He was an outlaw for many years and was involved in shootouts, knifings, robberies, high-speed car chases, dealt and used drugs, was a pimp, worked for an escort service, starred in porn movies, was a gambler, served four years in the Navy, and had other misadventures.

He's since taken a vow of poverty (became a writer) with nineteen books in print. Three of his novels have been sold to German publisher Pulpmaster for the German language rights. His memoir, *Adrenaline Junkie*, is currently being marketed. Work of his has been nominated for or won: the Pushcart Prize, O. Henry Award, Edgar Allan Poe Award (short story category), Derringer Award, PEN/Faulkner Award, Jesse Jones Book Award, Spinetingler Magazine Award for Best Novel (Legends category), and the Violet Crown Book Award, among others. Screenplays of his have placed as a semifinalist in the Nicholl's and as a finalist in the Best of Austin and Writer's Guild's competitions.

He holds a B.A. from I.U. and the MFA in Writing from Vermont College. He was the writer-in-residence for three years at the University of Toledo, for one year at Trine University, and taught writing classes for UCLA, St. Francis University, Phoenix College, Writer's Digest, Vermont College, the New York Writer's Workshop and other places. He currently teaches a private novel-writing class online. He lives in Ft. Wayne, Indiana, where he immigrated to some years ago from the U.S. and is currently learning the language and customs there. He writes because he hates...a lot...and hard. Injustice and bullying are what he hates the most.

lesedgertononwriting.blogspot.com
lesedgerton.net
Twitter @HookedOnNoir
Facebook – les.edgerton